Praise for Simon Wroe's *Chop Chop*

"At its best, food is a sensory pleasure that also fosters less tangible joys. At its worst, to paraphrase one of the many vivid characters in Simon Wroe's first novel, *Chop Chop*, watching someone eat is like watching a body convert food into waste before your eyes. The character phrases it less delicately, but many of the book's funniest moments—and they are plentiful—are also its most unprintable. That's as it should be. Wroe depicts the literal underworld of a restaurant kitchen with wit, vigor, and gleeful, necessary profanity. . . . His voice provides the second-greatest pleasure of the book after the sheer crackling energy of the setting." —*The New York Times Book Review*

"For evidence of Simon Wroe's talent, look no further than the first sentence of his first novel, *Chop Chop*: 'They arrive in pairs most weeks, blushing like schoolgirls in the kitchen heat.' Perfectly constructed, both beautiful and brutal (Wroe is describing pigs' heads arriving in a restaurant kitchen), written with great economy. Funny and dark and accurate. Teasing the reader to keep reading. All 276 pages of *Chop Chop* are this good. . . . Indeed, Wroe's kitchen scenes and their chefs jump off the page, crackling, alive." —*St. Louis Post-Dispatch*

"Lip-smacking . . . As shocking and witty as it is savage." —*Vogue* (UK)

"Darkly comical and full of surprising moments of fierce emotion. Wroe is an uninhibited writer who doesn't shy away from the grotesque or the rainbow of vocabulary used in the heat of a dinner service." —*The Rumpus*

"Brace yourself for this lively, amusing, and alarmingly informative novel. . . . The horribly plausible cast and foul-mouthed mania of the kitchen—described by a former chef who knows what he's writing about—give this book its energy and best laughs." —*Daily Mail* (London)

"*Kitchen Nightmares* has nothing on the horrors of The Swan, the fancy London restaurant in Wroe's darkly comic novel. . . . A first course worth savoring. Grade: B+" —*Entertainment Weekly*

"The kitchen and all its drama have found a home on television, but what about great kitchen novels? We have George Orwell's *Down and Out in London and Paris*, but besides that, the great books about the people and places that make your food tend to be nonfiction. . . . Orwell wrote that about his experiences working in Parisian kitchens as a *plongeur*, the guy who does all the dirty work. Simon Wroe, in his debut novel *Chop Chop*, gets hired for a somewhat similar position. . . . e, but The Swan's kitchen, full of 'hagg͏͏͏͏͏ ͏ring about an ad in the classifieds or a t ͏ had come from nowhere and would go ͏ *hop* a great kitchen novel. From describi͏ o the over-

all rhythm that goes into making every plate of food, Wroe (who has worked as a chef in London) makes this ugly world delicious." —*Flavorwire*

"Simon Wroe is a former chef, so it's no surprise that he set his debut novel in a kitchen. What is surprising about *Chop Chop*, though, is how little Wroe lets this fiendish little book get bogged down in the details of its setting. It's very much about the chaotic life of a kitchen, but this darkly comic narrative covers so much more, and the result is addictively entertaining. . . . Everything is amplified in this cramped, sweaty little space, but Wroe still leaves plenty of room for the unexpected, the uncomfortable, and the uncommonly funny. *Chop Chop* might be fiction, but the truth of the author's experience shines through. The result is a compelling debut from a mischievous new voice." —*BookPage*

"Savagery and violence are at the heart of *Chop Chop*; in the kitchen, in Monocle's past, and in the relationships between the characters, but, as in a perfectly baked molten chocolate cake, there's also a rich, gooey pool of dark comedy hiding beneath the surface. Despite straying into the realm of sabotage, blackmail, and secret dinner parties serving stomach-churning illegal fare, Wroe's novel makes for fresh, appetizing reading."
—*The Independent* (London)

"Wroe's imaginative metaphors and gritty kitchen colloquialisms are the key ingredients in a story that will appeal to anyone with a taste for the morbid and the whimsical." —*Publishers Weekly*

"A kitchen confessional that makes Anthony Bourdain's and Bill Buford's memoirs pale in comparison. Foodies will like this insider account of the London gastro scene, while others will appreciate a ripping good yarn."
—*Library Journal*

"A brutally funny look at the world of professional cooking. Sometimes the truth is so strange it needs to be sautéed in a pan of fiction."
—Gary Shteyngart, author of *Super Sad True Love Story*

"Furiously funny, fast, surreal, brutal—*Chop Chop* puts a Dickensian supercharge into the behind-the-scenes goings-on of a restaurant kitchen. The heat and the profanity feel painfully real; the prose, masterfully stylized, definitely the stuff of fiction. The vividly drawn characters stay with you for a long time. If *Chop Chop* were a dish, I'd keep craving more."
—Anya Von Bremzen, author *Mastering the Art of Soviet Cooking: A Memoir of Food and Longing*

"If like me, you've ever made your living from restaurant work, you'll recognize The Swan with a comical shiver. *Chop Chop* captures the combustible mix of sadism, gallows humor, machismo, and surprising perfectionism that powers many a professional kitchen. And it's all served up to us in great fun."
—Scott Hutchins, author of *A Working Theory of Love*

PENGUIN BOOKS

CHOP CHOP

Simon Wroe is a freelance journalist and former chef. He writes about food for *Prospect* magazine, art and culture for *The Economist*, and has contributed articles and features to a wide range of publications— including *Private Eye*, *The Times* (London), *The Guardian* (London), *The Telegraph* (UK), *The Independent* (London), and the *Evening Standard*. He is thirty-two years old and lives in London. This is his first novel.

CHOP CHOP

SIMON WROE

PENGUIN BOOKS

PENGUIN BOOKS
Published by the Penguin Group
Penguin Group (USA) LLC
375 Hudson Street
New York, New York 10014

USA · Canada · UK · Ireland · Australia
New Zealand · India · South Africa · China
penguin.com
A Penguin Random House Company

First published in the United States of America by The Penguin Press,
a member of Penguin Group (USA) LLC, 2014
Published in Penguin Books 2015

THE LIBRARY OF CONGRESS HAS CATALOGED THE HARDCOVER EDITION AS FOLLOWS:
Wroe, Simon.
Chop chop : a novel / Simon Wroe.
pages cm
ISBN 978-1-59420-579-8 (hc.)
ISBN 978-0-14-312700-0 (pbk.)
1. Restaurant—Employees—Fiction.   2. Cooks—Fiction.   3. Fathers and sons—Fiction.   I. Title.
PR6123.R64C46 2014
823'.92—dc23
2013028135

Printed in the United States of America
1 3 5 7 9 10 8 6 4 2

Designed by Gretchen Achilles

ACKNOWLEDGMENTS

I am greatly indebted to the professional chefs and restaurant kitchens that have chosen, at one time or another, to suffer my employment and let me into their stories. This book would not have been possible without them.

In my research, two memoirs of special value were *Heat* by Bill Buford and *Hotel Bemelmans* by Ludwig Bemelmans. E. T. Laing's book *Fakirs, Feluccas and Femme Fatales* provided me with the laws of the Kanun.

Of the family and friends who have shone their enthusiasm on the project, I am particularly grateful to my mother and father, Ann and Malcolm, and to my brothers, Tom and Pip. Also to Mark Studer, who instilled in me a love of food that I have never shaken, and to Dan Franklin and Bea Long, for their wise counsel through the knotty world of publishing.

Will Hammond and Colin Dickerman deserve huge thanks for being the editors of Monocle's dreams, and for so skillfully reining in his excesses. The insight and patience of Sue Armstrong, my agent, has likewise been essential.

Finally, I wish to thank Laura for her love, support and generosity in all things, for the inspiration she offers every single day.

CHOP CHOP

HEADS

They arrive in pairs most weeks, blushing like schoolgirls in the kitchen heat.

Their eyes follow you around the room.

Their tongues loll rudely from their mouths.

Their snouts are rough from rooting.

When you hold one and feel the hair and fat and clammy skin of it you wonder how different a person's head would feel dead in your hands. Sometimes when you pick one up from the peach paper your fingers get stuck in its nostrils, like a bowling ball. Sometimes you can still feel old boogers up there. A strange feeling, that this head must have been alive once, because only a living thing could produce something as useless as snot.

I've heard in fancy places they lather the snouts up and give them a gentleman's shave with a cutthroat razor. Most kitchens use a blowtorch and burn the hair. It gives off a dark smell, which maybe the fancy places won't stand for. We throw ours onto the burners and turn them with tongs until their eyes melt. Then we wrap them in a cloth and carry them over to the sink and wash the char off. We do it gently, like an apology. Ramilov, in one of his letters, says that's what all cooking is: a smart apology for a savage act.

Before the heads are brined and boiled, before they are torn apart at the jaws and the flesh is picked away from the gluey, shaking skin, we cut off the pigs' ears. A respite, I like to think, from the easy listening radio and the catcalls of the chefs. With those long rubbery ears gone the heads look naked and sort of comical, like two old men at the end of the pier who lost their toupees when the wind picked up.

I can't stop looking at how they were killed. I don't want to look. It makes me sick to my stomach. It makes me think I might not be cut out for this after all. A deep, yawning cleaver gash in the middle of each forehead, pushing the animal's tongue through its teeth with the force.

One chop. Sharp and swift.

One for each of them. Chop chop.

I suppose it's something I'll get used to in time.

Now into the pot with you, piggy.

Into the brine, swine.

PART I

TO START

Ramilov was in the fridge and he would stay there until he knew better.

"I want everyone to know," said Bob, dragging one fat sausage finger across the room, "that people will be punished for their lifestyle choices here."

"You can't ban love, chef," Ramilov said from inside the walk-in.

"I fucking can," said Bob.

And in that moment I personally believed, yes, Bob could ban love, he could do anything he pleased. Because when he said it, standing at the pass with a clutch of checks in his sweaty fist, in a pause between the demands for ravioli or onglet or potted prawns right fucking now and the constant haranguing and the whole "Generalissimo Bob marshaling the troops" act, Bob was the most powerful thing in the world. He was a giant, a blue whale, a Leviathan. On his colossal flanks we were mere flies. Bob was king of the universe. Thou shalt have no other god but Bob.

I say was, because even kings can topple. Even gods fade away. And as surely as one falls, another rises in its place.

"Get to the point, Monocle. We don't want your fucking life story."

This was Racist Dave's warning, or literary suggestion, when he heard I intended to write about what happened to us: how we suffered under Bob, how we were drawn past him into that cruel and shadowy world, how we made the mistakes we did. Dave said he didn't trust me to "make a beeline for the blood and gash," that I yakked on too much. It is true that I am different from my fellow chefs, one who is not afraid to employ words like *Leviathan* if the situation demands it. Apparently Dave considers this a stain on my character, for he has appointed himself as a sort of editor to me. I didn't mind showing him the drafts, I said, but let me handle the grammar. Dave said he didn't care about that stuff anyway. He just wanted to make sure I didn't get carried away with things, a continuation of a long-standing kitchen policy toward me. For many months, my mouth was barely open before the rebukes started flying: *You speak like an arsehole*, it has been observed. *Stop babbling or I will stab you in the face*—that was another one. *Monocle is always so fucking proper*. Well, pardon me if that is a crime.

"Monocle" was Dave's idea after Bob, with unconcealed glee, informed the kitchen of my English lit degree.

"Fucking university," said Dave. "That explains it."

Dave was proud of the nickname without good reason. Students do not wear monocles. I suggested he was thinking of a mortarboard. He suggested he was thinking of unspeakable acts with my mother. A rude man, Racist Dave, and an obtuse one. Whatever its origin, Dave used the nickname a lot, often several times in the same sentence, and with his sponsorship "Monocle" soon passed into the kitchen's common parlance. Only Ramilov was reluctant to use it. He was angling for either "An Unsuitable Boy" or "An Extraordinary Cunt." He was unhappy about a chiffonade of mint I had done that had bits of stalk in it. Ramilov was also unhappy about how much I talked, which he said, quote, was unbecoming in so shit a chef. And he was unhappy, like they all were, about my speed.

"If you were moving any slower," he said, "you would be going backward through time."

In his recent correspondence, Ramilov seconds Dave's support for the project I have undertaken. He too wants a little light on the dark heart. Often he asks that I tell this story with "the greater truth in mind" and reminds me of a promise I made under some duress. I have not forgotten it. But how can we ever hope to explain what we did without retracing our steps back to Bob? Without Bob there would be no Fat Man, perhaps no Ramilov either. Bob brought us all together. Without his tremendous cruelty, what would I be? He made me grow up fast. He forged my resolve. Here, in these early memories of The Swan, I can see all the markers for our decline and resurrection, our past and future trials; all the creases of character and thought that brought us to a single moment in time.

Ramilov was in the walk-in now because of a peluche, or the lack of a peluche. Bob had a grouse on order for 38 and it was customary, essential even, for there to be a peluche of watercress, or failing that some sprig of dressed greenery at the very least, in a salad bowl on the pass in front of Bob but not wilting under the lights when all else was plated up and ready to go. Bob called for it late and sometimes he did not call for it at all, but it was Ramilov's duty to know when a peluche was required and to have it standing by, and it was Ramilov's fault if it were not.

"*Peluche!*" came the cry for the grouse on 38 as the jus was sliding round the plate and the steam was rising into the hot lamps. No answer. No "*Oui, chef!*" Not a sniff.

"*Peluche!*" Again the cry. But only silence in reply. Everyone in the kitchen looked over to Ramilov's section because all cresses and leaves and salad gubbins were his responsibility, all cold starters and some of the hot ones too, but Ramilov had vanished.

Service hung in midair. The crashing and twisting and shouting and rushing and searing and flicking, the whole carnival, seemed to freeze. Every man there—and the quiet dark-eyed girl in the corner too—drew in his breath. The burners and ceiling vents and clamor of the KPs all faded into the background. Boorish laughter and snatches of conversation carried from the tables, it was so deathly still. Voices of people who were not chefs could be heard in the kitchen, and that is the worst sound in the world.

"Maybe he's in dry store, chef," offered Dave.

"Or the yard, chef," suggested Dibden.

But Ramilov was not in the dry store or the yard. Nor was he in the wine cellar or the downstairs office, and the game of Where's Ramilov? only ended at the bar, where Bob found him talking to the waitress with the button nose, halfway through his joke about how to dance to elevator Muzak. Bob was displeased, you could say, and expressed his displeasure to Ramilov in language that made the waitress's little nose turn white. Ramilov maintained that dinner services would come and go while this thing he had with what's-her-name here would last forever. He clicked his fingers and smiled at the girl.

"Really, though," he said. "What is your name?"

Alas, he did not hear her reply. Bob had hooked a finger into his collar and was yanking him back through into the kitchen outlining his intentions to injure him severely and telling him he was in for it now, by god. Ramilov was protesting all the while and even when the walk-in door was shut and the lock was turned you could still hear him arguing dimly about free will and the tortuous odyssey of the heart, though the words were mostly lost to everyone but himself.

Dave had sent the grouse to 38 before Bob could come back and make him plate it again out of spite, and Dibden had jumped from desserts over to Ramilov's section and was banging out plates to keep on top of the checks piling up on the grabber above the pass. From time to time he glanced anxiously at the fridge where Ramilov was trapped. It was not so pleasant being locked in there, 4 degrees Celsius in the pitch dark, trying not to knock over anyone's mise or you'd be in more trouble when you got out and might have to go straight back in again. Bob liked to call it his isolation tank or, if he was in a straight penal mood, the cooler. In the six weeks Ramilov had been in the kitchen he had made that fridge his own.

"I should be charging that cunt rent," Bob muttered, returning to the pass to make his announcement about lifestyle choices being punished.

Dibden was starting to look increasingly nervous. Those dolorous features, always suggestive of struggle, darkened as the pressure grew. His long hands were fumbling and his movements were becoming leathery and he was saying "Sugar . . . sugar . . ." under his breath like a nervous twitch. Dibden was of the opinion that cuss words made Mary Magdalene cry and it was wrong to make any woman cry, especially a woman as nice as Mary Magdalene.

"What is it, chef?" Bob had noticed his unrest and was glowering at him from the pass.

"I'm out . . . I'm out of lemon halves, chef," he replied.

The lemons were in the fridge with wicked Uncle Ramilov.

"Monocle," Bob said, "stick your massive face into that walk-in and ask him to pass out some lemons. Don't talk to the cunt or you'll be in there with him."

"Yes, chef."

I didn't know how to ask Ramilov for lemons without talking to him so I knocked on the door and kept my mouth shut.

"I know," said the voice of Ramilov. "Lemons."

I unlocked the door and opened it a fraction and a sinewy hand poked out with four lemons in it. Truly, it was the ugliest hand you ever saw. The kind of hand that comes up out of a grave at the end of a zombie film to claw dumbly at the sky. Every scar and welt and burn on it stood out against the whiteness of the skin. It was a crazed stump of hair and damaged tissue. Next to those smooth lemons it looked ridiculous. I held my cloth out like a hammock and the ugly hand dropped the lemons into it.

"Treats for fatty," Ramilov said in a sinister whisper only I was close enough to hear.

The hand disappeared. Ramilov was referring to Bob, of course. Bob was not just a giant in his power over us; he was an actual giant. Six foot four and as wide as a cheese trolley side-on, with blubber tight all around him like his body had started to melt and then decided halfway through to cool and set instead. Bob had worked hard on that fat, gorging himself on anything that he could get his hands on, his sausage fingers never far from a tasty morsel on an outgoing plate, always slick with the saliva from his greasy, slobbering mouth. His face was permanently red, as complexions of his standing and blood pressure often are. It looked like the swollen heart of an ox.

"Check on! Two chaka, one bass, one rav! Mains away!"

"Oui, chef!"

Bob turned and rigged the new check on the grabber in front of Dave, who was on sauce. With heavy-lidded eyes Dave studied the run of checks. The effort for him was in the reading, not the cooking.

"Five minutes on those two chaka, yeah?" he asked the quiet dark-eyed girl in his northern drone.

"Yeah," she said briskly, pulling two plates off a shelf above her head and dropping breaded cubes of pig's head terrine into the deep fat fryer.

"Coming up on that rav same time, yeah, Dibden?"

"Yeah." Dibden was rooting around in the service fridge. "Where does Ramilov keep everything in here? There's no order."

"Four and a half," said Dave. He banged a skillet on a burner.

The machinery was whirring again. Dibden huffed and puffed about Ramilov's setup, it wasn't human, no one could work like this, where was the remoulade anyway, why didn't he keep the gribiche out.

"Because it will spoil, you prick," Ramilov said from the walk-in.

It was just past eight on a Wednesday evening in late November. A reasonable time to lock Ramilov in the fridge. Several days of piercing winds and slushy rain, the kind of weather that turns Camden Town into a very low and uncaring sort of neighborhood, had put people off going out. The dining room of The Swan was half full; upstairs was shut. No office parties tonight. Forty on the books. A handful of walk-ins at most. But at some point in the next hour the dessert checks would start coming in from the early tables while the late tables were still ordering starters and mains, and Dibden, doing the splits between Ramilov's section and his own, would find himself greatly inconvenienced. "To sink like a sack of shit" is the correct terminology for this phenomenon, as Racist Dave often reminds me. Everyone was praying that Bob would change his mind about Ramilov and release him before the evening turned unpleasant.

"Fuck!" shouted Ramilov. "Something just bit me in here."

Bob grinned evilly from the pass.

"You found my little Christmas present, chef."

"Booboo?"

"Guess again."

"What *is* that?" shouted Ramilov.

"I let the lobsters out," said Bob. "And I took the bands off their claws."

He chuckled at the thought of Ramilov locked in a box with the lobsters angry and liberated, snapping at his ankles in the dark.

"If you damage any of them, chef, it's coming out of your wages." Ramilov's response was brief but heartfelt.

Whatever you say about Bob (and many things have been said), he was a master of cruelty. The man had an appreciation for a wide variety of punishments—spoons left on the burner until they were white-hot pressed into flesh, dish cloths soaked and twisted for whipping—though his favorites were the ones that messed with the mind, the psychological tortures. He would let a finished plate fall from his fingers and smash on the floor if he didn't like one aspect of the ensemble and sometimes for no reason at all, except presumably to teach us that life was as arbitrary as it was cruel. The fridge was quite a custom of Bob's. By forcing the other chefs to cover for HE WHO HAD SINNED, also known as Ramilov, it skewed the emotions and allegiances of the entire brigade. When the prisoner finally emerged, shivering and blinking into the fluorescent light, sympathy was in short supply. The sentence proved the crime. The lobsters were a new touch, but that was Bob: the man had an exquisite grasp of suffering; he was an innovator of pain. It was a rare genius that unleashed the lobsters before looking for the victim.

Aside from Dibden, who bore The Mark of Bob upon his hand and who, despite that, still defended him when the insults were swarming over pints in O'Reillys, there was not one man or quiet dark-eyed girl or kitchen porter in the place who did not hate Chef Bob. No one fought with him as Ramilov did, but I knew how they felt even if they never told a soul, because I am the commis. In the kitchen the commis is everywhere. Like a fly, he sees things that no one else sees, things he is not supposed to see. It is his job to buzz this way and that, from fridge to section to dry store to pass to wine cellar, fetching and prepping and chopping things the other chefs do not have time to fetch and prep and chop. I am the one beside the chef whom Bob is bollocking, topping up his herb bundles. I am the one sweeping the yard, unnoticed, when plots are being hatched over cigarette breaks. I am the one in the dry store trying to pull a fifteen-kilo sack of flour over your weeping body. I am the third who walks always beside you.

You are the one with the puckered arsehole—I can hear Racist Dave now—*fucking hurry up and tell the story.*

The bass was on the pass. The two charcuterie boards were up. Dibden, who had found the ravioli, scooped them from the chauffant of swirling jade water and slid them into a pan of butter browning with fried sage, tossing gently.

"*Where's that fucking rav?*"

"*Ten seconds, chef,*" he shouted, still tossing.

"If you toss that again, Dibden," said Bob, "I'll toss you."

Dibden stopped tossing and swiveled round with the pan to plate up, straight into Shahram the KP, hunched over the pot bin looking for washing up.

"*Backpleez!*" Shahram cried in fear and pain.

"*Sugar!*" Dibden shouted, managing to steady the pan. "Say '*Backs,*' Sharon! Always say '*Backs*'!"

"Fucking *chaud behind*, yeah, Sharon?" said Dave.

"*Backpleez,*" said Shahram again. He was terrified, dancing nervously from one leg to the other like he needed to piss, eyes goggling out of his skull, face twisted with incomprehension. Shahram's English was very respectable as far as it went—chauffant, moulis, ramekin, gastro, small spoons, more black pans, potato, backpleez, fucking chaud—only it did not go so far. He knew what a chinois was but not a chair.

Camp Charles, the maître d', stuck his head around the door.

"Table of eight just *entered*, chef."

This prompted roars of disapproval from the chefs, who had figured on a quiet service, a quick clean down and an early night. Curses were extended in the direction of Camp Charles.

"Out of my kitchen, gaylord," said Bob.

Camp Charles gasped in mock indignation.

"*So forceful,*" he mouthed. In the dining room he was charm itself, infinitely accommodating, always discreet. Away from the front of house he spoke entirely in sexual suggestion. Everything out of diners' earshot sounded like the purest filth. He could make the word *plate* sound so nasty you wouldn't have one in the house, let alone eat off it. "Give me two *beef,* darling," he would deadpan from the other side of the pass. "Where's my *meat,* you *bitch?*"

Now the ticket machine squawked.

"*Ça marche desserts! Two pear, two claf, one ganache! On and away!*"

"*Oui, chef,*" Dibden answered forlornly. It had started sooner than expected.

"What's the matter, chef?" sneered Bob.

"*Nothing, chef!*"

"*Monocle! More plate wipes!*"

"*Parsnip puree top up! In my tall!*"

"*Drop chips for an onglet!*"

"Little shit!" Ramilov cried in pain from the fridge.

The ticket machine exploded into a fit of squawks, refusing to be silent.

"The big 'un from Wigan," said Dave.

"*Ça marche! One chaka, one fish board, three rav, two bass, one onglet, one eel, ONE LOBSTER! All together, on and away!*"

"*Oui, chef!*"

"Monocle," said Dave, "ask Ramilov for a lobster. Now."

I knocked on the fridge door.

"I know," said the voice of Ramilov. "Lobster."

I cracked open the door and the sinewy zombie hand emerged again. Its index finger was extended, a little accusingly, I thought, in my direction. A large midnight-blue lobster was hanging from the second knuckle by a pincer.

"Take this one," Ramilov said in a tired voice.

The lobster had a good grip. As I struggled to pry it free, Ramilov called me many dark and impossible things. Then the door was shut and he was heard no more. Ramilov should have blamed Bob for his misfortune, or the lobster at a push, but who is it that gets the blame? The commis receives a lot of grief that is not deserved.

"*Coming up on the big 'un in seven!*" Dave shouted.

"*Oui!*"

Dibden was sweating now, heating sugar for a caramelized pear dish in one pan while he poured clafoutis batter into two floured ramekins and slid them into the combi oven. He pushed aside Dave's confit Jerusalem artichokes.

"Desserts on top," he said. "That's the rule."

"Such a pastry boy," said Dave.

Dibden ignored him and leaned across his section for the unsalted butter. He threw a few cubes into the pan of sugar and shook it, then turned again and grabbed three pears from his service fridge, quartered and cored them and chucked them into the pan with the caramel. One piece fell on the floor.

"Do another one, chef." Bob was watching from the pass, a wolf outside a pig's house.

Dibden rushed back to his service fridge, scrabbled for another pear, cut one quarter out of it and cored it sloppily, then threw it into the pan with the others. Now he was behind. He spun back to Ramilov's section, searching madly for the smoked eel mix, couldn't find it, cried out, then saw it, tore the plastic wrap from the top of it, grabbed two spoons and a clean plate from the rack beside him and began quenelling furiously, scraping the edge of one spoon into the hollow of the other, molding the mixture into a smooth oval. His hands were starting to shake. The kitchen watched him silently. Bob's eyes were hungry and sly.

"Your pears," said Dave.

Dibden ran to the stove and caught the caramel as it started to smoke, strained a glug of brandy into it and shook again, then swung over to the combi, tried to fit the pan on top but couldn't because of Dave's artichokes, muttered something under his breath and slammed them in below. Someone on the big table told a joke and there was a sudden burst of laughter, trailed by other subsidiary jokes and eddies of laughter. You couldn't hear what the jokes were in the kitchen, and you couldn't see the kitchen from where the table was, but the merriment seemed somehow, indisputably, directed at Dibden and his current misfortune.

"Dibden," said Bob, "that's not the plate for the eel."

Dibden looked about wildly.

"What is the plate for the eel, chef?"

"You should know that, chef," said Bob.

Please, everyone was thinking, please let Ramilov out.

"The square one," said Dave.

Dibden scraped the eel mix off the round plate and back into the container and started quenelling again. His hands shook so bad the mix was flying off the spoons, spilling all over the worktop.

"Three minutes on the big 'un."

Dibden remembered something and dropped the spoons and ducked back into the service fridge and pulled out a gastro of ravioli.

"How many rav was it?" he asked weakly.

"Three," said Dave. "In three minutes."

Dibden peeled nine raviolis from the gastro and ran over to the chauffant, where he dropped them into a waiting spaghetti basket. The scuzzy water swallowed. In the fifth circle of hell, sighs of the sullen frothed the vile broth. Then he slid back to Ramilov's section and started quenelling again.

"Don't forget that ganache, Dibden," said Bob. "I want everything looking fucking soigné."

Even a much-maligned commis such as myself could see by the way Dibden was comporting himself that things were going to end badly for all concerned. I was praying for Ramilov to be released. But you could not beg Bob; he was not a merciful man. You would have been handing the ax to the executioner, so to speak. Sometimes my hatred for Bob burned so fierce I feared he would see the flame and decide to stub me out once and for all. But Bob was so big and I was so small it seemed he did not notice me, and so I kept on with my bowing and scraping and burning and plotting, waiting for my moment, dreaming of a way that we, the chefs, might end him.

"*Check on! One rav, one pigeon, THREE EEL! That's four rav and four eel all day! And there's another dessert check on and away!*"

"Having fun, chef?" Bob asked Dibden.

"*Oui, chef,*" replied Dibden, who was not.

"How long on these first fucking desserts?"

"Two . . . Four minutes, chef."

"Four minutes?" Bob snarled. "You all right over there, chef?"

"Yes, chef."

"You look like you're going down."

"No, chef," said Dibden. You could never admit you were going down.

"D'you want I defrost the Russian?"

"If you want, chef," said Dibden, desperate.

Bob sighed and made a flick at some crumbs on the pass. He toyed with the idea, letting the kitchen squirm.

"All right," he said at last. "Let the cunt out."

I went straight over to the walk-in, unlocking it as fast as I could. Ramilov had been unnaturally quiet since the lobster. He was only in chef's whites in there—perhaps the cold had got to him. It was hard to know exactly how long he had been inside; time in the kitchen was like time nowhere else; no law governed its leaps and crawls. For a moment I thought I would find him curled up in the corner, a poor lump with lobsters feeding on his eyes. I opened the door, just a wedge at first. There was only darkness. No sound. No sign of life. Had Bob finally done it? Had he made good on his promise and killed Ramilov? I pulled the door open farther and the light clicked on and Ramilov pushed past me and out into the bright swelter of the kitchen looking almost all right, as almost all right as he ever looked, his arms outstretched like a homecoming hero, triumphant.

"Hello, bitches," he said. "Did you miss me?"

2. TRIAL

How did I end up here, chopping carrots on the back bench and daydreaming about destroying Bob? Ramilov and Racist Dave have often asked what a person like me was doing in a place like this, though perhaps in words less civil. This job, you should know, was not something I ever wanted. I took it when I was two months behind on the rent and the landlady cursed me in Portuguese whenever we passed on the steps. *Filho da puta, pentelho, good for nahting, polícia will know.* Dear Mrs. Molina, a study in black and gray. Stately, though prone to a quiver about the jaw when money was mentioned. Sweet Mrs. Molina, who had absorbed the colors and textures of the city until her look was solid concrete and her face like the back of a bus. A slight, short-sighted woman, you would never have expected the foul things that came out of her mouth in reference to your humble narrator. Aggressive in her cleaning too. Forever spraying that funereal air freshener. Squirting it through the keyhole of my room while I dozed, as if I were some monstrous bug. Gregor Samsa choking on the stench of roses.

It was not much of a setup, yet I had become sort of attached to this grimy Regency town house, its rubbish-strewn grilles out front protecting a rubbish-strewn basement, its scuffed gray door declaring NO JUNK MAIL OR FLYERS, the sooty shadows above. My bolthole lodgings, partitioned along one side to accommodate a minute communal bathroom, bore the pleasant wear and tear of previous tenants. Scuffs, burns, a bad stain on the carpet where someone might have sacrificed a goat. Perfect for the downtrodden creative.

Freckled mirror, chipped sink—all mod cons. Well-appointed view of strip between church and betting shop. Fragrant landlady seeks discreet and respectful professionals. No junk males or fly-by-nights.

Before The Swan, I would sit in an ancient armchair that smelled of hand lotion and read novels from the charity shop downstairs. Or I would watch, through the peeling sash window, the sleepless criminal bustle at the shabbier end of Camden Road. The chewed-up faces and hands cupped for change, the weathered ski jackets with bulging pockets, the stiff, brisk, kneeless walk. *Use so-and-so's mobile, tell him I want three, two white, tell him yourself, I've got no credit, hurry up.* The waiting, the fading into the background until they were no longer there, only to reemerge implausibly in a later act, like the crew of a Shakespearean shipwreck.

So often was I peering out of that window, observing the tireless tide of barter and exchange, I had begun to name these lurking, fading characters. There was Rosemary Baby, a tiny woman with the face of a very young girl and a hoarse, emaciated voice that rose, singsong, over the hubbub of the street. She had parted me from five valuable pounds on my first day—a labyrinthine sob story about catching a bus to hospital and a stolen handbag, *please mister serious mister honest to god mister*—and cackled now whenever she saw me. That well-dressed gentleman strolling leisurely through the crowds, hands behind his back, I knew as This Charming Man: the embodiment of good manners when he asked you for money, the devil himself when you refused. On the corner of a side street, a man I thought of as The Last Lehman Brother sometimes slept in a blood-red Porsche.

The person who most obsessed and terrified me, however, was a gnarled Rastafarian with one dead white eye who conducted his business from outside the betting shop. I called him One-Eyed Bruce. Oh, I had considered showier nicknames (Cyclops Dread?)

but the last thing anyone wants is a mythology they can't live up to. Best Burger opposite the Tube, for instance, whose grisly patties had me memorizing the Portuguese Lord's Prayer in Mrs. Molina's latrina. Such names are breeding grounds for disappointment, among other things.

Sometimes Bruce's solitary working eye, roving this way and that in search of customers or Babylon, would light upon me watching from the window above and he would crook a long, skeleton finger up and shout, loud enough for the whole street to hear, "*I see you, pussyclot! Come down, pussyclot!*"

On these occasions I would duck back out of sight, draw the curtains from a kneeling position and turn my attention to other matters. My reflection, for instance, which loomed back at me, wide-angled, morose, insistent without ever being so good as to tell me what it insisted. A face like this was how mirrors got broken. Peering into the tarnished oval over the little washbasin I would look for stray hairs growing between my eyebrows that I could tweeze or blackheads on my nose I could squeeze, and wonder, with no small allowance of self-pity, why One-Eyed Bruce had found it in his heart to hate me so. Why, with all this choice, all this competition, was it me he chose to torment?

Why too had I chosen Camden Town? Scene of a million teenage rebellions, where the anticonformist slogans are printed on sweatshop T-shirts, where punks eat in fast-food chains and the Rastas have only mixed herbs in their pockets. All these bold statements diluted. The iconoclasts posing for pictures. A muted, contrary, theme-park place. Yes, Camden Town was next to the zoo with good reason. It was a parade of denied impulses, of things reduced to type, of lions that could not remember how to hunt. It upset me to see it. Yet here I was at the center of it. What was I denying? What petty rebellion was I staging?

But I was not familiar with London and its neighborhoods when I arrived, a competent degree from a mid-table university to my name, a great career as a writer no doubt just around the corner. Camden Town was the only place I could remember. This was my excuse. I recalled a place of cheap food and sanitized vice, a place whose risks were minimal despite its claims to the contrary. The side of Camden away from the market, however, the side where Mrs. Molina's lodgings stood, was different. Its sleaze was real. Faces of young girls loomed out of doorways at me, calling to me sadly as I scurried past. No time, I would tell them, proud of how polite, how charming, I had been. No time for gratification, my dear. Not all of us are burdened by such needs. Some of us have loftier concerns, like the book I would soon begin to write. Besides, I had no money.

Money, or the lack of it, was how I ended up at The Swan. For a while there is a pleasure in economy—stealing toilet paper and ketchup packets from pubs, traveling the city on foot, obsessively tracking down the cheapest portion of chips, the most basic cup of coffee—but it soon becomes miserable trying to resist every tickling urge. By evening you are exhausted. You lie on your bed like a man with smallpox, aware of all the spots of want and desire about your body, listening to the cries of the city outside your window as other people realize those desires, unable to move because the slightest motion will inflame those itches a hundred times over. . . . It is a horrible condition. Not a pure form of poverty, but certainly its suburbs. Otherwise I believe I might have frittered away the rest of my existence in that overstuffed armchair. Given time the human creature can get used to just about anything, and my natural laziness had allowed me to adapt quickly. Even the *pentelho* and threats of *polícia* and *pussyclot* had started to take on a reassuring familiarity. But I needed money, needed it to avoid going home, so I put on my secondhand overcoat and went looking for a job.

What would I do? I was not against work. That was not my position at all. I considered work a very fine and noble endeavor. I just didn't want to do it myself. And under no circumstances would I do a McJob, because that's where he always said I'd end up. I toyed briefly with the idea of being a street cleaner. They earned good money, apparently. I could sweep the city and watch the people and let my mind wander. But a council gig would take an age to process: my scant savings were already gone and the hock money for my hi-fi was running out quicker than I had expected. Moreover, I could hear his mocking voice as my mother relayed the news that his youngest was sweeping the streets. *A cleaner? In a pinny or mopping turds?* I did not care too much for hospitality either. My poor brother had taken the sociable genes. But I reckoned, up against it, that I could stomach a few months behind a bar.

So I papered the public houses of Camden with my brief but thoughtful CV (three weeks as a script prompt for a university production of *Julius Caesar*; hobbies include walking and "being in nature"), and I waited. The Swan was the only place to reply, which made me immediately suspicious of it as an establishment. Why would anyone want to hire me? I had no bar experience, no kitchen experience, no waitering experience, no silver service training. I could not pull a pint. I could not serve a roast potato. I had a dissertation about modernist discourses between the individual and the city that a tutor had said was a good attempt. I had an A-level in medieval history and a hole in my trousers I couldn't afford to get patched. Any business that needed me had it pretty rough. In truth, I was already a little disappointed in The Swan before I got the job.

The Swan is on a street immediately parallel with Camden High Street that gets none of its big sister's traffic. Unless you have business on that street, or you take a wrong turn, you would never visit it. The market in Camden attracts the crowds of Italian tourists with Day-Glo backpacks, the teenage drug dealers and indie stragglers; the high street draws in the local shoppers and the area's more discerning bums. The Swan's street attracts a different type of pedestrian. The people you find on this street are guests at the boardinghouses at its far end, semirespectable places with names like The Star of Alexandria or Regency Court. You might see the odd door-to-door salesman in blazer and brown shoes still pounding the pavement, a foot-sore dinosaur in a digital age. Or you might spot a vagrant looking for a quiet place to shit or shoot up. With a favorable wind, this last kind might stumble upon an alleyway between a car park and a shabby terraced house halfway up to Mornington Crescent. When it is not being used as a toilet, this is the trade entrance to The Swan.

Here I arrived one morning in October, my hiking boots swinging by my side in a plastic bag, unsure what the hell I was doing. On the phone the man had told me to bring sensible footwear and knives if I had them. I didn't. My landlady did not permit me to use her kitchen because I was a *pentelho good for nahting*, but I wouldn't have even if I could. I was quite busy enough with all my street watching and novel reading and blackhead squeezing without worrying myself with cooking. Furthermore, some of Camden's kebab shops are very well regarded.

There was no answer to my knocking at the back gate in the alley. I found it was open, and wandering through into the yard I saw trays of stew and sauce and carcasses of mysterious meat covering every inch of a wooden picnic table. Deliveries of vegetables were stacked as tall as a man on the ground. Huge stockpots steamed like restive volcanoes. In front of me, sounds of music and conversation carried from an open doorway covered by a chain screen. I stuck my hand through this portal and stepped inside.

It was a small room packed to the gunwales with food and equipment and containers and cutlery of every imaginable kind and shape. Alien species of sieve and colander hung from the hooks in the ceiling next to gigantic ladles and slotted spoons and what looked like instruments of medieval torture. There were strange metal trays wrapped so many times in plastic wrap that the contents were opaque. On a long buckled shelf that ran the length of the left-hand wall, cookbooks and recipe cards sat beside a hi-fi of such age and decrepitude it seemed unkind to use it. A sign next to a large, glowing switch said, IF THIS IS OFF THEN WE ARE ALL FUCKED. A pair of stainless steel work surfaces stretched away from me, with stainless steel fridges beneath them, and where they ended another began, running across the top of them to form a giant π symbol. Behind that, at the far end of the room, a line of metal stoves pumped out a wall of heat I could feel from where I stood.

Two men were standing side by side in front of these stoves, prodding at pans on the burners and then turning to their work sections to chop and weigh and mix.

"I went to that Gourmet Burger the other day," one man was telling the other in flat northern tones. "All right, but what's gourmet about it? I still say you can't beat a Nando's."

"Nando's?" said the other man, stooping to read the measuring scales on account of his gangliness. "It's not chicken."

"Of course it is," said the first chef. "What is it, then? It's not fucking Poulet de Bresse, but it is chicken."

"Hello," I said. "I'm here about the job."

Both chefs looked up in unison. Their eyes were ringed with shadows, their faces gray and hollowed. I thought I saw, just possibly, the tiniest hint of amusement somewhere in their features, a dark and unknown joke slowly tickling them.

"You need to see the chef," said the northerner hereafter known as Racist Dave. "Have a look in the bar."

The taller man, who would later introduce himself as Dibden, nodded in sympathy or agreement.

They did not stop working, but their eyes followed me past the walk-in fridge and out of the room. The bar and restaurant area was at the end of a narrow corridor. To the left was a small box room stacked with rice and flour and pulses, the dry store. To the right were stairs leading to the cellar. Down there, I would soon learn, was the office where Bob reviewed the closed-circuit television system to see if his chefs were stealing from him; also the alcohol reserves, and the enormous chest freezers for storing meat and occasionally less reputable items.

The main room was a handsome old-fashioned saloon bar with frosted windows, dark chocolate wood and a sad, lingering smell of old beer and spilled coffee. Small taxidermied animals—a pheasant, an otter, a mangy-looking fox—sat around the room on high plinths. Above the till was a silver statue of a swan that looked expensive. In the middle of this room, his great bulk balanced ridiculously on a stool at the bar, Bob, my future tormentor, surveyed a sheaf of bills. He looked glum. His head, part bald, part shaved, stuck out of him like a bollard. Gravity had gathered the fat on his face into folds around his jowls and throat but left his cheeks and nose sheer. Eyes fell fast from that face, but they got a soft landing. His own eyes were large and liquid-dark, feminine. He regarded me unhappily as I explained why I was there.

"There's no bar work going," he said, "but I need more bodies in the kitchen. People keep leaving."

He looked at me as if daring me to say something about it. I remained silent.

"What do you know about The Swan?" he asked.

I knew it was a poem by Baudelaire. We had studied it in my modernism class.

. . . *its feet*
With finny palms on the harsh pavement scraped,
Trailing white plumage on the stony street,
In the dry gutter for fresh water gaped.

But something told me Bob would not appreciate the allusion.

"Not a lot," I said instead.

Bob dug about in the sheaf of papers and drew up my CV.

"This says you've got an English degree," he said, studying it briefly, "but it doesn't say anything about kitchen work."

I agreed. Bob looked at me. He was still unhappy, possibly bored.

"Let me see your hands," he said.

"Sorry?"

"Your hands. Let me see them."

Slowly I raised my hands to Bob. He looked and I looked with him. And I saw for the first time the soft frowning palms and feckless fingers, the creamy, pampered complexion of the skin. I felt ashamed and a little cheated. Could these really be mine? Bob grunted and held up his hands. They were huge misshapen clods, scorched and scarred by every blade and element known to man. Around the thumb and forefinger of each hand the skin was calloused and dead, the color and texture of pumice. On his left hand, a livid gash that ran the length of his heart line winked beneath a soggy blue Band-Aid. The tip of the middle finger had been sliced clean off. He turned his hands over leisurely, continuing the show. On the back of his other hand, a purple scar the size of an egg marked some old traumatic burn.

"These are the hands of a chef," he said. "The hands say everything."

I was to learn that Bob did not give a spit about a person's accomplishments or curriculum bloody vitae. His preferences were altogether more violent and arcane. Bob wanted soldiers, psychopaths and masochists. He wanted people who would do and suffer anything for him. To each new recruit he would raise his enormous fists, slowly twisting them open and closed, and show off the throng of welts and bruises and scars, scars within scars, that ran across them, as if each one were a medal. As if each wound made him a better man.

Bob had seen my hands and he knew what I was not, but if I could hack it in the kitchen, he said, I could still be of use to him. Fifteen minutes later I stood before him in a knackered T-shirt and a pair of Bob's enormous checkered chef's trousers, the elastic exhausted totally, held up with a plastic wrap belt. The ensemble was completed with a dusty black chef's cap and my hiking boots, last worn for a camping holiday in the Lake District where he (the other arsehole, not Bob) couldn't get the fire lit and drove off to the pub in a strop and we sat there for hours in the cold damp dark, waiting for him to return.

"Just the basics," Bob told Racist Dave. "He's green."

Dave looked at me. As if, in that outfit, there could have been any doubt.

"Fucking hell," he said. "I need backup. I need a chef de partie."

"I've got one coming in on trial next week," said Bob. "Russian name. Ramadov or something."

"So I'm on seven doubles," said Dave.

"Looks that way," Bob grinned. "I'll be in the office."

"You," Dave turned to me. "Do you know how to wash salad?"

I thought I did. I didn't. I removed too much of the dandelion leaves and too little of the watercress stalks. My hands kept going numb in the water. The salad came out of the spinner too wet and had to be put through again. I thought I knew how to chop onions too. Again, it turned out I did not.

"No," said Dave, already losing patience. "This is how."

He cut the onion in half and pulled out the root, then cut through it lengthways, in five-millimeter intervals, without cutting all the way, then drew the blade through horizontally, again not cutting all the way, then turned the onion half ninety degrees and brought the knife down in five-millimeter intervals once more, reducing the onion to a dice. He scrapped the cut onion deftly into a container and returned to his section.

It looked easy enough. I put the knife to the onion and cut downward in intervals. So far, so good. Growing in confidence, I turned the blade on its side and, holding the onion tightly, drew the knife decisively across the onion and straight into my waiting thumb. Dave's knife was very sharp. It sung through my flesh so cleanly that for a moment I thought I had got away with it. Just a nick after all. But then the blood began and no amount of persuasion would stop it. And as the blood drained out of me, the panic poured in. It was the day my brother found the wasps' nest all over again.

"I didn't ask for red onions," said Dave, looking over. This, I now realize, was very witty for him.

He sent me off to the dry store to look for a bandage, but the wound would not stop bleeding and the bandages kept slipping off. I have never been good with blood: since my brother, whenever I see the slightest cut I worry that it will not stop. I worry, and I am reminded of things I would rather forget. I was struggling with all of this when the quiet dark-eyed girl came in. She stood in the doorway, legs planted slightly apart, her eyes fixed upon me. They were extraordinarily clear and piercing, those eyes, possessed of a striking light up close. I noticed her nose had a strong Roman accent, not particularly ladylike, but certainly not ugly. The smells of the kitchen, the sweat and grease and smoke, seemed to part around her. She traveled with a lighter scent. Sighing, she extended a hand toward my huddled, bleeding form. I was feeling very wretched and thought this a great kindness.

"Thank you," I told her.

"Move," she said curtly. She pushed me aside and pulled a tub of mustard off the shelf. Then she left. A dark moment for the ego. There would be some vigorous tweezering in the mirror later.

A ferocious-looking man came in carrying a stack of pots. He regarded me in silence. Clearly, the look on his face said, You are something that does not belong here, a large and useless thing taking up valuable space, a beach ball in a bomb shelter. He put the pans down in a corner and left. I was left alone again to wonder what I was doing in this kitchen full of hard and hateful people. I didn't even like cooking. But a short while later the big silent man returned and threw me a plastic glove. It clung snugly to my damaged hand and, though it quickly filled with blood to resemble a set of diabolical udders, I found that if I angled my hand downward I could avoid bleeding all over the establishment. I thanked the kitchen porter, whose look had softened to a grim pity, pity for the useless object in the middle of a war.

Eventually I pulled myself together and returned to the kitchen

where the half-chopped onion sat mocking. I finished chopping it
and announced to Dave, with some pride, that the job was done. It
had been touch and go for a minute, indeed that vegetable had almost destroyed me, but I had won in the end.

"I don't want one onion chopped," he said. "What am I going to
do with one fucking onion? Do the whole bag."

The whole bag? It was the size of a turkey. I struggled to lift it.
No one in their right mind needed so many onions. That day I realized I knew nothing about food or cooking. Also, more worryingly,
nothing about people or communication. Months of fiction in that
armchair, and years of studying it before that, had left me dealing
with life at reading speed. Conversations passed me by while I was
still formulating a response. People here dealt with one another so
firmly, with no concerns for the nuances of situation. Violent, ugly
scenes were followed by swift resolves. A passage of action Dosto-
evsky might have covered in thirty pages was done and dusted in
thirty seconds.

A strange and terrifying world. A world for my brother, not
for me.

Later, as I was peeling garlic on the back bench, Dave asked me to
step into the yard with him. I was surprised to see it was dark out,
and I realized I had lost track of time. While I had been inside, the
day had drifted into a cool, starless night. The moment in the dry
store aside, I had not thought once about tweezering the spot between my eyebrows until I made it raw. At some point it had rained.
The bench and empty oil drums were damp with small archipelagos
of water. There were still trays of stew and pots of sauce and boxes
of vegetables sitting about, but they were different from the ones
that had been there that morning.

"Smoke?" He held out a cigarette. "You will," he said when I refused.

He lit his cigarette and tugged grimly at it. I had the job if I wanted it, he said. The commis post at The Swan was mine to turn down.

I felt the muscles in my back tightening as they cooled. I felt the arches of my feet dull as lead. I felt my hand on the frame of the kitchen door, gripping it tight, primed to pull myself through it or push myself from it and move in curt, decisive movements, to move like a chef. I looked down at my numbed and scarred hands. Not the same soft and feckless examples I had walked in with that morning. I thought of his face, sneering at the suggestion that I, Mr. Useless Streak of Piss, could get a job when he had never been able or willing to do likewise. I thought of that sneer falling clean off when he heard that not only had I got a job, but a man's job: I was a chef. By *he*, of course, I do not mean Bob. I mean my father.

"I think I will have one of those cigarettes," I said to Dave.

3. RACIST DAVE

acist Dave was the best chef in the kitchen. He has insisted I mention this prominently in my recounting. In front of the stove he was a master: his sauces never boiled, his toast never burned, his steaks were always just so. He moved faster than the naked eye, and could remember twenty checks at a time. He knew the order in which every element of every dish of every check needed to hit the pan or the water or the oil or the grill for it to be cooked perfectly. All this is true. However—and I can picture his low brow falling even farther as he reads this—there are other things to mention if this is to be a proper introduction to the man. Yes, he worked twelve moves ahead, like a great chess player, but he could barely read or write. He had left school at fourteen to work in kitchens and left the North four years later when he boshed a lot of drugs he was supposed to sell and roused the ire of some unsavory types. They would kill him if he ever went back, he claimed, so he was stuck in the South with all the South's overpriced lager and dry gash and faggy blokes. Dave hated the South and talked, gloomily and often, about how boss the North was by comparison. North till I die, he would say, which was true, but not in the way he meant it.

The only thing Dave liked as much as the North was musicals. He loved the swirling, seamless orchestration, which was how a kitchen should work but never quite did. He loved the colors and the razzmatazz, the voices poised at the edge of flight waiting for the soaring strings to lift them off the ground (my words, not his). He loved the outpouring of emotions, for he was a pretty phlegmatic sort himself and constantly amazed at how much feeling could be wrung from a simple lyric or a basic chord progression. Only a handful of occasions in life had the passion or the honesty of musicals: football matches, kitchens, certain "political" rallies. Dave loved them all. Being tuneless was no hindrance to him: he sang along to all the big numbers in his low Mancunian drawl no matter how busy the service. He knew he wasn't a poofter, so there. In Manchester his mates had struggled with the idea of a skinhead who quoted *Chitty Chitty Bang Bang*; in the South he had no mates to curb his enjoyment of song and dance. Even Bob tolerated it, and had made Dave's CD of the Broadway musical *Wicked* the mandatory soundtrack for Sunday lunches. It was generally agreed that it possessed the right spirit of triumph over adversity. Yet Bob's moods were mercurial, and too much musical grandstanding could make him suddenly furious. To make Dave furious you only had to mention foreigners or get him drunk.

The fucking Pakis are coming through the Channel Tunnel, he would announce over the third or fourth pint in O'Reillys. *We've got to close it now before we're overrun.*

Dave had a problem with Pakistanis and Bangladeshis, with African people and Chinese people, with Muslims and Jews and Indians and Eastern Europeans and French. He had been water-cannoned while trying to destroy a Turkish kebab shop at Euro 96, and had put a brick through the window of the Salford branch of Blacks before he realized it was a camping store. He did not read newspapers as that meant entering a corner shop and that meant giving money to terrorism. He wore his ignorance with pride and could get touchy if people tried to divest him of it. *I know what I know*, he would say if he suspected attempts were being made to educate him. *Prove me wrong*, he'd say, and then not listen. He was conscientious to a fault in his bigotry and inclusive of all minorities in his hatred. It was for these reasons, and others too numerous to mention, that he was known as Racist Dave.

He might have been an idiot (Dave, confused by this construction, says there is no "might" about it; for once we agree), but he could cook. That Neanderthal forehead held the secret to beautiful, light-as-air brioche and silky risotto. He created immaculate, complicated curries while propounding his theory of compulsory deportation for darkies. He prepared sublime turbot and lobster dishes for a hundred people, then went home, ate Pot Noodle, scratched his balls and watched *Mary Poppins*. Dave was a bundle of contradictions. Bob said he should see a shrink when he got a day off, but it was a throwaway statement since Bob did the rota and did not like giving Dave days off. It meant he had to work more hours himself. When Dave was off the whole place fell apart. Bob destroyed the walk-in looking for things and disappeared upstairs to visit his terrible wife when he should have been doing the mise.

Apart from his visit to Gourmet Burger when he had silently picked holes in every single aspect of their operation, Dave had not had a day off in three weeks by the time I arrived. Dibden, all nerves and Anglepoise articulation, was little help. Ramilov was yet to join us. Dave was, in effect, a slave, albeit one who swaggered into work in sunglasses and a gilet and considered slavery to be a good thing. He worked slave hours because people kept leaving. Bob said it was because these deserters were not true chefs, they couldn't hack it in a real kitchen. Dave, who was a true chef, was inclined to agree. But people kept leaving because Bob was a horrendous arsehole and only Dave was stupid enough (or "talented enough," as Dave calmly suggests) not to notice it.

So the kitchen struggled on, carried by Dave and the enormous Polish KP and the quiet dark-eyed girl on fryer whom Bob patronized for being a woman but did not bully for the same reason. Other chefs had come and gone with the seasons, I learned. The good ones never stayed once they saw how the place was run, and so the place was left with the rest. Dave has often told me what sorts these chefs were. Scruffy chefs, alcoholic chefs, agency chefs, arrogant chefs, flamboyant chefs, dull chefs, nervous chefs, troubled chefs, idle chefs, bored chefs, bullshitter chefs, young chefs who didn't know, old chefs who couldn't learn, chefs who spoke only French, chefs who played with knives, chefs who spent all their time trying to diddle the girls or boys behind the bar, chefs who dealt drugs, chefs who stole from the petty cash and sneaked steaks. Dave said that most of them didn't deserve to be called chefs. They were what you would call cooks.

A kitchen always got the workforce it deserved and The Swan, with its dim view of life and food and people, got only Dibdens, sincere but ill-suited, or the journeymen: haggard faces at the back gate inquiring about an ad in the classifieds or a boardinghouse window, oddballs who had come from nowhere and would go to nowhere, who had worked in thirty different places but never more than a couple of months in any one, telling the same war stories and the same old jokes each time, making the same enemies and the same mistakes and leaving in the same huff over some miscommunication or unfair accusation or murky rumor.

These men—the hopeless, slack-jawed cases are always men— form the backbone of the catering industry, though you will never see them on television or grinning from the cover of a cookbook. They are not champions of local produce or heroes of a certain gastronomic movement. They do not believe strongly in freshly ground black pepper or artisan bread. They are guided only by their indifference toward cooking and their antipathy toward everything else. Every year or so they will move to another town or city to "make a new start," telling anyone who will listen that this time will be different, that they have always wanted to live in _____ and never liked _____ anyway. You may see this type of chef smoking outside a cheap but still overpriced restaurant in, say, Victoria on any given day. A broken individual, leaning against the wall with ugly, lightless eyes and a miserable face that long ago stopped wondering where it all went wrong.

Dave, who has somewhat sniffily approved the chapter thus far (it fell off after the first couple of sentences, in his opinion), claims I had the attitude, if not the experience, of these chefs when I started at The Swan. In those first few months I was ready to quit every day. I hadn't known much about kitchens, and I was shocked that people could treat one another in such a way. From the moment the working day began the abuse was constant. The only way you learned anything in a kitchen, it seemed, was through humiliation, and the only way you asserted yourself was through sniping. The bitching knew no bounds. Not toward the customers, as people imagine—it's not as if anyone came into the kitchen and said, *Those people are a nightmare, spit in their food for me.* That never happened. It was all among the staff: everyone was constantly carping about everyone else. A snatched roll of the eyes when someone wasn't looking, a muttering under the breath when they stuck their heads into their fridges for something. Insults were thrown around openly too, at everyone except Bob and the quiet dark-eyed girl. It was no secret who hated whom.

A special brand of malice, however, had been earmarked for me, the new boy. In French, this position is called the commis. The English do not have their own word for it—"bitch chef" would be the most accurate translation. I was the person at the very bottom who did all the jobs no one else wanted to do. The onion chopping, the lemon squeezing, the garlic peeling, the cheese grating, the mopping, the labeling, the herb picking, the cleaning, the lugging, the repacking, the fetching, the shit. This chef at the bottom has no rights, no independent thought. I was a machine, turned to whatever use the other chefs wished. Today I was a cheese grater. Tomorrow I would be a potato peeler. Whole days passed when I did nothing except clean the fridges or wash mushrooms. Once, weevils were discovered in the dry store, and I had to go through every container, several hundred of them, sifting through the different flours and grains in search of these microscopic pests. If we received an order of game birds, the chances were that I would be the one sent out to pluck them, the feathers catching in my eyelids, the coldness of the yard impinging on my delicate health.

By the law of the kitchen, all blame lay with the commis. It filtered down: the chef shouted at a section leader who shouted at me and I, having no one beneath me to shout at, was forced to absorb it. And once I had acquired that scapegoat reputation I could do nothing right. Worse, I think I began acting up to their expectations. I made stupid, clumsy mistakes. I became paranoid. When I came back into the kitchen from elsewhere it felt like the other chefs had just finished talking about me—a crazy suspicion, because there was nothing they couldn't, and didn't, say to my face. Not that I ever said anything back. That was the first rule I learned at The Swan: never challenge the person in charge. They could make your life more hellish than you could imagine. This, incidentally, is true of families as well as kitchens.

On bad days I felt as if one more thing would push me over the edge. Most of the time though it was merely a sense of confusion—about how I had ended up in this place, and how I could dig myself out. One thing I knew for certain: chefing was an awful job done by ingrates and arseholes, shit-out-of-luck people unqualified to do anything else. Every part of the job was awful, even the cooking, which was only about 2 percent of it. It was backbreaking, terribly paid, dangerous, bullying, stressful, ridiculously houred, freezing, scalding, finger-slicing work. Surely this wasn't me. A man who had read the great works, who had spent time in the company of Shakespeare and Joyce. As I reminded Racist Dave, I had an English literature degree.

"Well, it's not making you peel those spuds no faster," he said.

Potatoes? Double negatives? It wasn't me. I wasn't me. My body smelled of the kitchen: a creamy, rotten vegetable matter smell. My sweat was spicier. Hours after I had left I could feel the heat of the ovens continuing to cook me. In the mornings I felt poisoned when I woke. The skin of my fingertips was so ringed with permanent dirt it looked like wood grain. No matter how much I scrubbed I could not get it clean. In the few waking hours between shifts I would stand at my washbasin in my little bolt-hole room and scrub and scrub like Lady bloody Macbeth. But of all the agonies of being a chef, none are so painful as the legs. You are standing the entire time, for sixteen or seventeen hours straight. I don't know how beefeaters do it, or soldiers outside palaces, but I have never got used to it. When I was not scrubbing or asleep I lay in a torpor upon my bed, my legs buzzing bluntly, watching beadlets of rainwater gather on the electricity wires outside my window, slowly getting fatter until they fell.

The tiredness, and the stress of having to get up and go back regardless, soon eclipsed all else. I lost track of current affairs and the outside world. I barely even noticed the announcement of a new Tod Brightman book. Really, I barely noticed. Who cared that he'd already published his second book, at the age of twenty-three? I was too busy with work to think about that overhyped young nobody, that two-bit Amis whom I, at some unknown juncture, had made my literary nemesis. And those late-night missed calls from my father, they also somehow passed me by.

After two weeks of this I had tried to phone in sick.

"You don't get sick days," Bob informed me. "Get your fucking arse in here now."

Many times I imagined telling him I was quitting.

Bob, I am leaving to take up another job offer.

Where? Who would take me?

Bob, I am leaving to concentrate on my blossoming writing career.

My last weeks would be unbearable.

Bob, I am leaving to look after my ailing mother.

But I didn't want to talk about my mother. Let's leave her out of it.

Bob, I am leaving to look after my ailing father.

As if I would. I'd rather stay here with Bob.

Sometimes, while shredding cabbage or cutting carrots into batons, I found myself tracing the corridors of my parents' house in my mind without wishing to or knowing why, visiting each room in turn and looking in, testing little parts of my memory to see how faithful it was. I remembered there were hardly any pictures on the walls although they had lived there since before I was born, and I remembered the damp, unlived-in smell the house always had when you came back from anywhere, like it had been rotting quietly in your absence. I thought the glass on the front door might have been striated. I remembered the large oak tree that towered over the back garden and cast the living room in perpetual darkness. In the kitchen I saw the spot where I had dropped a pint of milk on the floor and he had chased me and cornered me with blows. I felt the carpet between my toes as I made my way up the stairs to the bedrooms. I was cold, remembering, because my father considered heating an unnecessary expense. Betting on the 3.30 horse race at Newmarket, apparently, was another matter.

On the landing I could see the rest of the cul-de-sac, with other cars parked in front of other drives. *Cul-de-sac* sounds fancy, but it is actually a medical word for a cavity near the rectum. Then I am at the top of the stairs and there is the bathroom off to the left and my brother's room directly in front, untouched ever since. My fingers, reaching for the door handle, feel metal—it is the cool blade of the knife, the face of the mandoline, and I am back in the kitchen once more.

However lousy and tired I felt, Racist Dave had it worse. Dibden was barely able to look after his own responsibilities, so Dave had been working seven-day weeks since the last chef de partie's breakdown. Christof had been a decent chef, competent and quick on the checks, and Dave had hoped he was going to last. But something in him was blown: his nerves were shot by years of services and close calls; he coiled in fear every time Bob spoke. He would stand mournfully at the fryer, looking out into the restaurant with such profound sorrow that a few diners complained he was putting them off their food. He was thirty-four, which was too old for a jobbing chef de partie in a pub kitchen. Dave said if you weren't sous or head chef or in a place with a star by the time you hit thirty, something had gone wrong. Maybe it was drugs or prison or that journeyman transience, maybe you just weren't up to scratch. Whatever it had been in Christof's case, he was marked from the start. I didn't meet the man, he was gone three weeks before I arrived, but Bob's hatred of him was well documented.

I never trusted him, he would say. *Did you see his hands?*

Dave had seen Christof's hands, and they were beautiful. Lilac white, with carefully manicured cuticles, as unblemished as Italian meringue. They were, as Mary Poppins would have put it, practically perfect in every way. They were impossible. How could a chef, in and out of ovens and freezers and brine, in daily commune with knives and graters and mandolines, keep his hands like that? It was witchcraft. Bob could not conceal his disgust. He tried to burn them every chance he got, brushing past him with hot pans or trying to push his hands into the lamps when he was plating up. He covered the inside of Christof's service fridge with pictures, torn from his terrible wife's magazines, of painted nails and feminine fingers. He urged him to chop faster, hoping to push him into an accident with a blade. He worked him like a dog, yet Christof's hands remained annoyingly, agonizingly perfect. Christof's mind was not made of the same stuff, however, and he flipped halfway through a Sunday lunch, storming out of the kitchen when Bob poured boiling gravy on his knuckles in an apparent slip of the hand. Dave found him sitting on the curb halfway down the road, sawing back and forth, glassy-eyed, oblivious to the traffic.

"Don't worry about that fat prick," he told Christof. "Just push on."

But Christof did worry. He would work no more at The Swan.

Before Christof there was Nick from the agency who never cleaned down and talked more than he chopped. Before Nick there was Leon, who turned up late and took three sick days in two weeks and had an excuse for everything. Before Leon there was Pavul, who had poured the old fryer oil into the pumpkin soup in an act of either immense stupidity or brilliant sabotage. Before him, no one could remember. There had been so many. And before and after every one there had been Dave pulling hundred-hour weeks, a cart horse, a machine. He acted like a superstar, but he felt like a heel. No matter how mad or bad the soon-to-arrive chef with the Russian name was, Dave had already decided to hire him. Bob wouldn't care. He would run them into the ground regardless. Besides, after The Swan's run of chefs, how much trouble could this new guy be?

Things were grim before Ramilov arrived, but it took his turning up for the rest of the kitchen to realize just how grim they were. Ramilov rode in on a storm and brought a reckoning. He welcomed wolves in sheep's clothing and bit sleeping dogs. He picked roses by their thorns. He washed his dirty linen in public. He let butter melt in his mouth. He taught grandmothers to suck eggs and thought it proper. He danced all night but paid no fiddlers. He lay down with beasts and got up with fleas. He dug his own grave. He foamed at the mouth when anyone said "organic." He built a house for virtue and vice and made them live together. He praised his own broth. He was at war with everybody and everything. And it is now a matter of recorded fact that he was the instigator, if not the architect, of Bob's demise. Ramilov, in those letters where he seeks to alter and correct these pages, has confirmed as much to me.

Before Ramilov, Bob was unruffled and unconquerable. Untouchable. He pulled the wings off flies like us for fun. When Ramilov arrived Bob tortured him too, as was his custom, but Ramilov made him do it to keep order, not for recreation. Ramilov got under his skin. (This, Ramilov writes, is one thing I've not messed up in the telling so far. He is keen for the world to know his gift for chaos and dissent.)

I had been at The Swan only a week when Ramilov came for his trial. My salad washing was not much improved. I was holding my hands under the hot tap to bring the feeling back when who should appear at the back door but this dark and stocky stranger, our hero.

He slid seedily through the fly chain and stood watching us with a grin pasted across his face, like he had just transgressed in some way and greatly enjoyed it. Without doubt he was a strange-looking creature. His bulbous head flared outward at his shaved temples and bulged off the back. His arms hung limply at his sides like a decommissioned robot. His jaw jutted in some secret mischief. He looked like a skull. He said nothing.

"You must be Ramilov," said Dave.

The stranger kept up his silent grinning act. An optimist might have said he seemed "engaged in contemplation." Crazy was more like it.

"You all right?" asked Dave.

The stranger looked at him with pinprick pupils set in eyes that never blinked.

"I'm all right," he said finally. "It's the others, isn't it?"

"What others?" said Dave.

"Yeah," said Ramilov. "What others. Good one."

Racist Dave looked confused.

"I'm Dibden," said Dibden, leaning over to shake his hand.

"You look a bit like the bloke from Coldplay," said Ramilov.

"Really?" said Dibden, flattered.

"Yeah," said Ramilov. "You've got the same kind of dickhead face."

"I like him already," Bob announced from the pass. And he liked Ramilov even more when he saw his hands.

"Fucking horrible," he told the rest of the kitchen later. "And his eyes? He looked as if he was going to kick off any minute."

Ramilov was the chef Bob had been waiting for: a dyed-in-the-wool psycho, a universal soldier. At this stage in my recounting Dave thinks I'm building Ramilov up too much. Perhaps—the man had his faults, and I'm not condoning what he did—but it's true that at the time Bob thought Ramilov was the answer to his prayers. He should have been more careful what he wished for.

Actually, the storm took a while to muster. Ramilov was the great white hope when he started at The Swan in the second week of October and it wasn't until he was locked in the walk-in with the lobsters in late November that his fall from grace was complete. In those intervening weeks I did not see much of our new champion. The kitchen was too small for a five-man brigade to do mise en place, there were only four work surfaces, so on busy shifts when there was a full team I was sent to work in the plonge until I was needed for service.

The plonge, or dish pit, is the twilight hovel of the kitchen porters. It is a small square grotto of pots and pans and plastic containers. Its ceiling is dark with grease and elaborate blossoms of mold. Its walls are lachrymose. In the middle of this cave, cloaked in a swelter of steam and spray, one or both of the KPs work tirelessly, hacking at the caked char on the bottom of the pans, scraping the stockpot sump, blasting cutlery with the high-powered jet that hangs in coils above the two stainless steel sinks, hauling great trays of washing up to and from the industrial cleaner, sorting plates into giddy, groaning stacks. The Swan plonge adjoins the kitchen, down two steps that are usually taken in a single frantic bound, with no door or screen between. Everything that happens in the plonge can be heard in the kitchen. It is obvious when Shahram is chanting or when the enormous Polish KP laughs his unnerving piggy laugh. But in the plonge the noise of the kitchen is a muddle. The KPs know only that for every moment they breathe there are dirty pans and plates building up and that they must work faster, always faster.

The enormous Polish KP was called Darik. His biceps were bigger than a man's head. He had a trick of crushing a potato while he looked at you that gave everyone the willies except Shahram, who was terrified and confused by everybody in the kitchen except Darik. The two men communicated via some pidgin language only they understood, Shahram jiving around the bigger man with his goggling eyes and skittish, edgy dance while Darik threw his massive head back and squealed, huge and delighted like a hippo being cleaned by an oxpecker bird. The chefs believed that Darik harbored an awful secret. He had never mentioned he had a secret, and the kitchen had decided, collectively, that this proved he had one. Dibden, who trumped everyone else for sheer terror of life, said Darik had murdered a man in Poland. This rumor quickly spread, with accessories. Bob heard he had killed a drunk in a bar brawl by breaking his skull with his bare hands like it was a potato. Dave was certain he had pushed the woman he loved from a bridge when he found out she was sleeping with a black man. Ramilov claimed Darik was a pastry boy who murdered nothing except Gloria Gaynor songs.

"*Can you give me this wishywashyback, Darik,*" he'd singsong in a lousy Baltic accent as he slung pots into the plonge, "*or are you maybe too much gay?*"

Ramilov, we would learn, was very much taken with homosexuality and its abuses. He fondled everyone in the kitchen except the quiet dark-eyed girl, whom he judged correctly was not a man and would stab him if he tried. He cupped his hand to each man's arse as he passed or rubbed their earlobes between his thumb and forefinger when they were trying to tell him what to do. The ultimate prize for Ramilov, however, was "the gooch," the line of folded skin between a man's balls and his anus, and he would sneak up behind the working chefs and porters and try to reach in between the forest of legs to stroke this rare treasure whenever he could.

"Its medical name is the perineum," he informed Dibden as Dibden shied away from his molesting hand. "Its sensuality is renowned in many cultures."

Dibden was not interested in its sensual renown.

"He's trying to violate my bum hole," he complained to Bob.

"You whine like a little fag, Dibden," replied Bob, who at this stage was still in love with Ramilov.

Poor Dibden, the lowest of the low before I arrived, recipient of all abuse. My appearance had moved him up in the world—away from drab commis tasks, to the glamour of pastry and larder—though it had done little to change people's attitudes toward him.

Every day Ramilov was in the kitchen his confidence grew. He was a Molotov cocktail of filth and kink who was actually from Albania, via Birmingham, and not Russian at all. There was no man in the brigade with whom he would not simulate buggery, no waitress he did not try to flash. His hoarse, delirious crowing carried over the hubbub into the plonge where I labored; an excitable bragging about what ladyboys could do with their cervixes and the collective term for waitresses and how many drugs you had to take to shit yourself. His motto was "It is easier to ask forgiveness than permission." His speech was peppered with strange slang and snatches of rap.

Man dun' know, I'm straight cake.
Bitch give brain, work hard at the ramp shop.

This was what I knew of Ramilov in the first few weeks. Tall claims and short bursts of obscenity, grammatical anomalies and promises of sodomy.

No doubt this confession will delight Ramilov, but here it is: in those early days I resented him. No one questioned his place in the kitchen. He had the swagger and bluster of a chef. I worked hard, I stroked no gooches, yet my approval rating was a solid zero. And though I had been there longer and could spell pigeon correctly on the prep labels, Ramilov instantly asserted himself as my superior and tormentor. He called me "Bumfuck" even after I had explained that that was not my name. When I prepped vegetables he made jokes about a family reunion. Once he sent me to the dry store for "a long wait" and would have had me looking in there all night if Bob had not needed me to grate horseradish. Worst of all, he accused me of being useless on purpose.

"Just leave if you don't give a shit," he told me in the walk-in one morning, less than a month after his arrival.

That I, who had sweated so much for this place, should be told I didn't care by a clown who spent his days groping arses: it was almost more than I could stomach. And the other chefs would chuckle as he ordered me to chop flour and fillet whitebait. Would they be laughing, I wondered, if I suffered some hideous accident? If I lost my hand in the meat slicer, that would shut them up. Then they would be sorry for all the things they had said and done to me. They would have to cut their own chips and work overtime and they would see how much I had done for them and they would say, "That Monocle, he really was something after all, and we were too blind to see it." And the tears would run down their faces at the injustice of life.

That's what would happen: I would be cutting ham one day and one of them—Ramilov, no doubt—would come by with a shout of *"Behind you with a knife!"* and prod me with his finger, another favorite joke of his, and I would leap forward in shock and somehow bring my wrist into contact with the exposed whirling blade and it would slice clean through, squealing as it found the bone. My poor hand would be hanging on by a flap of skin, blood spurting everywhere, the gray tendons inside pulsing and flailing like headless snakes. Such senseless tragedy. And I so young and promising. Rachel Parker, the girl who had spurned me at university (who had by chance walked into The Swan that very moment) would see the error of her ways and throw herself upon me in grief. Dibden would faint. Ramilov would for once be silent, and as white as a sheet. I would be stoic, of course, and refuse to blame anyone for the misfortune. In certain versions of this fantasy I finished slicing the ham one-handed, to rounds of rapturous applause.

These were the noble tragedies I dreamed of when I was sent to chop carrot batons and blitz parsnips in the plonge where the walls wept and the air was muggy with bad spores and the floorboards of the first-floor restaurant buckled above your head as fat full diners shuffled in their seats, where there was no quiet dark-eyed girl to look at, where the pipes kept on with an almighty whistling like they were about to explode while Darik and Shahram cooed at each other in their strange nonsense tongue. *Backpleez. No you backs. Backpleez. No you backs.*

Ramilov was invincible in those early days, and if he had limited himself to tormenting me and Dibden and the KPs he might have remained so. But Ramilov had no notion of the lines he should not cross. This was demonstrated by his shameless carry-on with Bob's terrible wife and his friendship with the tramp who was Bob's sworn enemy.

If Ramilov were here now he would tell you that a restaurant's regulars are its best customers. If Bob were here, however, he would say a fellow can show up at a restaurant with straw in his pockets and a powerful urge to release his bowels as often as he pleases but until he buys something he is not a customer. (The Fat Man, with his "give me one of everything" attitude, was Bob's idea of a model customer, extravagant in his tastes, generous with his tips, ceaseless in his appetite. Though ill rumors surrounded him, and all who had served him shuddered at his name, his money was the right color.) But the tramp came every day to groom his reflection with a gap-toothed plastic pocket comb in the darkened glass of the restaurant windows while the diners inside tried to ignore him, and he liked to use the public alleyway at the back of the premises as his personal toilet. Bob had been chasing the tramp away since the restaurant opened. Ramilov committed the cardinal sin of supplying him with napkins.

Bob's wife, who lived with Bob above The Swan, was another matter. She didn't have a job because she had enough things to worry about, like why did the Internet sometimes not work in their flat and when was Bob, whom she called Booboo, going to come upstairs and cuddle and where had her yappy Chihuahua, which she also called Booboo, got to now. Several times a day she would clomp into the kitchen in her heels to ask the whereabouts of her Booboo, meaning either the dog or her husband. The dog was an evil-tempered midget that sowed misery far and wide in its relent-less pursuit of food. It broke out of the flat at any opportunity and made its way down the stairs on its stubby little legs to snap at scraps in the plonge or nibble at the edges of trays left out in the yard. It destroyed the mise and snarled most ungraciously when anyone except Bob's terrible wife came close to it. It was a pest and every chef in the place wished for its demise. "The rude fiend who so yells on souls," Dante said of a similar hound. "Someone should shoot the fucking thing," said Racist Dave.

Each time it got out, Booboo's reign of terror ended only when Bob's wife found it and pressed it to her enormous breasts and administered a blithe, affectionate scolding in the middle of the kitchen while the chefs desperately ducked and twisted around her trying to keep the whole show afloat.

"I envy that dog," Ramilov told her the first time he saw her burying the dog's face in her cleavage. "I can get lost too you know."

Bob's wife flushed and arched her neck indignantly. Her eyes, however, flashed with excitement. She did not come down to the kitchen in boob tubes and wedges just to catch dogs. Bob's wife had a face like a garden trowel, a stupid mouth and spongy, necrotic skin. She was vain and whingeing and fiercely possessive of Bob, and her jealousy toward the waitresses was magisterial and absolute. Bob was her Booboo, her meal ticket, and she would claw out the bright little eyes of anyone who thought Bob could be their Booboo. And yet she saw no irony in coming down to the kitchen in her tiny Lycra outfits and flaunting herself in front of every other man there. Whenever she appeared, Ramilov would howl and paw at the floor and generally act up in a way that was shameful to witness. When she asked if Booboo was ready to come upstairs Ramilov would say yes, thank you, he was always ready for a fine creature like her.

Bob was confused by Ramilov's behavior at first, because his wife was anything but fine. No man had ever expressed an interest before—even Racist Dave, who was joyfully unburdened by standards when it came to women, secretly described her as "Predator with Tits"—and this made Bob suspicious. He began to think Ramilov was taking the piss.

"He should be a gentleman about it," he told Dave gloomily, "and shag her or shut up."

"You should be a gentleman about it and shag her," Dave told Ramilov in O'Reillys, "or you should shut up." It was early November and Ramilov's tempestuous streak was becoming dangerously apparent.

"I can't shag her," said Ramilov, swilling his mouth with bitter. "She looks like a trowel."

"Bob's getting pissy about it," said Dave. "He asked me for reasons to lock you in the fridge."

"I'm not sexually aroused by garden implements," said Ramilov. "Ask Dibden."

"What?" said Dibden, who was trying to pat down a cowlick in his hair and was not listening.

"You've got to shag Bob's missus," Ramilov told him.

Dibden looked worried.

"Does Bob know about this?"

"It was his idea," said Ramilov.

"Oh."

Dibden looked as if he were trying to imagine it: what he and Bob's terrible wife would do by way of small talk, how the seduction would unfold, whether there would be music playing or Bob standing over them and shouting for him to hurry up. He shuddered.

"I can't," he said.

"Go on." Ramilov flicked bitter at him.

"Why me?" Dibden asked. "Why not Monocle?"

"Monocle would take too damn long," said Ramilov, "and he might hurt his massive face. You look like Coldplay. You've got to take what you can get."

"If you don't want her, why do you keep fucking howling at her?" Dave asked Ramilov.

Ramilov shrugged without interest and looked around the pub. O'Reillys was the only place open when the chefs finished work. It was an Irish bar that Nora, the cross-eyed matron of the house, ran like a hostel for inebriates, which was more or less what it was. At the back, where the chefs usually sat, there was a dartboard positioned to test the wits of those visiting the toilets, a few low tables and a jukebox full of folk music from the old country. The bar and Nora stood in the middle of the room where a cross-eye could be kept on the rowdier customers, which was most of them. Toward the front was a raggedy pool table that played to a slant on one corner pocket, beneath a chandelier no one could explain. The pictures, insofar as they fit that description, were covered with cellophane instead of glass so they could not be smashed over people's heads satisfactorily. Every so often one of the regulars would stagger over to the jukebox and pick a song and start to dance and sing. Sometimes they would notice the tired bunch of chefs huddled in the corner and become incensed by the lack of patriotism on show.

Jig, you bastards! Jig! they would cry, or words to that effect, and Nora would tell them to hush the feck up.

"Whose round is it?" asked Ramilov.

"Yours," said Dave.

"Same again?" Ramilov said. "Isn't it past your bedtime, Monocle?"

I did not immediately reply. The talk of Bob's wife had set my mind off in another direction, toward the quiet dark-eyed girl. In the kitchen I could not stop looking at her, out of it I could not stop thinking of her. I had not forgotten how she had pushed me aside in the dry store while I was bleeding, or the profile of her nose up close. No, there was nothing sophisticated about her. Yet something about the way she held herself in this world of men transfixed me. The gravity of bigger planets like Bob did not affect her. Ordinary, forgettable acts seemed important when she did them. Small details stayed with me. That brisk, high voice above the male grunt, so far beyond me, so removed from the earthly concerns of Ramilov and Racist Dave. The cool skin of an upper arm glimpsed beyond a rolled sleeve. (Well, I imagined it would be cool.) A slight sigh as she pulled a pan from the shelf above the stove. Minute feminine betrayals. I wondered how I could possibly approach her.

"Monocle?"

"He's fallen into a fucking coma," I heard Ramilov say.

"I'm not tired," I said. I was, but I did not want any of them to know it, least of all him. I would have liked nothing more than to take my daydreams of the quiet dark-eyed girl back to my shabby room and hold the thought of her, but these chefs thought I could not hack it, so I would show them otherwise. It's been a quirk of mine since childhood. When people talk down to me, I stick my neck out further. When they express their irritation, I buzz louder. When someone suggests they know what's best for me, I do the opposite. Perhaps that's why I never quit in those first horrible weeks at The Swan. I would not give those bastards the satisfaction. It's contrary, I know. It has not always served me well, but I learned it at my father's knee and the habit has stuck. Now I sat upright in my chair and tried to look like my colleagues, awake but dispirited.

"All right," said Ramilov. "A nightcap for Monocle."

He sidled up to the bar, where Nora watched him with experienced disapproval.

"Nora, my dear, we'll have the same again."

She lined up four glasses of slopping amber liquid and pertly took his outstretched money.

"And Jesus Christ," said Ramilov, returning to the table, "why isn't Bob shagging his missus? Why should I or numbnuts here do his work for him? On top of the hours we're already putting in? Treat the worker like a dog and he'll work like a dog, is that it? I'm sick of that shit. That's not man's nature. We did not come into this dark place crying for a shovel or a fucking briefcase! No! We cried out and looked for the nearest breast to clamp ourselves to and by god that's all we would have done ever since if not for the burden of money"—here he sipped emphatically—"the where to find it and the how to get it. . . . We're ruled by the bloody coin, breaking our backs for it. . . . That's the real shitter. That's our curse. I'm already poisoning the choicest days of my life for that fat prick and now he wants me to fuck his wife into the fucking bargain! Fuck!"

The table mulled it over in silence.

"Stop howling at her, then," Dave said at last.

"I'll howl at whoever I damn well want," said Ramilov. "It's a free country."

And soon the beer was gone and it was late and the cross-eyed landlady let us out into the night, calling after us, "*Safe home. Safe home.*"

It might have been a free country, but The Swan was not a free state, and Ramilov's luck finally ran out a few weeks later when Gavin, The Swan's meat supplier, sent Bob the calendar.

Gavin was Bob's comrade in cruelty: his idea of a joke was giving chicken bones to dogs to watch them choke, while Bob liked burning people with spoons. When he came by to deliver something in person or settle an invoice, he and Bob would call Shahram out from the plonge and command him to bring them impossible things. "*Pig eggs now!*" "*More left-handed spoons!*" "*Chicken lips!*" It was rumored that the two men had killed a cow together with a bronze mantelpiece clock belonging to Gavin's mother-in-law. Secretly, Gavin thought Bob was a lousy chef and Bob thought Gavin uncultured. Both men liked to talk about it when the other wasn't around. But each man's sense of superiority over the other seemed only to strengthen their friendship. Men are odd like that.

The calendar, an inauspicious gift, was in the kitchen less than a day, but in that time it managed to almost wreck Bob's marriage and succeeded in destroying what was left of Ramilov's good name (even before peluches or button-nosed waitresses came into the equation). Entitled "The Girls of Upfront Meat," it featured a series of nubile beauties in pornographic poses beside loins of pork and ribs of beef. Bob loved it. He told the kitchen he might have

been wrong about Gavin being uncultured after all. Miss July was
his favorite: a, quote, filthy-looking blonde with a gash like a cheeseburger. Until the beginning of that evening's dinner service Miss
July hung in pride of place on the pastry rack next to Dibden, who
didn't know where to look. No one could ask Bob anything until
he had picked his favorite girl from the calendar and discussed the
shape of her genitals. At seven P.M., when Bob had to write the rota
for next week, he took the calendar downstairs with him. Four
hours later he had not emerged.

Shortly after eleven Bob's terrible wife clip-clopped into the
kitchen demanding her Booboo. Her nostrils flared with suspicion.
Ramilov, unable to resist, directed her to the office under the stairs.

"Go quietly, my love," he told her. "I think he's working."

The ensuing ruckus confirmed that Predator had found the
filthy cheeseburger. For a moment the chefs stopped their cleaning
down and their bluster and listened, rapt, as the banshee cries of
Bob's terrible wife rose up the stairs. It seemed to pierce the very
walls; it was the sweetest music. Racist Dave's heavy eyes flickered.
Dibden looked about to cry. Ramilov turned the radio off so that
no accusation or groveling defense was lost to human ears. But the
happiness was short-lived. After Bob's wife had clomped back upstairs, Bob climbed the stairs alone. His look was murderous.

"Who told her?" he asked quietly.

"Little joke, chef," Ramilov said.

Bob nodded.

"No harm done," he said, forcing an unpleasant grin. He moved
over to the pass and asked Ramilov, quite politely, to fetch him
some beef jus from the walk-in. As soon as Ramilov stepped inside
Bob rushed over and locked him tight within. No word of explanation. He'd made up his mind about Ramilov and his intentions.

From that day on Ramilov's goose was ringed. When he put

something on the stove—a parsley sauce, slivers of almonds to toast—Bob would turn the heat up on it when he wasn't looking, then shout at him when it burned. He sent Ramilov's plates back, saying they looked like shit, when they looked the same as they always had. Any chance he got after that he would lock Ramilov in the fridge, including, but by no means limited to, the occasion with the lobsters in late November where this story began. At first Ramilov was confused and muttered how it was a dirty fucking stitch, but slowly the clouds of 'wilderment parted and he saw how it truly was. Then he stopped muttering and started plotting.

5. THE GREENS

Don't *shit a shitter*. One of the many nuggets of wisdom Ramilov was fond of sharing with the kitchen, now repeated in his latest letter. Apparently it is not enough for these opening chapters to set the scene or take us beyond where we began. I am hiding something, Ramilov writes. Something personal. As someone who has made a career of obscuring his past, he can sense when others are at it. Hence his advice not to shit a shitter. He wants to know what I am not telling. He wants to know, he says, about home.

Home. There's a hard concept to put a finger on. London is not my home. I am not used to its volume, its noise creeping in from all corners. The strains of Mrs. Molina's telenovelas trickling through the ceiling. "*O senhor! Meu coração!*" At night, the drunks in the street below infuriate me. Those boorish fools, resonating on a wavelength I do not understand. I am from a quiet place, a place where learner drivers come to reverse park, where small tangles of wasteland hide beneath the flyovers and pavements run out abruptly. A place of golf courses and other manicured turfs. Proximity to those links appealed to my father, I think. His dream was always to be a pro in the golf world.

It would have happened, he used to say, *if your brother hadn't taken ill the way he did.*

A convenient excuse, though if we are being honest his career had already dried up by the time Sam got sick. Not that I ever challenged him on this point. My father has insulated himself in many layers of denial. Also he is spiteful, with a long memory for acts of treason against him. It is a very tough thing to accept that your dreams did not happen because you were not good enough. And even though he has become a sort of nemesis to me (he sits on the list with Tod Brightman, that disgustingly young novelist), when it comes down to it, a sympathetic urge stops me from picking apart all his fabrications.

My father was a born winner who worked his way down. Great-grandfather Charles, a cattle auctioneer, made a fortune when the railways arrived. The business expanded. Randall's, the Midlands' quality supplier. Ten thousand head of cattle through the door every week. Millionaires with shit on their boots. In his ruddy cheeks and lumbering stride you could see my father's country stock, though he was of the greens, not the fields. A natural with the stick. Single-figure player from the age of ten. A consistent par-frightener. As a cadet, he hit drives so cleanly he did not disturb the tee. His swing was effortless, or so he tells it. At nineteen, when he met my mother at a country ball, he was already amateur county champion. Why should she be impressed? Golf meant nothing to her. But the potential coursing through him was obvious to all. Such people seem to shimmer, like water about to boil.

But grandmother didn't want heat and light. She wanted some security for her only daughter. "A game for idlers," was how she put it. "You can't eat trophies." She sulked through the wedding. The band was too loud. The icing was margarine. He was a dubious character in her eyes, not much in the way of a provider. How did she know this then, of a young man with the easy confidence of one who believes it's all coming to him? A young man, ostensibly, of means: his own car, roofless but roadworthy; his own lodgings, restricted but respectable. To my mother he always behaved the gentleman. When Sam was born my father moved the family out of the bedsit to the new development at Silver Hills. Sponsorship deals took care of half, and there would be more in time to pay off the mortgage. They were so young; they had not had time to accumulate things, or to cultivate their own tastes. So they bought the show home. Right down to the doormat. They used to joke about the photo of the woman that had come with the picture frame on my father's side of the bed. He would kiss the picture good night and my mother would scold him happily.

The neighbors liked them at the beginning, my mother claims. Jean next door was a keen gardener, and she and my mother became quite competitive as to whose borders were the straightest, whose begonias bloomed first. Over the fence they traded cuttings and tips. Jean explained what sort of thing was proper in Silver Hills. The lawn in the center of our garden was always trimmed short and watered every evening. My father began teaching Sam to putt out there when my brother wasn't much taller than the golf club. He never bothered to teach me though. I was left to help mother with her gardening. *Nasturtium. Rhododendron. Love lies bleeding. Chrysanthemum.* She taught me the names. She intoxicated me with language first. Her pruning away at the clematis while I watched father and Sam. A happy scene, from the outside.

But Grandma had a hunch about my father. His easy confidence pinched her.

"See who's laughing when the checks stop," she said, running her hand along the hem of a bedroom curtain.

"Look how he eats," she'd say loudly across the dinner table as my father wolfed down helping after helping. At which Mother would shush her crossly and Father would grin, because there was plenty, and what did it matter what the old woman thought?

But Grandma was proved right. A horrible type of validation, at her daughter's expense. She could take no joy from it. Seven years after the wedding, top three finish on the cards at The Open, a comfortable half million predicted in sponsorship deals that year alone, and my father forgot how to play golf. Forgot, or perhaps remembered too much. Applied too much focus, monitored those delicate, implicit sporting movements too closely. The familiar suddenly became unfamiliar. A misfiring of neurons somewhere in his brain stopped him from converting thought into action. He locked up. Hooked a shot off the tee on the eighteenth. Dropped another shot in the bunker. Then couldn't putt a two-footer to close it. The damn club would not connect with the ball. His impulses denied. Eventually he dragged it wide. A spectacular choke. My father preferred to say he had lost his rhythm. A one-off, he told his young family, but the touch never returned. Even in training his swing was labored; even when it meant nothing he played as if it meant everything. He tried the overlap grip, changed his posture, but his thinking had become too rational, too analytical. Too sensitive. Who'd have thought that would be my father's tragedy?

As he fell down the rankings, the tournaments stopped calling. He ceased playing professionally. For a while he poured his ambitions into my brother and dragged him round the holes, but his expectations were too high; there was anger on both sides. *A Randall never quits*, he would shout at Sam, though that was exactly what he had done. Unable to face his colleagues at the club, he canceled his membership and looked to sell up. But the jerry-built homes of Silver Hills had paled next to newer, slicker developments and my father could not afford to take the loss. So beside the golf course we remained, its cool expansive greens looking in, mocking quietly. Sometimes the sliced shots landed in our garden: a bright white ball sitting in judgment on the lawn. These my brother and I hid. Well, my brother hid them. I watched. I was always watching him, waiting for his lead. Sam had that effect over all the neighborhood children: they fell in line behind my brother, those kids I toiled after.

Weeds came up. Jean stopped talking about what was proper in Silver Hills, started talking about what wasn't. My brother changed to a school where you didn't wear a cap. In the scrublands next to the golf course, previously unanimous decisions about water fights or bike races met with mumbles of dissent. Some gang members suddenly became studious, and could not be extracted from their homes. Our TV got smaller, our family unfamiliar.

My mother, who had believed in my father even more than he had, was forced to take a job at a nearby nursing home. Her girlish mannerisms became tired and prim. She watched the bitterness growing inside my father. His ruddy cheeks blotched and scowling, those athletic limbs setting thickly. That exuberant appetite now selfish, parasitic. The mother's daughter, observing. She watched him become the man he is today. Lying on the sofa eating dry cereal with a bent pound shop spoon (miserly with the shopping yet prodigal at the bookmaker's), cutting his toenails (still oddly vain, my father, though disheveled in spirit), muttering at The Masters on TV, unwilling to find work since that short stint as a double-glazing salesman when people kept asking if they had seen him somewhere before. You could call it a tragedy. But let's be clear: it's not the tragedy of how things change. It's the tragedy of those little parts that stay the same. How what we took for emblems now look tawdry, now spell shame.

6. BOB AND BEYOND

F*ucking soufflé!*"

But these family troubles are ancient history, all behind me. Or a hundred miles away, at least. (At my back now, Racist Dave is telling me to press on. If it is not Ramilov raising editorial quibbles, it is Dave.) On a heaving Saturday evening at the beginning of December—three days after Ramilov, in search of a loving touch, ended up fridge-bound in the company of lobsters—the ogre is demanding a soufflé. Dibden's section is once more sprayed with bits of fruit and crumb and peel. Spilled sauces and dark reductions are clotting like blood. The mint leaves tremble in his hands. His mouth is slack and open, his movements awry. His head folds one way, then the other. There is no use left in him. He is a punch-drunk boxer, a spavined horse, a former umbrella. We watch in silence.

"*I want it now, spastic! Get it on the plate!*"

Originally this account of Dibden's collapse was going to give him the benefit of the doubt: wrong-footed by one horrific service, an unfortunate soul who flew too close to the sun. He has suffered enough, I feel, without having to be tarred and feathered again in these pages. My editors think otherwise, however, and they have offered various unflattering insights, counterclaims, to the effect that our companion's demise was inevitable. Ramilov, in a frenzied missive, suggests Dibden is "less use than a velvet prick." Dave claims that Dibden was the longest-serving commis The Swan had ever had. It was a year, he says, before Bob let him reheat soup. And only when I arrived, when there was absolutely no excuse, did Dibden finally receive promotion to the larder section. By then, Dibden had been at The Swan for almost two years, and still inspired such little confidence that the day Ramilov started he was essentially demoted again, exiled to pastry.

"A raspberry soufflé, you dopey fuck!"

The truth is that the pastry section is seen as an easy gig. A kingdom of one, where scorned but aloof chefs twiddle their thumbs while sauce and larder get shafted. Desserts are an afterthought in most restaurants. As Dave likes to observe, everyone needs a main— only fat bastards *need* a pudding. It is an extravagance. Some nights The Swan did not sell one dessert. So it seemed reasonable, in one sense, for a man of Dibden's capabilities to fill the post. Nor did he require any practice acting scorned but aloof.

"Soufflé, cunt?"

Bob would like a raspberry soufflé that has been on for half an hour. He leans on his palms at the pass, poking his jowly, sweating head beneath the hot lamps to shout at Dibden. Big Bob, in all his petty, weaselly majesty. Cocktail sausage fingers, huffing like a spoiled child. The tyrant. The buffoon. The prick. Where are you now, Bob? Who are you terrorizing? I ask, but I do not want to know.

"Soufflé!"

People say we never should have taken all this from Bob, that we should have walked out the minute he raised his voice to us or treated us in an unprofessional manner. But those people don't understand. In the kitchen, shouting and bullying *is* the professional manner. I know most places don't take it as far as Bob did, but I've also heard tales of worse from Ramilov and Racist Dave, of chefs they have heard about, or other places they have worked. Chefs are

very partial to this game, I have found. It gives them a warm and
cozy feeling about their job while it confirms the horror of it.

Did you hear about so-and-so?

I heard . . .

Total fucking psycho . . .

Apparently at _____ he doesn't let them use the loo during ser-
vice. Blocks the door with a chair. If they piss themselves they just got to
carry on. Two stars, plating foie gras and truffles with piss running
down their legs.

At _____ _____, the chef put specials on that we didn't know
about. I got an order for pig's head ravioli with pickled apple and he
said, "That's you, chef." I had to make the whole thing from scratch.
Get out the pasta machine and roll ravioli. All for one order. It fucked
up the whole service.

He put a commis in the bin and poured fryer oil over him.

Eighteen hours every day. He makes them all take coke to stay on top
of it.

His sous went mad and topped himself, I heard . . .

At _____ the chefs aren't allowed to speak.

I heard he stabbed a guy and had him finish his shift.

I heard he had him clean up his own blood.

The chefs at The Swan told these tales with relish, claiming they
were lucky by comparison. This, they'd say, this was nothing. They
held Bob up against the scare stories and tried to tell themselves he
was a decent sort after all. But they knew also that there were other
chefs in other kitchens not so far away playing the same game, having the same conversation, with Bob's name included.

Or if you left, what then? You traded one hell for another, a different kitchen with another head chef who might or might not be a
cokehead or a drunk or just a good old-fashioned arsehole like Bob.
There were a few good places, of course, where service was all pre-

cise movements and clean surfaces and classical music and the chef never shouted because the shame of being asked why you had done something a certain way or why it was not ready was humiliation enough. These places chefs liked to talk dreamily about.

At Hospital Road every section has their own induction stove under the worktop, with spotlighting like on film sets.

They pass all their sauces four times, till they're superfine.

Everything is made to order, à la minute . . .

He lent one of his chefs de partie the money to start his own place . . .

Everyone sits down to eat together, before service, like a family. It's the rule.

Yet such places were hard to find, according to Ramilov and Dave. There are no universal rules about kitchens and the sadism, or lack of it, therein. It is impossible to know the atmosphere of a kitchen from reading reviews or even eating in the dining room. At this very moment there are hapless, tortured chefs in some of the best restaurants in the city trying not to get their tears in the sorbet. And there are hapless, tortured chefs in some of the worst too.

Dibden, now flailing desperately on pastry, was one of those chefs. Six feet five inches of gangly misery, in his late twenties but with the hard-won sorrow of a much older man. He wanted to wow the world with his cooking, to be a great artist on the plate in the style of Pierre Gagnaire or Juan Mari Arzak. Unfortunately, he was inept.

"Soufflé, cockbreath!"

Dibden was from a rich family, a fact he was desperate to hide though there were too many other things to mock him about for anyone to care. Dave reminds me that in the end this revelation came out of its own accord when Dibden was sincerely, emphatically high on cheap soapy pills and bad chalky coke the night we all went to Mr. Michael's for the first time. His family even had their own legend, Dibden confessed with unblinking, moon-eyed urgency. It was emblazoned in gothic capitals on the back of every chair around the dining table: "SUFFER." Not the "suffer the little children" type of suffer. The "suffer" type of suffer. He had spent his whole life trying to escape that motto. This Saturday in particular, as Bob pummeled his fists in fury, it was fair to say he had failed spectacularly.

"*Soufflé!*"

The evening had begun so pleasantly too. An expectation bubbling over from the afternoon, laughter tinkling off the dining room glass, a curl of cinnamon and clove in the air, the warmth and camaraderie of Saturdays all around. In the kitchen, Ramilov was telling Dibden how shit he was.

"You are so shit, Dibden," he said. "I'm going to get you a Jamie Oliver cookbook for Christmas."

"But I don't like Jamie Oliver," said Dibden.

"That's the point," said Ramilov. "No one does."

"I'll have you know," said Dibden defensively, drawing himself up to his full spindly height, "that I was taught by the best. Chef Ducasse at The Dorchester, no less."

Dibden returned to the tart cases he was attempting, in vain, not to break. The pastry was too crumbly. What was a mild annoyance at five o'clock could be a disaster by nine, but on this occasion Dibden in his great foolishness had chosen to overlook it. Perhaps that family motto hung too heavily about his neck; it seemed he could not resist it. Lurking in his service fridges, ready for the night ahead, a whole catalog of bodged mise awaited him: soufflé mix made with overbeaten egg whites that would explode when baked, a chocolate ganache at least three weeks old, overripe raspberries, underripe pears, quince jam that would not set, fondants that would not rise, and a crème anglaise that tasted faintly but unmistakably of garlic.

His mise en place was a ticking bomb; yet after a quiet lunch, before the madness of Saturday dinner, it looked just fine. I remember learning at university about the Russian formalists, who said, in a nod to Chekhov's gun, that if a man hammers a nail into the wall in the first act he must be hanged from it by the third. Well, Dibden was that man and he had been busy with the hammer.

"I'm going to take your mum on a package holiday to Tenerife," said Ramilov.

"That's not even a nice place," Dibden protested.

"*Exactly!*" shouted Ramilov. "*Exactly!*"

The problem with pastry was that whoever worked it was unregulated. All the other sections straddled starters and mains; they had to work together on every check, which kept them in time with one another. Ramilov couldn't drag his feet over a ravioli order if it was coming up with one of Dave's steaks. Each cog kept the other cogs turning. But pastry was alone in the wilderness.

At five thirty Bob walked purposefully into the kitchen doing up his apron.

"Right, gentlemen, we are entering the power hour. You all know what that means. Chop chop."

He pointed to the clock on the wall above Dibden. One hour before service began.

"You ready, shithead?" he asked.

Dibden did not have a nickname, but there was no shortage of suggestions. Ramilov thought he should be called "Bumble Stumblefuck" but it was too hard to shout quickly. In retrospect I think Ramilov was actually very fond of Dibden.

"*Yes, chef!*" Dibden replied. He paused and examined Bob's countenance to see if he might be amenable to further discussion this evening. Bob liked to say that he was always there if anyone needed to talk about anything, that he welcomed questions and suggestions on all aspects of the operation. Dibden decided to try his luck.

"I'm thinking of doing some apple crisps, chef," he said. "I thought they'd go well with the soufflé."

"Shut up, you prick," Bob said. Wolfishly he turned his attention to a gastro of braised pork cheeks. But he had hardly begun chewing when a sound in the plonge made him freeze. Hopping, terrified Shahram, obliged on Saturdays to work more than his customary nine hours, had turned to song.

"Mhut va fuck iffat?" he bellowed at the little man. *"Are you praying?"*

Through the doorway, Shahram gave Bob an edgy smile that made it clear he understood nothing that had been said to him.

"You're not doing that in here," shouted Bob, swallowing painfully. *"I'll have no praying in this kitchen. No pray. Get it?"*

"Chef." Shahram pulled at his crotch nervously and showed his small gappy teeth.

"And stop looking so fucking nervous," said Bob.

"Probably wants to blow us up," said Racist Dave.

An olive flew across the kitchen, striking Dave in the eye, causing him to cry out. Ramilov, the thrower, chuckled to himself. "Racist Dave" was another nickname he refused to endorse. *What's Dave about him?* he used to say.

"Right," Bob said, ignoring them. "Power hour. Let's have 'The Cage of Pure Emotion.'"

Dave, groaning quietly, wiped the oil from his eye and reached for a broken CD case next to the hi-fi. The CD was scratched to pieces, and when the hi-fi finally recognized it, it seemed to groan too. Mercilessly, it played the song all the same.

Trapped in a cage,
A cage of pure emotion.

Bob clapped his hands and bellowed the words loudly.

"Come on, chefs!" he cried. There was Bob for you—Mr. Good Times.

With some reluctance the other chefs joined in. Ramilov added a low hoarse baritone, Dave droned loudly and tunelessly, Dibden mumbled like a posh person making an excuse. The quiet dark-eyed girl watched in silent disgust.

This was the power hour. The last chance to make everything right. Had you done enough to keep your head above it? Were you set? At every section chefs were topping up their service fridges, cadging chopping boards, filling the squeezy bottles with olive oil and wine vinegar, dicing butter, refreshing the water in their spoon washes, sprinkling salt on the ice cubes in the deep steel trays to slow their melting, laying damp paper towels on top of the herbs to stop them from wilting. Ramilov was demanding kisses from the waitresses in return for the complimentary bread. This was the hour to eat, if you had time, or it was the hour to get your head down and blitz through any mise outstanding. This was the hour when the slow chefs worked fastest and the fast chefs smoked. This was the hour when every chef took a gamble. Would they have enough of this or that to last them the night? How busy would their section be? Would the great collective unconsciousness that governed all their fates be in the mood for the steak or the fish pie?

On other nights of the week this in-between hour might pass unnoticed, with service dawning slowly while life, and mise, continued around it. Saturday night was different. There were no quiet sections, no empty tables. Everyone front and back of house got short shrift. At six thirty the squabbling, shit-talking kitchen fell quiet in anticipation. The radio was switched off. This was the moment when those head chefs with a taste for the grandiose might choose to give a short rallying speech to the brigade. One for all, all for one, that sort of thing. Bob rarely did, though occasionally he would remind the chefs that if he said anything personal about them during service it was not a heat-of-the-moment thing, he really did mean it.

And then . . . silence. The kitchen stood at attention like an army in the moment before battle, awaiting the first volley of arrows, listening for the first signs of attack. As the silence grew, so too did the anxiety. A deluge was coming. The longer this silence went on, the harder the deluge would be. It was an awkward, sleazy wink sort of silence; not, in fact, a silence at all, but a digest of many small noises, each lacking the particular accompanying sound that made them whole. It was the sound of absence: the absence of pans clunking on the blazing burners, of chefs' cries bouncing off the tiled walls, of plates clattering on the work surfaces. Such stillness hung about the place, one struggled to imagine that bodies had ever whirled and jagged about it. The sheer and total industry of the kitchen was at a standstill. Ice melted slowly in the trays.

Croak!

Then, suddenly, there it was. The sound everyone was waiting for. A *croak croak* cutting through the empty noise. The ticket machine hacking up the first check of a long night and Bob tearing the paper off to cry . . . "*Ça marche! Check on!*"

This was how it always began.

The night Dibden went down, the night The Fat Man came to dinner, was no different. The early, breathless anticipation; the first rush gathering momentum as one by one each section joined the fight; the strange little bubbles of calm between the frenzies. Dibden did not get a dessert check on until seven thirty, a single order for caramelized pears and ice cream. And though the pears were harder than they should have been and took an age to cook, he produced the dish with only cosmetic mumblings from Bob about how shit he was and how he needed to play the game.

Then it got worse. Around eight there was a brief flurry of dessert checks from the early tables and suddenly Dibden had four different tickets on his grabber and was trying to cook twenty different things at once. Then Bob, as wolfish as ever, stuck his fat finger in the garlicky crème anglaise Dibden was heating on the side of the solid top and declared it fucking gash. The whole lot went in the bin and Dibden found himself in the inconvenient position of having to separate egg whites from yolks and heat cream and split vanilla pods with twenty dishes still to make while a very fat and unfriendly chef bawled in his ear about the ingenious things he was going to do to his intimate parts.

"Dibden's sweating like a nun in a fish market," Ramilov observed.

Dibden did not even have time to object that this was offensive to nuns.

Then it got worse. A raspberry soufflé burst in the oven and had to go in the bin and Dibden had to get another in fucking ASAP but he could not send the other desserts for the soufflé table because the soufflé would be twenty minutes and everyone else would have finished by the time it arrived. He managed to fob off a flat fondant and caramelized pears onto another table that was waiting, pushing the fondant through the pass to the waitress with the button nose before Bob, momentarily distracted by a table of mains, could speculate on its lack of height. He flicked the first spores of white mold from the top of the ganache tartlets and prayed to the god of the kitchen, a most unobliging god by all accounts, that Bob would not notice.

As Dibden was scooping some runny quince membrillo into a ramekin for a cheese plate, Camp Charles ran in asking about the desserts for the soufflé table that had now been waiting for thirty minutes. It seemed a reasonable question. Bob, particularly, was impressed by its reasonableness and began to demand an answer to it in language that was less reasonable. Now the mint was trembling in Dibden's hands, his mouth was slack and his head lolling one way and then the other. Punch drunk. Spavined. Former. And all the while the machine hacked out dessert checks and everyone else was too busy with their own drastic situations to improve Dibden's and soon Bob's greedy fingers would poke their way into a ganache and deduce that all was not well there and his keen eyes would spy the crumbling pastry tarts and exhausted fondants and stewed raspberries and there would be separate, clearly labeled portions of hell to pay for each of them. The more mistakes Bob spotted, the more particular he became, until Dibden could not hold a plate without provoking his ire. In time there were so many orders to do and mistakes waiting to be made that Dibden did not even know where to begin and only stood there paralyzed in the middle of the kitchen, a latter-day Buridan's ass, dying of indecision between the proverbial stack of hay and pail of water while Bob screamed blue fury at him.

In the middle of this shitstorm something happened that made everyone, Bob included, forget for a moment about Dibden and his ongoing torture. Camp Charles appeared once more at the back of the kitchen, this time in a state of great anxiety. Ordinarily the maître d' was an unchanging façade of civility. No one, customers or staff, could tell what he was really thinking, which was a great boon in the service industry, where people were usually thinking the worst thing imaginable. Now his plump face bore signs of strain. One hand wrung the other.

"What's the matter with you, gay boy?" said Ramilov, who loved Camp Charles unconditionally, for his constant innuendo and the professionalism he wore so effortlessly alongside it. "Why don't you touch my arse? It'll cheer you up."

Under normal circumstances Camp Charles would have been delighted to take him up on the offer—though he maintained he was not actually gay, just very unimpressed. "I've sucked enough dicks to know I'm straight," he once told Ramilov, which was the only time I ever saw Ramilov lost for a response. But now the maître d' ignored the invitation. "The Fat Man's here," was all he said.

Dave stared at Camp Charles in horror.

"What did you say?" he asked.

"*The Fat Man is here*," Camp Charles repeated.

The kitchen fell silent. Bob, midway through a complicated volley of abuse to do with Dibden's parentage, seemed to turn to stone. I craned my neck past him and saw what looked at first like a moderately sized marquee blocking the dining room doorway. As my eyes recalibrated I realized it was the largest man I had ever seen. He spotted the table the front of house was fussing over for him and began moving toward us like a ship pulls out of harbor, its movements slow but possessed of absolute authority, the great sails of fabric that were his clothes tightening and slackening with the motion. I would have remained transfixed had Dibden not made a plaintive cry for eggs and sent me off at a scramble for the dry store.

The Fat Man! A legend in the considerable flesh, here at The Swan! My hands trembled as I turned the speckled shells from their seats. I had heard all the stories. Dave said The Fat Man controlled Camden's vast and sprawling underworld. Camp Charles said he had heard from a busboy at The Crown who had heard from the maître d' at The Castle that The Fat Man ran a secret dining club, a club with exotic tastes. The maître d' had been Waiter of the Year 2008, and he knew things. Others suggested he was a food critic, but Bob was not scared of critics. He bitched about them and everyone else, yet he would say nothing about The Fat Man except that his food had better be fucking soigné. Everyone had a theory on this corpulent mystery, but no one knew anything for certain, not even his real name. The only thing we knew for sure was that he had a remarkable effect on Bob, indeed on anyone who had heard of him. Several caustic senior chefs, and one sardonic maître d', now started falling over themselves to do his bidding.

The rest of that evening Bob bowed and scraped as if his enormous guest were the king of Spain. The Saturday rush paled in comparison. Smiling broadly, oozing with convivial menace, The Fat Man eclipsed all else as he ate. And how he could eat! Three or four starters, and every main going. Tremendous amounts were consumed, seemingly without limit or pleasure. Despite his booming bonhomie and the sharp smiles he flashed at Bob or the nervous front of house staff, his face bore no trace of joy or appreciation as he ate. He had an aggressively friendly manner of complaining that became more sinister the longer it went on.

"*Dear boy!*" he shouted at Camp Charles. "*Are you trying to starve me with these portions? Do you wish me to waste away? Where is the seasoning on this beef? Where is its soul? Am I not a good customer? Why do you hate me? You must hate me to serve me this. What's the wait, friend? A little morsel of piglet is all I ask. A little bloody liver to whet my whistle. A smidgeon of pigeon. Something with flavor for a change. Something with taste.*"

Yet every morsel was devoured, every plate wiped clean. He treated food as billionaires treat money, as showgirls treat presents from admirers. An entitlement he claimed even though it disgusted

him. His size—limitless, free-form, overspilling in a way that made
Bob look like an old stick—confirmed his attitude. I kept forgetting whom I was running errands for or what I was supposed to be
fetching, it was impossible not to stop everything and just watch
him eat. Also I felt uneasy ignoring him. You didn't turn your back
on *that*.

When the dessert menu was put in front of him, The Fat Man
ordered the lot. Camp Charles said he didn't even read the list. Poor
Dibden, already quite sunk, gripped the service fridge as the check
came through. He gulped. He wobbled. A drowned man's pallor
crept over him. The flailing that ensued, not helped by Bob's
screams for "perfection or death," was the worst yet. Those long
hands had aged a hundred years in an evening. They stumbled over
simple dishes, dishes plated a thousand times before. That small sad
head of his looked farther away than ever, pushed out of the top of
his body like toothpaste from a tube. His chin, subjected to such
inward pressure, such violent disappointment, had receded completely; it had vacated his face. Dave, seeing how broken he was,
came over to garnish and decorate the plates.

Toward the end of the evening, as I was changing the cloths on the
pass one final time, I witnessed The Fat Man at close quarters.
Having annihilated his last dish of the evening, he pushed the table
away and hoisted himself from his seat for a word with Bob.

"Everything all right with the food?" Bob cringed.

"You did the best you could, Bobby," The Fat Man replied. "But
I know you'll do better with the Christmas feast."

"It's a lot of people." Bob sounded nervous.

"A lot of people owe me," The Fat Man answered.

"I mean . . . it's a lot of people to cook for."

The Fat Man widened his eyes. "Well, Bobby, you'll have to work extra hard then, won't you?"

"Couldn't we cut the numbers slightly?" Bob pleaded. "The weekend before Christmas will be crazy."

"You busy, are you?" The Fat Man smiled.

"I am a bit," said Bob.

"Busy Bobby," said The Fat Man, still quietly taunting. "Always hard at work. It amazes me you have the time to make those tapes. . . . Requires a lot of dedication, I imagine. A *dogged* approach. . . . You making another anytime soon? Pets Win Prizes?"

"All right," Bob hissed.

"Have you forgotten how this works?" said The Fat Man. "Do I need to remind you?"

"All right, all right." Bob had started sweating. He looked like death. "We'll keep the numbers as they are."

"That's it, Bobby," said The Fat Man. "That's it."

When The Fat Man left, Bob turned to the kitchen. Clearly, he was keen to pay the threats forward. His fury fell on Dibden, leaning, ghostly and broken, against the pastry fridge. In a pathetic attempt at cleaning down, the exhausted chef flopped a damp sponge about the surface.

"And you were a fucking disgrace this evening," Bob snarled at him. "*Again*," he added, a reference to the Wednesday evening just passed when Dibden had sunk on larder and Ramilov had had to be released from the fridge sooner than Bob might have wished. "I'm putting you on donkey jobs for the next fucking year. Right now I wouldn't trust you to peel a carrot, you cunt."

Dibden hung his head. From the outset he had shown a potential for failure, and he had made good on his promise. What would become of the rest of us remained to be seen.

7. GLOSSARY

At the insistence of Ramilov and Racist Dave, I have included a glossary of kitchen terms. I should point out that this list is unique to The Swan; every restaurant kitchen has its own particular idiom. Yet there is also a universal language of chefs, represented here by the French words and phrases, which you might hear in the back of any decent restaurant from New York to Bombay. And there are still other phrases that every restaurant has a version of, out of necessity, such as *chaud behind*. These may vary from place to place, or region to region, but they will always be present in some form.

I have explained to Ramilov and Dave that a glossary traditionally appears before or after the main body of work, but they were adamant it should go here because, quote, it looks less boring and people will feel like they have to read it. I should also point out that neither Ramilov nor Dave has an English literature degree, or any academic qualification beyond GCSE.

ALL DAY: Across all checks.

AWAY: Re an order. When the check or course is away, the customer is waiting.

BLAZE UP: *Slang.* To start cooking.

ÇA MARCHE: Pronounced "summ-age." The French means something like "It's walking." In the kitchen it means the order is on and away.

CHAUD BEHIND: Coming past and carrying something hot. Also Backs, Chaud (pronounced "sho"), Chaud backs, Behind, Hot pan.

CHECK: A table's order, and its printed counterpart.

CHINOIS: French term for a conical strainer, similar to a sieve.

COOKING ON GAS: Statement of fact, repeated loudly.

FIX UP: *Slang.* Sort yourself out.

FUCKING OUI: Expression of strong approval.

GASH: Expression of strong disapproval; female genitals.

GO DOWN: Due to how few women chefs meet, and the language they use when they do, this phrase rarely has anything to do with the above definition. Instead, it is almost always used to describe the physical and/or mental collapse of a chef during service.

GRABBER: A rail, usually placed at eye level on the sauce section, pastry section and pass, that holds the relevant checks in the order they are "coming up."

JAMIE OLIVER: *Derogatory.* Term used by chefs de partie to describe someone who is paid lots of money to talk about food but knows no more about food than they do, while they are paid pennies. Clear case of sour grapes.

MAURICE: This is what Bob used to call a spatula. It is not French for spatula and I have no idea why he did it.

MISE EN PLACE: Sometimes shortened to mise or abbreviated to MEP. Literally, the putting in place. The daily, inglorious task of getting one's dishes, utensils and setup ready for the shitfight ahead. Kitchen work is more mise than anything else.

NICE BOY: *Derogatory.* A homosexual.

PASTRY CHEF: *Derogatory.* A homosexual.

PART TIMER: *Derogatory.* A chef who does, or is perceived to do, less work than other chefs.

PASS: The place that all food must go before it leaves the kitchen, where every plate must "pass" the scrutiny of the head chef or his representative on earth. Final garnishes may be added, sauces tried, stains expunged.

PLONGEUR: Someone who works in the plonge. A kitchen porter.

POOMPLEX: *Slang. Derogatory.* An idiot.

SOIGNÉ: Pronounced "swan-yay," by Bob at least. French word meaning elegant or sophisticated. In the kitchen usually preceded by the English word *fucking*, meaning "very" or "extremely."

SOLID TOP: The sheer metal hot plate; source of great heat, as my elbow can attest.

WASTEMAN: *Slang. Derogatory.* A useless person; Dibden.

YOUR COCK-UP, MY ARSE: A favorite expression of chefs that touches all the bases: profanity, homoeroticism and accusation.

Ramilov has also asked me to include a short section on nouns of assemblage. I am very happy to do so. It is easy to forget Ramilov's flashes of learning amid the many loud reports of his baser nature. His education, so far as I know, was slight, but somewhere in his carousing he has picked up certain facts and details of philosophical interest—his sexual theory based on Kissinger's foreign policy, for instance (*that* should have been a warning)—which he is fond of presenting and employing. The nouns of assemblage is one such area. He clutches like a jackdaw at these shiny items. Yet that does not quite do him justice. I have come to believe there are elements of deep wisdom secreted about Ramilov's person, wisdom of a sort I do not fully understand. This is balanced, though not canceled out, by some extremely poor calls of judgment, of which we shall see more later. The list our wise fool has prepared is below.

A Band of Men

An Ogle of Waitresses

A Wince of Lobsters

A Tirade of Chefs

It is a Skein of Geese in flight, a Gaggle of Geese on water.

A Buzz of Barflies

A Blarney of Bartenders

A Skulk of Foxes

A Peep of Poultry

A Business of Flies

An Unholiness of Ortolans

A Slaver of Gluttons

A Snarl of Tigers

A Fighting of Beggars

A Colony of Ants

A Horror of Apes

I wrote to Ramilov to tell him that I do not think all of these are correct. He wrote back to say they were, and to remind me of my promise.

8. THE QUIET DARK-EYED GIRL

The quiet dark-eyed girl was sullen and moody and not my type at all. The quiet dark-eyed girl was possessive of her containers and tough and once watched me fall on the solid top and burn my elbow without lifting a finger to help me. The quiet dark-eyed girl was unamused by the banter of the chefs. She was especially unamused by Ramilov's habit of leaning in front of the pass with his penis in the plate cupboard beneath and asking one or other of the waitresses to fetch him a plate. The quiet dark-eyed girl did not drink in O'Reillys after work with the rest of us. Nor did she brag like Dave or fuck up like Dibden or bully like Bob. The quiet dark-eyed girl prepared a special vegetarian meal for Shahram. The quiet dark-eyed girl was called Harmony. And Harmony was beautiful.

Everything she said or did was decisive, forceful, pushing the action on. She moved like a tree in a gentle breeze, her legs rooted, her long torso swaying this way and that to the demands of service. At five thirty every afternoon she would take her only cigarette break of the day, sitting on the bench in the yard, for exactly three minutes. Never did she stoop to chitchat. Her demeanor was cool, willowy, composed. She raised her chin to exhale. Brave was the chef who inquired of her private life; it was somehow, implicitly, off-limits. To consider it was dangerous. Deliverymen did not wolf whistle at her, Ramilov did not flash her or pretend to hump her with a carrot or reach slyly between her legs. Even Dave tried to put some other words between his obscenities when she was around. He curbed his bigotry in her presence too, though her olive skin and strong features hinted at Jewish or Arabic blood that would ordinarily have set him off at a rant. She existed in her own private universe within the kitchen, untouched by the dirt around her, untroubled by its school yard sadism.

The kitchen, being predisposed to types—the cocksure joker, the northern goon, the scorned but aloof pastry section, the foreign and uncomprehending kitchen porters—did not know what to make of this bold, immovable female and warily omitted her from classification. Maybe it is the case that any woman in a professional kitchen, juxtaposed against the hardness and testosterone and bitchery of men, will appear a goddess. But no, I think she appeared a goddess because she was one. A goddess who scowled at me and told me I couldn't use the medium balloon whisk because she needed it in two hours' time. A goddess who refused to share her one-liter plastics and deep sixes and lids, kitchen items that seemed to exist only in theory, items a commis could spend his whole life searching for. Only Dave was better at hoarding kitchen equipment. All over the restaurant these two had secret stashes, in places no one would even think of looking: behind the mise in their service fridges, in the shaft for the dumbwaiter, underneath the combi oven covered by specially placed gastro trays.

(The other thing about Harmony: her hands did not bear The Mark of Bob. When it came to women Bob was at once chivalrous and craven, sexist and submissive. During service he never gave her grief, never so much as raised his voice to her. Women were unstable, emotional commodities that Bob did not understand or trust. As he knew from his own beloved and terrible wife, a woman's will was absolute, and her fury when crossed was awful to behold. For Bob, "The Missus" was a mysterious and sacred institution that should never be disrespected or contradicted. He of all people knew

how a woman could make a man suffer, and even he, the connoisseur of suffering, would not wish it upon others. When his own
wife demanded her "Booboo," Bob became a simpering fool, switch-
ing in an instant from brutal tyranny to baby talk. Such language
sounded very undignified coming from a first-rate arsehole of Bob's
standing, and in those moments, to the great surprise of all the
chefs, we found ourselves wishing for the petty, heartless bastard
we knew and despised. This other Bob, this "Booboo," was just depressing, like a toothless crocodile or a clean rat.)

Harmony was callous because the environment demanded it. Or
perhaps she had sought the kitchens because her character would
brook no shit. Whatever the truth, she was the only chef who seemed
comfortable in The Swan's turmoil. Everyone else had about them
the look of caged beasts: one-hundred-hour-a-week Dave, jabbering
Shahram, shifty Darik, cloistered Dibden—to make no mention of
Ramilov the iconoclast, winking at blind horses and pulling fiercely
at weak ropes. Harmony alone belonged. It was wrong to say, as I
did earlier, that she existed in her own orbit. We existed within hers.
Primarily, she belonged because she retained an independence from
the place. As I slaved week after week in that pit of despair I came
to see how that singular, star-bright quality, silently relayed from
the corner fryer, was worth a thousand macho brags. The other
chefs might talk about how they were ready to up and leave, how
they wouldn't take any more of Bob's cruelty, but none of them
would do it. Most had no other qualifications, no professional experience beyond kitchens. No life beyond. Some had spent so long in
front of the burners that just the thought of getting on the Tube or
walking down the street put them on edge.

Inexorably, as the weeks wore on and we slogged deeper into
December, I felt myself slipping toward the same condition. Even
to step outside the back door and see the small square of sky above

the yard was unnerving: it suggested there was something beyond cooking, a world outside the kitchen, and that led the mind down unpleasant lines of inquiry. As Ramilov, our very own Book of Wisdom, writes, fear is the great nut squeeze. The kitchen was all chefs knew. Something made them pick up the knife afresh each day. Something chained them to it. Like flies, they were enslaved to the pursuit of food, to the fulfillment of their urges, and, like flies, their single-mindedness could be read as brainless, as cowardly, or as noble. I, however, had no wish to pick up the knife or suffer for food; I did not care one way or the other about any of it, yet somehow I had become trapped.

Harmony gave me hope. Dave will scoff and Ramilov will explode with ridicule, but I am not ashamed to admit it: I looked to her with growing desperation. She became a sort of crutch to me, and I gleaned much inspiration from observing the way she held herself beyond the kitchen's consumptive, libidinous grasp. Yet—and this is the funny thing about it—the more I watched her, the harder it was to leave.

I must confess my thoughts of her were not entirely pure. My dictionary explains, with a leer, that crutch and crotch share the same root, as if all succor has carnal implications. This is what you get, I suppose, when hundreds of men compile a book together. (I can only hope the editorial influence of Ramilov and Racist Dave does not drag this book the same way.) But on this occasion, on the subject of Harmony, those learned men were quite correct. I daydreamed about her soft lips and sweet caresses, her warm dark eyes. I prayed for a way past her defenses. Perhaps one service she would be up against it and I would ride in on a white horse, so to speak, to save her from the onslaught of checks. We would beat the dinner rush together, side by side, anticipating each other's movements, spinning gracefully around each other. Then she would see that I wasn't useless or small of self. Then she would see that I was capable and strong and considerate and that she had been wrong about me after all. After that we would be inseparable, and there would be no more cold Harmony, no Harmony who watched me fall on the solid top and burn myself without lifting a finger to help, who pushed me out of the way of the mustard as I bled.

I should stress that I was encouraged in these fantasies. For Harmony was not always cold toward me. Sometimes, quite unexpectedly, she might say hello to me in the morning, or let me use the large mixing bowl. On more than one occasion she offered me chips that were going spare. Small things, admittedly, but I, unused to the civility, made them seem bigger than they were. I can see now that I read too much into these gestures. I confused sympathy with interest, and the two are not the same. In my defense, I was not much fortified against the smiles of beautiful women.

At the time, however, I felt sure romance was afoot. I put the memory of Rachel Parker, my university heartache, behind me and planned my approach. I knew from my excessive consumption of fiction that women were won by either chivalry, bravery or tremendous cruelty. If you defended their honor, they pretty much had to kiss you. If they hated you at first, it was practically a given that they would fall in love with you later—or that they had really loved you all along. By that rule, the true reason for Harmony's meanness toward me was embarrassingly obvious. Now she needed to notice my thoughtful and modest nature, to see that I was not of the Ramilovs of this world. But there was no place for poetic sentiment in the daily kitchen bustle, with the pans clanging and the prep list building and Racist Dave singing and Ramilov flicking chauffant water in my ear.

One afternoon, a week or so after Dibden's soufflé collapsed, I found myself with a rare half hour to spare. I decided to ask her if she wanted to go to the park with me.

"Why?" was her blunt response.

I did not know what to say.

"We could have a walk . . ." I mumbled.

"You want to have a walk?" The concept sounded ridiculous when she said it, and perhaps it was. It wasn't what I really wanted, after all. From her mouth I could hear how vague and deceitful my statement had been. I realized she was operating on a different scale of honesty. It wasn't new to me, that honesty: my brother was the same. Everything said in a very clear and plain way that left you nowhere to hide. An intimidating trait, one I never sought to emulate. I needed a little foliage. I wasn't that honest with myself.

"Haven't you got any jobs?" she wanted to know.

In a somewhat cavalier fashion I explained I did not.

"Then you can make this mayonnaise for me," she replied.

All right, I would win her heart with work. I made her mayonnaise. On another occasion, in the hope of impressing her, I volunteered to slice courgette ribbons for her. But she threw them all in the trash and told me to do them again "but less shit." I no longer had the time and got behind on my own work. In the rush, I nicked my fingers on the mandoline and got blood on some of the courgettes, which also had to be thrown away. She got her ribbons in the end, but only half what she would have got if she had done them herself. This did not endear me to her any further.

The miserable memory of Rachel Parker flared up again. Why, I wondered, did women have to be this way? I had given all my modernism essays to that girl and, after the initial gratitude, it was all why was I so slow at writing them and why was her mark lower than mine. After all those essays bequeathed in good faith, all those "good words" a friend had put in for me with her, all those study sessions where our knees touched under the table, where I was close enough to sense her body moving beneath her clothes, look where that had ended up. Tragedy on the university bus back from Brighton. She began telling me about this new guy she had met, and I, with the fatal clarity that comes of a few drinks, realized she would never be mine.

"He's just so sexy," she said, combing her hair. As if I were one of her girlfriends. As if I didn't possess the same appendages as Lover Boy. I smiled sickly while she talked of their "crazy" date at the roller disco. I tried, weakly, to ask questions. What was his situation? Was he older? No, he was the same age as us. At our uni.

"If you like him, you should follow your heart," I replied. *Follow your heart?* I was hurt, confused. It is an unfortunate defect of human beings that they slip into cliché at their emotional extremes. I realized I had played it all wrong trying to make friends with pretty, bland Rachel. We had nothing in common. Sometimes two knees touching was just that. Those feminine mysteries she had let me get close to—applying makeup in front of me, asking my opinion on her outfits—had taken me further away from my goal. And I, too sensitive, too obscure in my intentions, had sidelined myself.

"What about me?" I asked.

"You? What about you?"

"I thought we had something."

"Us?" She did not stop combing her hair. "I've never thought of you like that."

This was one of those polite ways of punching you in the face that I encountered a lot at university, and which I grew to despise passionately. If you have ever been told you weren't invited to a party because there wasn't enough room, you will know what I mean. But at the time I wasn't familiar with this construct, didn't understand that I should let it lie. Duped by how reasonable her response sounded, I imagined our divide could still be bridged.

"Why not?" I asked.

Some deeper cruelty flickered in her cold blue eyes, but whatever observation it accompanied she chose not to express. She kept quiet. Still combing her hair, delighted by my agony. In a white shirt and a blue V-necked sweater. I remember exactly. Pristine, her full lips freshly done. If I could kiss those lips just once, would she melt into me like in the romance novels, and realize she had loved me all along? Something told me no.

"I'm not begging," I said to make it clear. "I'm not begging."

In hindsight this was a mistake. I had lost her, I would never have her, but putting this match to my dignity was unnecessary. Chiefly, I think, I was mortified with myself, for confusing acceptance with interest, for mistaking beauty for goodness.

Still nothing from Rachel. As if my declaration were not worthy of a response. Suddenly I realized I had lost, lost everything, and my temper went the same way.

"Why are you being such a bitch?" I shouted angrily.

That shattered her cool façade. She scowled at me, curling her mouth in contempt.

"Oh, fuck off, you little shit," she said. "Why would I be interested in you?"

She moved to a seat at the front. The bus became loud with whispers. We got off at the same stop and I feigned interest in a bush so we would not have to walk back to halls together. *You see what you missed out on, Rachel?* the subtext ran. *This man can find inspiration anywhere, even in this bush.*

I tried to avoid her for the rest of the term. We stood at opposite ends of parties. In the library I pretended I hadn't seen her. We never spoke again. I still thought about her often, though they were angry thoughts, free of lust. When lips are used to curse you it is necessary to imagine their kisses differently. And this friend of mine, not so much of a friend as all that, it turned out, bought me a drink in the union bar the next week and listened sympathetically to my story, putting in the odd word about the evils of women and the perils of love. Only later did I realize this act was an admission of guilt on his part. He, I discovered, was the guy Rachel was seeing. It seems that is my fate. Forever finding out wrongs committed against me after the fact, in sideways and roundabout ways. Not hurt by the presence of the firing squad, but by the sight of one soldier among them who has not bothered to shave.

Reluctantly, I put my thoughts of Harmony into the same box. I was too proud, or too insecure, to let such a debacle happen again. I accepted, as best I could, that she was not interested in me. I had shown weakness, that was why. It wasn't just women either—it was everyone. All animals could smell it. All animals despised it. My own dear father, whose number often flashed up on my phone late at night as I drifted into sleep, was a case in point. To whomever invented the mute function, I give daily thanks.

And yet, trapped in this loveless kitchen, I did begin to miss home. Things had been simpler there. I hesitate to say better, but my status had certainly been higher, at least with one of my parents. In the end, nagged by memories I had no control over, I wrote my mother a short e-mail three weeks before Christmas saying that I was well, that I had found work and would not be able to visit over the festive season. I affected a breezy style. London was full of interest, and I had made many new friends. *Pentelho. Pussyclot. Bumfuck.*

I asked how they were and if she had got any further with the garden after I'd left. When I had been there that summer the two of them were going to Lindy Hop classes in the gym opposite the train station. I asked how it was coming along. I didn't know what else to ask them. The Internet café down by Chalk Farm seemed like too public a place to ask them if they were still arguing at night, or if my father was still sneaking off to the bookie's with the grocery money. I couldn't ask if my mother still hated working in that care home or if the tree still blocked out the sitting room light or if the spoons were still bent. I couldn't ask because I knew the answers. So I asked how the neighbors were, whom I hadn't spoken to in five years. Looking back, I realize this might have come across as desperate.

The next day I received a reply from my mother. All my attempted breeziness had been read as sincerity. The phrase "full of interest" had obviously worried her. It's also full of pollution and people looking to take advantage of you, she wrote, as if a boy, a man, of almost twenty-three couldn't look after himself. Still, I appreciated her concern. On that second point, particularly, she had a lot of experience.

I'm sorry to say the garden has fallen back a little since your visit—a nice way to describe my four months of purposeless regression—I've been out a few times with the gloves when I'm not at the Grove but those weeds will keep coming. There was an incident at Lindy Hop with your father and we won't be going back. It's all "he said, she said" and I shan't bore you with the details. The tutor has agreed not to press charges. Your father insists it was a misunderstanding. The group was of the opinion that, whatever exactly happened, personal property and personal space should always be respected. I've given up trying to defend that man. All I know is it's a shame, as we never went out anywhere as it was, and this is what happens when we do.

I keep trying to remember what granny used to say about marriage, as a deal two people struck. She said it so often I never bothered to listen. I only remember the bit about love having nothing to do with it. But there was a deal, she said, and you both had to keep your end up. I've stopped expecting that of your father. Maybe when that happens, when someone can't change, the deal is off.

Sorry to end on a sad note, dear, the restaurant really does sound exciting. Are you the sous chef?

Love, Mum.

P.S. The neighbors are still arseholes.

Those tangled, tenacious weeds. My mother among them, forthright, embattled, with scything flourishes of personal disclosure. I had forgotten that about her. How she could announce, over the breakfast table, that there was no female receptionist at the mechanics and my father would be out on his ear if he ever lied about who was calling again. You could see where Sam had got his plain speaking.

Yet this message did not comfort me as I had hoped. In fact, I regretted ever starting the correspondence. Nothing had changed. It was hard enough carrying around one set of anxieties as it was. Sending that e-mail had been a moment of weakness; I tried to put its words from my mind. But I kept thinking of my mother, sitting down in that hardly used study to write to me, my father's sports channels blaring from the next room, and I saw the clouds of sadness that lagged beneath the surface of her handsome face as she typed, in that big overcast house, she and him, the two of them alone. Knocking about in an old life that no longer fitted them. Unable to let go of what they were before they were strangers to each other.

Inevitably I found myself retracing further, back to my elder brother, Sam. That was when we had all become strangers to one another. When my mother sent me up with his dinner, the hot bowl of soup wrapped in a tea towel so I did not burn my tender hands, and I would place it on his bedside table slightly too far away, just a little out of his reach, so he would have to stretch for his supper. I don't know why I did it; I worshipped my brother. Every time I climbed those stairs I wanted only to help him, to make him well again. But—and here was that cruelty again, the moment weakness was revealed—when I saw those dim eyes, that forehead beaded with sweat, the limp limbs beneath the covers, I was filled with disgust. This sad specimen was not the Sam I wanted to help. He was an impostor in Sam's bed, in his body. Let him get his own soup. Let him strain. Perhaps I wanted to test him, or to test myself: to see if I could ignore the groans of someone I loved, to see if I was strong enough. Whatever the reason, it plagues me still. There are many other moments when I was kind to him, but that's not the way memory works. Only this, and what it led to, feels real.

9. A NEST OF WASPS

Tolstoy says that happy families are all alike, while every unhappy family is unhappy in its own way. I'm not saying he got it wrong, but it's the kind of sentence that makes more sense in a book than it does when you try to hold it up against your own life. I mean, it has a pure sense, as an axiom that makes people nod their heads and say, "Old Tolstoy's nailed it again." It's exactly the right side of conspiratorial: everyone feels included and everyone feels unique. But when I look at my own family I can't separate it so easily into happy and unhappy, good and bad. I don't see it in terms of light and shadow, like those oil paintings you find in Catholic churches, The Randall Clan Cast Out of Paradise and such. Our happiness was never a concrete state; the unhappiness was built into it. Grandmother saw that, the cataractic old sage. Part of my parents' joy in those early years, I am sure, was knowing exactly what misery they had so far dodged. And part of their misery today, I have no doubt, is knowing the specific joy they once had.

Ramilov and Racist Dave know where this story ends: The Fat Man giving me the look of death, a locked door reverberating with shouts and whacks, blood that will not stop. Images that will remain with me, I expect, no matter what I do. But my self-appointed editors do not know the history that precedes those moments, the images from my family album that still sneak up to slit my throat. We can't choose what we remember or what we forget—for me, these early memories keep floating to the surface. Ramilov accuses me of being cagey about my home life—well, this snapshot of my family

is for his benefit. But it is also for mine: I need to set this all down
if I am going to explain what happened.

It was the summer of my eighth birthday, the summer before
everything really fell apart. My brother and I ruled the footpaths
and backwaters, charging around them on our bikes, he always
ahead of me, a blur of motion, his reddish-brown hair already au-
tumnal against the deep summer greens. In woodland clearings we
would throw our bikes to the ground and build great forts and dens
from fallen boughs, camping out until dusk, when we knew the golf
would end and our father would look up from the television and
realize we were not there.

I have happy memories of those early summers. Yet remembering them brings me no joy. Perhaps all memories are inherently sad,
even the happy ones, and should for that reason be avoided. Nostal-
gia is not so much the recollection of things past as the recollection
of things you are no longer connected to.

Sometimes on those long childhood afternoons my brother
would build a fire and we would sit up against it, enjoying the unnecessary warmth, while he told me about his new school. He'd
swapped the coat-of-arms place for a secondary with its welcome
sign in three languages. This was very sad news to me at the time. I
was a smart little boy, who wore a shirt and tie with his shorts, and
I wanted desperately to wear the cap of that fancy school. (I never
did get the chance. I went to the multilingual state, where they
locked me in the cleaning cupboard during break.) But always with
my brother this sort of information was given without bias. Instead
of prayers, now he had assembly. Instead of Latin, it was now sex
education. He told me about his new classmates and teachers: the
girl whose mother provided a tin of cold baked beans for her field
trip packed lunch, the boy with a library of video nasties in his

room, the time Mrs. So-and-so started crying in class and the head-mistress had to finish the lesson. He and his new friend Josh Phillips fighting the whole school in the playground after lunch.

I remember, even at that age, being struck by how my brother spoke about people, infinitely more generous and forgiving than I was. He was twelve, with a sneering father and hormones to boot. He had no business being such a saint, such a bold and upright specimen. I, by contrast, was a weak plant: I straggled and crept. To this day I look up to that twelve-year-old, still wiser than me though I am nearly twice his age. Isn't that also strange? That I have grown older than my older brother. That one day a child might be older than his parents or grandparents. Perhaps this is why I still look up to Sam. I have been compromised by time; he has been preserved by it.

On such a summer's day we found the wasps' nest. We were tearing through the scrub behind the golf course when my brother brought his bike suddenly to a halt and pointed at a large, dirty-white bulb hanging from a tree in front of us. It bulged obscenely, its wedding cake tiers swollen and lopsided. A veil of wasps surrounded it, buzzing, teeming, darting this way and that on their errands. Naturally I was afraid and told Sam we should go, our father would be missing us. A strange phrase that, which can be true and false at the same time. Sam, however, was not afraid.

"Look," he said, holding his face right up to it. "Look, it's fine."

And the wasps flew about him, unbothered by his presence. A miracle to little me: my saintly brother at one with the perils of nature. But when he pulled his face back from the nest and into view again there was blood running down it. His nose was pouring with the stuff. "Untold claret," as Ramilov would say.

"What?" he said, seeing my look. "What's wrong?"

Then he put his hand to his nose and felt the gushing blood, saw it falling in long, stretching drips onto his football shirt. Just a nose-bleed, he said at first, it did not matter. But the nosebleed would not stop, it was coming thick and fast, and I could see that my brother was worried now. That really scared me, as my brother was never worried about anything. So we pedaled back to the house as fast as we could, my brother bleeding all the way, and found our father in his usual spot, trying to eat his milkless cornflakes with a bent spoon from a supine position. When he saw the blood on Sam's face he leaped up, the quickest I have ever seen my father move.

"What's happened?" he cried. "Did your brother do this?"

A nice assumption, which says a lot about my father's attitude toward me.

As he blocked Sam's nose I told him about the nest in the woods, how the nosebleed had come on all of a sudden. *"Bey neber dutched me,"* my brother kept saying through the clods of tissue. But my father was adamant the two events were connected. The wasps had harmed Sam in some way, and had to pay. At his insistence we led him back to the nest, with Sam bleeding all the way. Through the fence beside it you could see the golf course he used to visit with such regularity, a few argyle sweaters doing the rounds not so far away. Now the golf club was once more in our father's hand—I believe he had selected a nine iron for this shot—and he was lining himself up for a long, unorthodox swing. We pleaded, my brother and I, for him to leave the nest alone. The wasps had done nothing, we begged. The argyle sweaters had stopped and were looking over at us.

"Go on, Marty!" one of them shouted. "This one's for the cup!"

We hoped our father might recognize them and recoil in shame. We prayed for the yips to strike him at the moment of his swing. But our father had no such hang-ups with destruction. Order must be restored. He swung cleanly, brutally; a shattering hit. A pro might have been proud of that strike. The wasp nest exploded into a million pieces, blanching us with dust, to sarcastic cheers from the argyles. Inside the wedding cake shell you could see the most elaborate and incredible tunnels, a complex network of connection and information. And there was my father, Big Chief Pale Face, blinking stupidly beside it. It made you wonder who knew more about order.

Then the wasps were upon us. They were, no finer point on it, pissed. Their buzzing had gone up three notches, like a chainsaw hitting wood. They came for my father mostly, they seemed to have a pretty good idea what sort he was, but for my brother and me too, stinging wherever they could, a furious cloud, a biblical plague crawling under our shirt collars and up our shorts. We ran from those forsaken links with the laughter of the argyles at our heels, a tribe of jerky hollering vandals, a family united at last. My mother put us in the shower one by one, and when we emerged our new welts shone like medals.

Of course my father would not hear a word about it. He had played the right shot, made the right call. He knew all about wasps. This was how you dealt with them. On the subject of Sam, however, he was less certain. Sam, who did not stop bleeding all day, growing whiter and wilder, his eyes stretching with fear, until it became clear he needed medical attention. In an instant he became the disputed territory between my parents, a shorthand for all that was tainted and unresolved. Those two have been collapsing in slow motion ever since. It will not be long now.

10. CROQUEMBOUCHE

Very soon Bob will fade from this story, swallowed by a bigger creature. But in my head his tyranny lives on. Often in my dreams my skin is cauterized and traumatized in fresh and terrible ways. Sometimes when I shut my eyes I see the skin coming off like orange peel, or a blade sliding smoothly and firmly down the bridge of my nose, opening it up to the white beneath. I can still hear Bob's horribly blunt knife—a present from Marco Pierre White that he refused to throw away—causing tremendous grief to the shallots. *Borkunch*, it goes. *Borkunch*. And when I open my eyes, there are reminders all around me. Everything in the kitchen is designed to damage flesh. Lean boning knives that hew through sinew, razor-sharp mandolines that nibble the fingers. We have fire and boiling oil. We could defend a city against the Ottoman army. With these weapons we could fight a monster, and we shall.

The Mark of Bob was placed upon me the weekend after Dibden sank, two Sundays before Christmas and The Fat Man's fateful party. Racist Dave says I am not making this bit clear, that I am buzzing around this story in a way that makes him want to cause me harm. Fine. To make things clearer for Dave, the Mark of Bob was placed upon me on the day of the croquembouche. It was, I like to think, the event that set the wheels in motion; a cruelty too far, which led to the fall of Bob and the rise of something worse. This is how the tree of blood grows. New limbs keep sprouting. What warrants a plaster in December needs a gurney in April.

The croquembouche was Bob's idea. A wedding reception had

booked upstairs and Bob had offered to make the cake. What he meant was that Dave would make the cake—disgraced Dibden was not considered—so Bob offered the happy bride and groom the most difficult and elaborate cake he could think of.

"A fucking what, chef?" was Dave's response.

"A croquembouche," explained Bob. "It's French. Lots of little éclairs stacked up and stuck together with caramel. It is very fucking soigné."

"Oh."

"On a nougatine base."

"Right."

"With sugared almonds."

"Yeah."

"And royal icing."

"Yeah?"

"And spun sugar."

"Okay."

"And chocolate sauce."

"All right."

"And each éclair is filled with brandy crème patissière," said Bob. "About three hundred éclairs should do it."

"Fuck!"

Dave saw his day off disappear in a cloud of sugar. But he made it, and a traffic cone was stolen from the roadworks on the high street to contain the towering spectacle. An hour before the guests were due the croquembouche was freed to appreciative gasps from the chefs. Great was Bob's joy, for it was every bit as preposterous as he had envisaged it. Too tall to fit on a shelf, too precarious to sit out in the kitchen, it was left on the walk-in floor. When the moment came to bring the croquembouche forth, however, a terrible discovery was made. The dessert had collapsed. Éclairs covered the fridge floor soaking up boggy black kitchen muck. The proud tower was now more of a bungalow. Dave went into battle mode, saving what he could of the éclairs and trying to rebuild and disguise the ruined structure with new caramel and sauce. Bob stalked the aisles of the kitchen, his face harder than I had ever seen it, silent and furious, looking for blood.

"Someone knocked it," he muttered to Dave.

"It doesn't matter," Dave replied. "Let's just bang it out."

"Someone knocked it," Bob muttered again.

"Can I take it now?" Camp Charles rushed in. "The bride is looking *daggers*."

"Over my Gary Rhodes," said Dave. "You've got to have icing sugar dusting."

Eventually the croquembouche was dusted and sent. It was no longer soigné, or pristine, but it looked like whoever had eaten it first had been delicate about it. Bob was still livid, brooding dangerously in the corner of the kitchen. The chefs watched him fearfully. He grabbed the pan of caramel Dave had been using to conceal the flaws and took it back over to the solid top and stood there, stirring quietly. Cautiously, the kitchen returned to its tasks. The silence was terrible. After a minute or so, Bob spoke.

"Monocle, come over here."

I put down the lemon I was juicing and looked around at my fellow chefs. Ramilov, quenelling eel beignets at his section, did not seem to notice. Harmony looked up for the briefest moment and her dark eyes met mine. Was that concern in her face? I was wary of trying to read her expressions. I saw Racist Dave watching through the chain screen as he smoked in the yard. Dibden, who had been reacquainted with the lowly job of grating cabbage, was staring at me, frozen to the spot. His mouth was drawn tight. Very slowly and slightly he shook his head.

"*Oui, chef.*" I walked toward the stove.

"Hold out your hand," commanded Bob.

What else could I do? It seemed a reasonable request. I didn't know what would happen next. I didn't know Bob. I held out my hand, palm up.

"Other side," said Bob.

I turned my hand over. Dumbly I watched him gather a spoonful of the bubbling caramel. How stupid I was! Just watching him like that, with my hand outstretched . . . When I think about that moment, I do not see Bob in my memories. Only me, standing there like an idiot, waiting patiently for the saucepan's boiling contents to be tipped onto the back of my hand, waiting for the heat . . .

Oh god, the heat.

I'm not sure if *boiling* is the right word. For I know now that sugar changes state at a much higher temperature than water, between 140 and 160 degrees Celsius. The pain takes your breath away. It matures and swells. It finds new ways to express itself. And I know now that molten sugar hardens quickly when it hits the skin, like plastic does, so that when you try in panic to remove the searing heat you pull your skin off with it, leaving raw, damaged tissue behind. It makes you somehow to blame. I didn't appreciate that at the time, but I'm sure Bob did. Like I said, the man had an exquisite grasp of suffering.

And only now can I appreciate the profound sense of empathy Bob also possessed: he was cruel exactly to the point each chef would tolerate. He possessed an innate knowledge of whom he could and couldn't burn. He knew he could lock Ramilov in the fridge with lobsters and make Racist Dave work forty hours' unpaid overtime every week, but he was keenly, brilliantly aware that if he harmed their persons he would have a war on his hands. He knew he could scar me and I wouldn't leave, that I would thank guests for their custom even as I tried to soothe the wound. He knew that before I did. What Bob did not realize, what none of us did at the time, was that his cruelty pulled the odd and ornery chefs of The Swan together. He made it him against us.

"Everyone likes stories," Bob was saying. "Now you'll have a story to tell. Anytime someone mentions sugar, you'll think of me."

My hand was pulsing and raw right across the back where the caramel had been, a plastic pink jewel set in a clenched fist. I ran to the back sink to cool my tortured flesh under water but the sink was full of salmon defrosting and I knew I would be in more trouble if I got blood on the mise. So I dashed upstairs to the toilet that the kitchen shared with the function room on the first floor. Bob didn't like the chefs going up there when there were guests but sometimes, such as now, it couldn't be helped. I pressed my shaking hand beneath the cold tap and felt the shock of the water hitting it. I shut my eyes and cursed Bob silently for all the pain and misery he had put me through. Those long months in the plonge I had dreamed of succumbing to a terrible accident, a severed hand or the like that would cause the rest of the kitchen to gnash their teeth and wail at the injustice of it all. Well, here was the injured hand, the great agony, yet no sympathy was forthcoming. Nor was it an accident.

As I stood at the sink the toilet door swung open and a young man with blond hair careered in from the wedding party, laughing about something he had shouted to someone outside. His face was red with drink. He looked at me, a little surprised, and I could see what he saw: a young chef with a fresh scar on his hand who had not seen daylight for months, a haggard youth in checkered trousers stained with expensive food he never got to eat. I looked at him and saw someone my age, who might have gone to my university, his skin scrubbed pink and fresh, his fingernails free of dirt, without a care in the world. His office would have beanbags and smoothies. A foosball table for creative inspiration. Or perhaps he was another writer type, like my nemesis Tod Brightman. Drunk by four P.M. was a hallmark of literary talent. This encounter might feature in his next novel. *The Mysterious Tale of Ted Brickman. The Baghdad Birdspotters' Club. Strawberry Picking in Sarajevo.* Instinctively, I hated him.

"Awesome work on the food, man," he said in a posh voice. His breath was harsh with champagne.

"Thank you," I said, pulling my hand out of the sink and hiding it behind my back. "I'm glad you liked it, sir."

I grimaced humbly and ducked past him. *Sir?* I had wanted to throttle him, but instead I had called him "sir." Moreover, I felt proud. Even with my hand still pulsing like mad I was proud he liked the food cooked by the kitchen I worked in. I was proud of the place I hated. I could have shown the young man my wound and told him what kitchen life was really like and ruined that reception, I could have walked out of the restaurant then and there, I could have sued Bob. But I did none of those things. I hid my hand and bowed and scraped and called the customer "sir." I thought about the mise that still needed to be done before the dinner service, and how if I didn't do it chefs would be unhappy and betrayed and customers would have to wait. I headed back to the kitchen. It's a funny thing—I can't explain it. You want to leave every day; in your head you plan handing in your notice while you sweep the yard or carry the potatoes to the cellar, what you will say, how you will break the news. But something always stops you. It is never the right time. There is always work to be done.

Racist Dave observes it is only a burn and says I should stop feeling so sorry for myself. He advises me to jog on with the story and

asks if we are going to get to the gash and drugs and trouble soon. I
have reminded him what Walter Benjamin said about storytelling,
that "boredom is the dream bird that hatches the egg of experience." This argument has failed to impress him.

Downstairs, Bob greeted me triumphantly.

"Oh, Monocle. Welcome back. I got you a good one, didn't I?"

The rest of the kitchen said nothing. Bob was the chef. Backchat
was not appreciated. "Come not between the dragon and his wrath,"
the mad old king warns. All-powerful Bob, who held our fates
under his third chin. What could these flies say to him?

"That fucking bastard's got a nerve," was what Ramilov said later in
the pub. "Hot spoons are one thing, but caramel's not a joke. That's
just nasty. That's unpleasant."

"What are you going to do?" said Dave. "He does that to half the
chefs that walk through the door."

"Well, he better not try and do it to me," said Ramilov. "I'll
fucking ruin him."

Dave shrugged and turned to me.

"Elizabeth Arden Eight Hour cream," he advised. "It's fucking
boss for burns."

"Don't worry, kid," Ramilov whispered to me. "Very soon, we'll
get him."

"And it makes you smell like a new BMW," said Dave.

"Don't you worry, mate," Ramilov whispered again.

Mate? This was a change from the Ramilov I knew, the Ramilov
who had been campaigning for my name to be changed to "An Extraordinary Cunt." With a craven gratitude, as a beaten dog returns
to its master's side, I decided that Ramilov might not be such a bad

sort after all. Weeks of abuse wiped off the slate by one "mate." Perhaps there was more to the guy than cock jokes and horseplay. If I had been less busy marveling at this shred of pleasantness, I might have paid more attention to the intent in Ramilov's voice.

The tramp who was Bob's sworn enemy had spotted us through the beveled glass and come in through a side door.

"Gentlemen," he said in a groggy but ringmasterly manner, extending a crumpled paper cup. "A contribution to the cause?"

His long and slender fingers played upon the cup. A tune from another time.

"Not now, Glen," said Ramilov. "We're up to our necks in it."

"Glen Roberts, you're still barred!" Nora shouted from behind the pumps. She pointed to a faded sign on the wall, really several faded signs fixed together, that said in handwritten capitals: DO NOT ASK ME FOR CREDIT. IT UPSETS ME.

Then, farther down: NEITHER A BORROWER NOR A MONEY LENDER BE. I DID IT ONCE AND NOW I AM BROKE.

With a wistful look at Nora, Glen slunk out.

"It's not right," Dibden said quietly. The way he held his glass his own Mark of Bob was visible, a cruel privilege only he and I enjoyed. "I mean, I think Bob means well"—here Ramilov barked derisively into his beer—"but we shouldn't have to take this. I mean, I've been taught by the master, Chef Ducasse of The Dorchester."

"This again," said Ramilov. "One day your mouth will eat itself."

"At The Dorchester," Dibden went on, ignoring him, "it was hard but fair. Military precision, yes, but no violence. We started at five in the morning for the breakfast shift and more than once if I worked late the night before I would curl up on my section and sleep there. There was no time to go home, you see, no time. Every morning a team of chefs would set to making the pastries, there was a team to prep the fruits, a team to make the breads and so on. It was an immense operation, grueling, but when the chef gave you that little nod you knew you'd done well."

"Hotel chefing is the last insult to the human spirit," said Ramilov. "You can cut my dick off before I become a banquet chef."

"It requires skill and organization," said Dibden, "which you know nothing about. How do you get a hundred and fifty soufflés to the table before a single one collapses? How do you keep the ice cream frozen in the middle of two hundred Baked Alaskas? This is beyond your comprehension."

"If it was so good," said Ramilov, "why did you leave?"

"The new head chef was different," said Dibden. "He didn't care as much as I did."

"And flamingos stand on one leg to prove they're not drunk," said Ramilov. He downed his pint, stood unsteadily on one leg to demonstrate his point and fell face-first into the lap of an angry Irish pensioner on the next table.

"Dibden!" he called from the floor. "I have fallen! What an amateur I am! How did you sink so gracefully, like the sack that is filled with shit?"

Picking himself up without another word, he strode off to the bar for more beer. I thought it prudent to go over and help him with the drinks. Besides, it was depressing listening to Dibden lie about his glory days.

At the bar, two regulars conversed with the cross-eyed proprietress.

"He's a wrong 'un," one of the men was telling the other. "Owes so many people money he can't walk down the high street. Has to go all the back routes."

"He's another George," said the second man.

"You know the worst thing about George?" said Nora. "He'll be out soon."

"Christ, it's true," said the second man. "How many was it?"

"A pair of 'em," said the first man. "But in the eyes of the law it's only destruction of private property. Park wardens were steaming."

"Christ," said his colleague again.

"You'd get worse for stealing a sofa," said the first man. "In the eyes of the law."

"I was up at that park the other week," said the second man, "and there were hundreds of Canada geese."

"Well, they migrate here, don't they?" said his friend.

"There's a shitload there now."

"Gaggle," said Ramilov, who was waiting to be served.

The two men looked at him suspiciously.

"What?" said the man who had seen the geese.

"It's a gaggle of geese, not a shitload," Ramilov explained woozily.

"What the fuck are you talking about?" the man asked Ramilov in a less than friendly manner.

"And it's a skein of geese if they're in the sky," Ramilov added helpfully. I would venture the word *skein* had never been heard in O'Reillys before that night, and I was secretly impressed.

"Are you taking the fucking piss?" said the first man.

"Abs'lutely not," Ramilov slurred, looking grievously offended. "I never joke about collective nouns."

"Who is this cunt?" the other man asked Nora.

"Now you." Nora rounded on Ramilov in cross-eyed fury.

"Ah, Nora, I was just telling these gentlemen about collective nouns."

"I don't give a feck," said Nora. "We'll have less of it."

Ramilov could not understand why anyone would want less of collective nouns.

"It's an effective description of types," he explained indignantly.

"For instance, Nora, were you aware it's a *blarney* of bartenders? Blarney is Irish for nonsense or bollocks . . ."

"Stop talking, man!" cried Nora.

"You seem a little stressed, Nora," Ramilov observed with blurry but genuine concern, wagging a finger at the lady of the house. "I think your work-life balance might be out of sync."

"*Right!*" shouted Nora. "*I've had enough of your lip for one evening. Get out and take your poxy friends with you.*"

"Nice one, Ramilov," said Dave when we were turned out in the rain and shivering like wet dogs. "We'll never get another pint in at this hour."

"Let's go see Mr. Michael," Ramilov said.

11. DELICACIES

We were in need of cheering up, Ramilov shouted at us through the rain as he led us to the modest lodgings of Mr. Michael, the neighborhood drug dealer. Between my wounded hand and my more general melancholy, I agreed with that much of what he said. Mr. Michael was regarded as a most obliging sort by one and all, Ramilov went on, leaping a puddle with surprising grace, as long as you did not owe him money. Since none of us apart from Ramilov had met Mr. Michael before, or even heard of him, we were quietly confident that we were square on this account. Our confidence proved unfounded.

"Aha!" came the cry as the door opened. "You owe me money, you owe me money, you owe me money!" Mr. Michael pointed at me, then Racist Dave, and then, possibly correctly, at Ramilov. "And you," he said, spotting Dibden hiding at the back, "owe me lots of money."

"I don't think this is a good idea," Dibden whispered to Ramilov as Mr. Michael led us inside. The same idea had occurred to me also.

Ramilov was shocked.

"Come on, Dibden," he said. "What else are you going to do?"

"Sleep?"

Ramilov dismissed this suggestion with contempt.

"What's the chef's motto, Dibden?" he asked.

"Hurry up?" said Dibden.

"No," said Ramilov. "It's *'Here for a good time, not a long time.'*"

The corridor opened into a sparse kitchen and living room. At the far end, a very small and shriveled man was curled up in a fetal position on a large leather sofa, his eyes shut tight. Mr. Michael sat down beside the man without paying him any attention and busied himself undoing an ingeniously knotted plastic bag on the coffee table in front of him. He sat with a very upright posture, a short fellow with a head too large for his body. The features of his face were set in a friendly expression, though still a little scary at that.

"What brings you gentlemen calling at such an hour?" he asked magnanimously.

"We've had a shit day," said Ramilov bluntly. "We need cheering up."

"This I can facilitate," Mr. Michael proclaimed happily. His pronunciation was glottal, particular.

Ramilov and Mr. Michael proceeded to discuss the particulars with occasional suggestions or haggles from Racist Dave, who it turned out was something of a connoisseur when it came to narcotics.

"We shouldn't be doing this," Dibden moaned to me. "We've got work tomorrow and I'm already in the sugar before the day has started."

This last part was certainly true and I felt very sorry for Dibden, since it was entirely his fault that he was useless and he did not have a soul in the world to blame for his misfortunes. And I too was somewhat skeptical about the wisdom of starting on a drugs bender at midnight with work the next day. What I really wanted, above all else, was to go back to my room and lie on my bed with my pulsing hand wrapped in a cold damp flannel and let my mind wander into forbidden thoughts about Harmony, tracing scars, lulled by the creaks of the radiator as it cooled and the casual cries of violence from the street below, not so different from the kitchen sounds perhaps but turned down a few notches, until sleep ran up on me.

Sleep was a friend I seldom saw. I had no business with these pills and powders and you-owe-me-money types. Was I now a drug fiend like those lost souls beneath my window? Was this, like the whole process of moving to Camden, another petty act of rebellion?

Ramilov, perhaps sensing my trepidation, was shooting long, measured stares in my direction as he negotiated the finer points of business with Mr. Michael and Dave. It felt very much like I was being sounded out, as if this were a marker or test of some sort. Not whether I was a man, but maybe whether I was a chef, whether I had that love of self-destruction, that willful pursuit of sensation and oblivion, that natural inclination to the path of most resistance, that appetite, insatiable and pestilential in its scope, which overrode everything. And I realized I wanted to pass Ramilov's test, to impress him, more than I ever had my father. From Ramilov I had learned the praising of waitresses, the giving of oracles, the taming of men. From my father, what had I learned? The ignoring of phone calls, the squeezing of spots, the passing of blame.

"So it's decided," said Ramilov at last. "Those two cunts over there will have a pill each and Dave and I will take four between us and we'll split a gram of that horrible mersh for a nudge in the right direction."

"You are doubly in luck then," said Mr. Michael, "as I am currently running a buy-four-get-one-free promotion on pills, which makes the tally five for you two."

"Grand," said Ramilov. He looked at the shriveled comatose man in the corner of the sofa. "What's up with him?"

"Rossi," said Mr. Michael, "shall not be partaking of any more delicacies tonight."

"Rossi?" said Ramilov, then leaned toward the shriveled man and shouted at him. "*Va bene, ragazzo? Tutti apposto?*"

"I wouldn't bovver with that, mate," said Mr. Michael with disinterest. "Rossi does not speak Italian. Rossi does not speak much."

The shriveled Rossi opened his eyes a fraction and looked forlornly at Mr. Michael, then Ramilov, who grinned and gave him the thumbs-up. This seemed to make Rossi even more anxious, and he swiftly squeezed his eyes shut again.

While Mr. Michael weighed and sorted the drugs, Ramilov collected the money from the rest of us. Dibden was still making a fuss but Ramilov explained that Mr. Michael's drugs were quite shit and would wear off in a couple of hours. Mr. Michael took exception to this argument and Dibden did not seem much convinced by it either but in the end the chef handed over money and the dealer handed over delicacies and we all partook.

As I remember it, the waiting was the longest part of that night, sitting in a strange flat with a drug dealer and a comatose Italian who did not speak Italian, waiting for it all to seem like a normal, even pleasant, thing; for this quite awkward situation to change from within. While we waited, Mr. Michael informed us of the harem he was cultivating, an exercise pitched somewhere in the middle of Ramilov's suggested work-life balance. The harem was keeping Mr. Michael very busy. The women were doing his bloody nut, he explained, and when they did that you had to give them a bit of time to cool off, then they were happy to see you again. Ramilov nodded vigorously in agreement.

"Do you gentlemen know any girls?" Mr. Michael asked.

Ramilov thought about this and replied with another question.

"Would we be here if we did?" he asked.

Mr. Michael shook his head. There were a number of good brothels he could recommend, all quite reasonable. Not as many as there used to be, of course. Whoring was not as recession-proof as you might think. Likewise with dealing. He'd had to adapt his business model. Hence the coke for thirty pounds a gram—"the mersh," as he called it, the commercial stuff. Sure, it was shit, cut to buggery, but people wanted a budget option. He was also doing an eighty-pound gram, for the luxury market.

"It's like how you used to have Mars bars and that was it," he explained. "Now you've got fun size, king size, twin pack, minia-tures, Mars drinks, Mars dark, Mars ice cream, Mars Planets, and *then* your Mars bar. These days you've got to give the consumer choice across the board or you're dead in the water."

He spoke of the rival business in Camden. A Mr. Big character had flooded the streets with some disgracefully bad product.

"Should be ashamed to call himself a dealer," he declared. "Brings the whole profession into disrepute. But I welcome the competition. That's the free market, innit." He paused to accept a joint from Ramilov before adding darkly, "Plus he's only got one eye. Visually he's in trouble. He's got blind spots."

As he spoke, I felt the rush begin. Not the dinner service sort of rush exactly but a relation of it, a cavernous cousin, a sickly light-ness, a blur in the edges of vision. My stomach was in turmoil, as if I had eaten a crow. Its sharp bones folded and unfolded in the re-cesses of my gut. Its soft dry feathers against my insides made my senses bristle. I realized it was trying to spread its wings. In the darkness its black beak opened and shut. The air about me seemed to be concentrating with special, intoxicating powers; I was excited just to breathe it. Then my pupils started to breathe the air too, to see what they'd been missing, and it was so strong, that air, so fresh. . . . Before long I was chain-smoking Ramilov's Marlboros and telling Racist Dave about love.

"We have to satisfy ourselves with the idea of love, you know?

Not loving things—we might not even care about the things—but loving the loving of things."

Dave said he did not know what I was talking about.

"Some writer said it," I told him. "I can't remember who. Love must be the object of our love."

"Monocle, I will give you ten pounds if you shut the fuck up right now," said Dave, who had ingested a not insignificant amount of drugs and was looking somewhat peaky.

"Take me, for instance," I said. "I love loving love. Love loves loving, you know?"

"Please shut up," Dave groaned.

"What I'm saying," I explained, "is that our love for things is not so great as our love for our love for things."

"Make him stop," cried Dave, rolling his eyes into the back of his head and trying to crawl inside the sofa.

"*Oi!*" shouted Ramilov. "Don't talk bollocks to Racist Dave when his brain is cake. Use your English lit degree for good, not evil."

"My parents never showed me any love," Dibden exclaimed with big moon eyes. "They never gave a . . . a sugar."

Wincing at the mention of that scorching word, I thought not of Bob but of my father, with his own very particular brand of affection. And even through the pills and their talk of love's loves I could not disregard his rare ability to disparage. But at least I had escaped and found other people to mock me and be disparaging, people who were not supposed to love me in the first place and had built no such intricate fencing around the concept.

"I think I'm going to call you 'Sugar Tits' from now on, Dibden," said Ramilov, "because it's ruder in your language than in mine."

"Thanks, mate," said Dibden fondly.

"Don't call me mate, Sugar Tits," replied Ramilov. "Our relationship and this drug binge are purely professional."

"Not for much longer it won't be," said Dibden. "I'm going to quit."

This comment prompted much groaning and general ill feeling toward Dibden.

"*Are Subway hiring?*" Ramilov shouted, even though Dibden was sitting right next to him.

Dibden explained it was nothing personal against any of us, just that kitchens did not have to be run this way and we all deserved better. Ramilov grew quiet at that and muttered that Bob would get his soon enough, but the crows in our bellies were in full flight now and hardly had the subject of Bob's crimes been raised than someone shouted for music and there was a collective surge for Mr. Michael's computer, where a series of increasingly frantic numbers were found and played until they lost their punch somewhere around the minute mark, at which time they were abandoned in favor of something else that absolutely had to be played this instant, and so forth, with bodies rising or falling according to musical preference and Mr. Michael's oversized head grinning along at the madness he had sown, occasionally nudging poor Rossi into consciousness to witness one chef or another making a fool out of himself.

Scarcely had the dancing begun, it seemed, than Ramilov cried out for booze and cigarettes and on prosthetic legs we skidded down the stairs and out into the streets where the air was alive and the lights held conversations with our eyes and here now was a wrinkled street busker, strumming "Wonderwall," whom Ramilov snarled at and accused of "trying to kill him with his fucking oboe." The fellow was aggrieved and pointed out that he was playing a guitar but this denial only made Ramilov more suspicious and he was suggesting that Carlos Sultana was a smart arse when we dragged him down the street away from danger. And soon we were in the late-night supermarket and the dark South Asian faces were watching us with fear and fascination and the juice cartons were a wall of colors in my eyes, the brightest reds and pinks and purpley blues and yellowy greens, and this was so wonderful to me that I did not know how to express it, there were not words enough to tell it, though I thought I must try.

"My soul is overwrought with petals of wonderment," I told Ramilov.

Ramilov made his face into a wall of teeth and glanced left and right in great concern.

"Please don't talk like that," he said. "Someone might hear you."

The next thing anyone knew we were back at Mr. Michael's and dancing once more and then the music had grown old again and we were talking, gabbling long excited stanzas, and again the subject turned to love and Dave, much recovered, widened his ink-blot pupils as he declared undying ardor for a girl back in Manchester whom he had had to leave behind when he boshed all the drugs he was supposed to sell and thereby chafed the criminal element.

"That was five years ago," he explained sadly. "We don't talk anymore, but I still think about her all the time. I fucking loved her."

To which Ramilov, Mr. Compassion, replied thoughtfully that five years was a lot of sex.

Dave began to cry at that, which was a departure for him emotionally, and Ramilov pulled his mouth into a wince and rubbed his eyeball socket with the palm of his hand and said, "Don't cry, mate, don't cry," but that did not seem to have any effect on Dave who was really going for it with long wracking sobs. Dave, reviewing this chapter, disputes this account, but I have found that despite his hard exterior Dave can be quite inclined to the sentimental when the mood takes him. Soft elements live about him; others will break your hand. I suppose no one is quite the right balance. Ramilov put out his cigarette and leaned over and gave him a hug, then he shouted that everyone should be hugging Racist Dave, which seemed like a good idea so we all came over and hugged Dave who smelled strongly of Lynx and gum and he told us how grateful he was to have such a good group of friends around him. That was what chefs had to do, he said. They had to stick together. They were family.

This comment, from the mouth of Racist Dave, no less, should have filled me with horror. Yet for some reason it felt, and continues to feel, true. This was my family now.

12. GLORIANA

I don't regret what happened next, Bob got what was coming to him, but at the time it seemed like very bad luck that everything came together the way it did. "A huge shitstorm" is how Racist Dave describes it. Though I do not often agree with Dave's choice of vocabulary, it being somewhat limited, I am inclined to concur with him on this occasion.

Bob's demise was brought about by many factors, of which he was one, but it will forever be symbolized by the Gloriana. What, you may ask, is a Gloriana? Picture one of those Russian dolls with another smaller doll inside it, and another inside that and so on. Well, a Gloriana is a Russian doll made with birds. A quail inside a guinea fowl inside a duck inside a chicken inside a turkey or some such. You've got to bone each bird and splay it open to wrap the next smallest bird within. Then you cook the whole monstrous thing and some poor devil tries to eat it.

According to Dave, Bob had read about the Gloriana in a book, one with leather binding and color pictures and a name like *Great Dishes of Antiquity* or *The Taste of Luxurious Yesteryear*. Dave says he saw this book and it was like another world. Everything was set in jelly and the potatoes were as smooth and white as eggs. There were recipes for animals he'd never heard of. The one that got Bob dribbling was called the Rôti Sans Pareil, a type of Gloriana made for a French king with bustard, pheasant, teal, woodcock, plover, lapwing, linnet, lark, and a garden warbler; seventeen birds in all. He got his head chopped off, the king, but I think that was for something else.

Dave says that Bob was beside himself grieving when Gavin at Upfront Meat informed him that half the species in the recipe were as good as extinct. Bob was desperate to cause a sensation at The Fat Man's Christmas feast, and he had got it into his head that only a Gloriana would do. Gavin saw how tearful Bob was about his Gloriana and said he would see what he could rustle up.

So the day before the grand dinner, as I washed salad in the back sink, The Mark of Bob shimmering darkly beneath the water like some rare fish, Gavin and one of his meat lackeys came puffing into the kitchen with a large package wrapped in greaseproof paper. Ordinarily Bob let the commis bear the weight of the deliveries, but on this occasion he insisted on helping haul it onto the tabletop.

"Right," Gavin said to Bob when they got it up onto the counter. "There she is, then."

"She doesn't look too bad either." Bob was peering through a hole in the bag like a cheap pornographer.

"She's a beauty, all right," said Gavin. "You know what she needs?"

"Course I do," said Bob. "Nothing to it."

This Frankenstein's monster took up so much space in the oven that Bob decided to cook it halfway through on the Friday and finish it off ahead of the dinner on Saturday. As much as I hated Bob, I freely admit that when he removed the Gloriana from the oven that Friday evening, with the juices spitting and sizzling, it was a thing of beauty. We were all called over to admire it. Then Bob's wife emerged and demanded her Booboo come upstairs and he hurried off, leaving instructions for the Gloriana to go in the fridge and to make sure everything was ready for tomorrow.

When the clean down was finished Ramilov said he needed to catch up on some mise before the big dinner. He could lock up, he told Dave. Ramilov had been somewhat taciturn since he had been locked in the fridge with the lobsters and since Bob had put his mark upon me, so the offer came as a surprise. But as Dave has helpfully explained, he wasn't going to wait around for Ramilov to finish when he had *Fiddler on the Roof* waiting for him at home, so he handed over the keys.

The next morning Ramilov was in before the rest of the kitchen, working studiously on the menu preparations. Again this was odd: it was as unusual for Ramilov to be early as it was for him to volunteer for extra work. Yet everything seemed to be in place and the Gloriana in the fridge looked golden and succulent. That afternoon Bob put it back in the oven to warm through and resumed his bragging.

You could tell it meant a lot to him. He even gave the staff a predinner talk, front and back of house gathered together, to impress upon us all the importance of the event.

"This is the biggest night of the year," he said. "Some powerful people are going to be here, and it's vital we show them a good time. I mean really vital. Life or death . . . But we get this right and we're free."

I was less than sure about the phrasing, or how much this speech was for us. It seemed as if Bob had gone into himself a bit. Perhaps he sensed this, for his next words were quite consciously for our benefit.

"I know you've all worked hard, and I know you're tired. And we are so nearly there. This is the last push before we go off to spend time with our families. . . ."

This part of Bob's little speech elicited snorts of merriment from some of the restaurant staff. I suppose they were snorting at the suggestion that getting Christmas Day and Boxing Day off counted as a holiday, but they might equally well have been snorting at the idea of Bob modeling a scarf his mother had knitted him or Bob and Trowelface watching the Queen's Speech, for the thought of the man spending time with his family was like envisioning a dog trying to walk on its hind legs—the humanity it conferred was preposterous. I snorted for another reason altogether. I snorted at the idea of family.

"If we get this right, we'll put this place on the map," said Bob. "And what's good for The Swan is good for every single one of you. . . ."

On he went, making a big deal of how this dinner was going to lift all our fortunes and change our lives and so forth. The amount of significance he had placed on that Frankenstein bird was almost touching. An unpleasant individual, certainly, but also a hopeful one. He did want things to be better, and that was worth something.

Dibden was also buoyed by Bob's optimism, and as the meeting adjourned he approached with a suggested improvement to the great dinner.

"Chef, how about some apple crisps for the Christmas pudding?" he asked.

Bob must have had other things on his mind because he told Dibden he was going to cut his balls off and hang them on the Christmas tree if he mentioned apple crisps again.

Camp Charles also had a query for Bob: "Chef, there's the small matter of that *filthy fox*." The maître d' was always trying to get rid of the molting fox above the bar. He felt it spoiled the ambience of the establishment.

Bob groaned. He had bought the fox at a flea market and now it had moths. There was a cheap irony for you.

Camp Charles stood awaiting an answer.

"It's *crawling* with *beasts*," he explained.

"Then put it in the freezer to kill the eggs, gaylord," Bob said at last. "Why do I have to think of everything?"

So Camp Charles took Bob's advice and lugged the skanky creature down to the chest freezers in the basement and cleared a space for it in one of them. After fitting it in among the jowls of beef and solid gray ox tails he must have looked again at the wretched beast, its teeth permanently bared, and decided it would not do for the restaurant staff to come across it unannounced. Those of a nervous disposition might not appreciate it. So he wrote a note in bold black marker: BEWARE! FOX INSIDE.

The next part is now the stuff of legend, told by chefs who like to scare other chefs with bogeyman stories of crime and punishment. If you don't watch out, they say, you could make this place another Swan. Any chef who gets a kick out of another kitchen's misery repeats this story, so it's told a lot.

About an hour before dinner, an awful smell started to creep out from beneath the oven doors as The Fat Man's guests gathered in the bar. We noticed it first—an acrid yellow stink crawling into the nostrils.

"What is that?" I asked Dave.

He gave me a strange look and said nothing.

"Shouldn't we tell Bob?" I asked.

"Leave it alone, Monocle," was all he said.

Dave, my personal revisionist, denies this exchange. He says if he spoke to me it was because I was talking again when I should have been working. He says he smelled nothing. Bob, running back and forth between his minions in the kitchen and his new friends in the bar, did not seem to catch it either. Nor, it seemed, did The Fat Man's guests. They made their way up the back staircase, chattering about the surprise in store while the fog gathered in the near room.

Bob was shouting at all of us over the kitchen swelter now. I think he was anxious too: The Fat Man seemed to bring it out in him.

In the midst of this excitement, a small and inconspicuous man appeared at the back door of the kitchen. I'm trying to remember what the man was wearing or what he looked like but I can't. He was sort of hard to focus on, like the patterns on the seats in public transport. You got bored if you looked at him too long. When he walked into the room it felt like someone had just left. None of the other chefs seemed to notice the man, for he walked unchecked into the frantic gangway and was caught smack in the chest by Harmony, spinning round from the back sink to chuck a hotel tray into the plonge.

"Say '*Backs!*'" she shouted, glowering at the man. "Always say '*Backs!*'"

"Or you could watch where you're going," said the little man smartly. "It's not a good way to start an inspection."

"What?" said Harmony.

"I am the restaurant inspector," announced the man.

Harmony flushed a deep red. I would be lying if I said I did not enjoy seeing her squirm a little.

"Really?" she asked.

"Really."

"*Chef!*" Harmony turned her neck and yelled to Bob, who was gauging the suitability of some nibbles at the pass.

"*What?*" Bob shouted back, mouth full.

"*There's a man here. . . . A restaurant inspector!*"

From round the corner Bob appeared, swallowing hard and wiping his hands on his apron.

"Really?" he said. "Now?"

"Yes," said the inspector. His quick eyes appraised Bob. "Now."

"It's just we've got a massive party upstairs, we're serving up any minute," Bob explained, his voice caught halfway between kitchen bully and whining Booboo. "Can't you come back another time?"

"We've had a tip-off about this place," said the inspector. "We like to act on these things as fast as possible."

"A tip-off?" Bob scoffed. "I think there's been some mistake. We're at the top of our game. Look at this. . . ."

He gave Dave a nod and together they pulled down the oven door. The miraculous bird was brought forth shining like the Ark of the Covenant.

"You won't find any problems here," Bob informed the inspector. The power was creeping back into his voice again, drop by drop.

"It smells odd," said the inspector, and wrote something down on his clipboard.

Bob flashed him a patronizing grin.

"You come upstairs," he said. "See how they lap it up."

It took four of us to carry the Gloriana upstairs, all in great ceremony with Bob following behind with a silly new tall hat on, the nondescript inspector behind him, slight and precise in his movements, full of animal intelligence. The room, I noticed, was strangely quiet for a party of thirty or so guests, though a general gasp still went up when the bird came in. No one had ever seen such a thing. Was it real? Had the dodo been rediscovered? Could it be eaten? I also noticed—it was hard not to—The Fat Man's threatening circumference at the head of the table. Even he looked impressed. We set the bird down in front of him and fanned out along the walls, hands behind our backs. The inspector stood in the corner in his drab suit, his drab little eyes blinking in the glamour of the occasion. The Fat Man rose from his seat and cleared his throat to speak. Immediately, the room fell silent.

"Well, well," he said. "Here we all are. So glad you could all make it. So nice to see everyone without sheets over their heads."

A few of the rich guests smiled uncomfortably. Others looked away. At the time I don't think any of us chefs paid much attention to The Fat Man's speech, or to the anxiety he seemed to instill in his supposed friends. Not that it would have made much difference. When you are already in the web, it does not help to have it pointed out to you.

"Your donations have been most generous," The Fat Man continued. "Wonderful how charitable people can be given the right incentive. . . . But it's not about that tonight. No. Tonight we're all friends. That stuff is forgotten. So don't look so nervous! This isn't one of *those* dinners. Enjoy yourselves! Eat! Drink! Take full advantage of the hospitality of Bob here, who's cooked this fantastic creature for us. . . . Isn't that right, Bobby?"

Bob's face, which had paled slightly as The Fat Man spoke, resumed its impersonation of a proud plum. All those rich and privileged eyes, on him! He took his place next to The Fat Man and stood over the enormous beast, carving knife raised. Poised in anticipation, he was. He never looked more gluttonous.

"That's right," he said.

"Tell us, then, Bobby," said The Fat Man, taking his seat. "What's this treat you've made for us?"

I remember Bob's next words so clearly. The hubris makes my toes curl even now.

"Ladies and gentlemen," he said, clearing his throat for effect. "It gives me enormous pleasure to introduce my pride and joy, a creation of my own devising . . . *the Gloriana*." There was a pause, in which Bob looked slyly at the inspector, then at The Fat Man. "If I might say something else?"

"Of course," said The Fat Man. "Help yourself."

"We've also got a special guest in our midst this evening," Bob continued with a sarcastic nod in the direction of the little man. "A restaurant inspector."

The guests laughed uncertainly and swiveled in their seats.

"He's here to check I'm not poisoning any of you," said Bob, drawing more laughter from the crowd. Even The Fat Man gave a little smile. "What do you think, everyone?" Bob gestured smugly at the golden beast in front of him. "How am I doing so far?"

He allowed himself a last triumphant chuckle at the inspector and angled his knife to pierce the side of the bird. It's a way to tell if the meat is cooked, as much as anything, if the juices run clear. If there's blood it means it's not done yet. The Romans did it to Christ too, when he was on the cross. Pierced him with a spear and blood and water came out. Maybe that's why Christ rose from the tomb the way he did. He wasn't done yet. Into the monstrous bird went Bob's knife. Into the flesh it sliced. . . .

But to Bob's great surprise there was neither blood nor water in the Gloriana. As the knife went in a great jet of clotted pus sprayed out from the bird. The stench of rotten flesh hit the guests. Some of the pus hit them too. It was too raw and sudden for some of the diners; for all their good breeding they were overwhelmed. They couldn't control themselves. One lady vomited where she sat. Another rushed from the room with her hand clasped to her mouth, then staggered on her heels, lost her balance and fell down the stairs with a terrible racket. We chefs had to put our hands over our faces, which did not look at all proper. It looked as if we were laughing. Even Harmony was trying not to smile. I noted, to my chagrin, that happiness looked marvelous on her.

Bob did not move. He stood fixed in this dumb pose, like a hunter with his catch, except without the grin. Oh, that look! When I get sad thinking about the misery he inflicted upon us or the injustice of what happened to Ramilov and the storm clouds seem never-ending, I have only to recall that look to cheer myself up. Bob's color was puce or darker. I stood in the corner unnoticed, drinking it in.

All eyes turned toward The Fat Man. His breath was coming deep and heavy. With a napkin he dabbed stiffly at some pus on his suit. He did not say a word. After a moment or a lifetime he rose and fixed Bob with a look of such cruelty, such profound disgust, that it quite took your breath away. He threw the napkin down on the Gloriana.

"You owe me, Bobby," he said. He looked around at the other chefs and the guests who had lowered their heads. "Remember that, all of you!" he shouted. "You owe me!" With that he sailed hugely out.

At his exit the room awakened as if from a spell. The guests began to talk again; some phoned taxis. Beside me, the restaurant inspector was looking somewhat disappointed and making little tut-tut noises under his breath.

"Rancid meat, risk of botulism, salmonella," he said, shaking his head. He leaned forward to the table and scraped a sample of something unpleasant into a petri dish.

"*Get them out of here!*" Bob was hissing loudly to Camp Charles over the heads of the shell-shocked guests. "*And you, Monocle!*" He beckoned me over. "*Take that fucking inspector downstairs right now, I don't care where.*"

So I led the inspector downstairs to look at the kitchen, where Ramilov took it upon himself to tell him at some length how he too was a great one for standards. I thought Ramilov made too much of this myself, especially in light of the Armageddon unfolding upstairs, and I sensed the inspector thought so too because he kept right on examining the bread bins and running his finger along the bottom of the ovens and peeking over the top of the shelves saying "Oh really?" and "Is that so?" while Ramilov talked, as if he were not really listening to any of it.

The inspector's mood was stable if not sunny until we navigated the perilously steep steps down to the basement and I showed him the whereabouts of the chest freezers.

"What's this sign?" he asked me. "*Beware! Fox inside.*"

For a long and horrible moment my mind raced through possible explanations I could give the inspector, but none of them was good enough to say out loud. A number of bad things were happening quite fast. I cannot speak for the inspector here but personally my nerves were very raw at this point.

The inspector opened the freezer cabinet and let out a howl of horror.

"I am sure I do not need to tell you this is a hotbed for germs," he said. "Disease germs," he added, as if there were any other kind, before resuming his tut-tutting with vigor.

When we emerged into the kitchen once more Bob was waiting for us with a shit-eating grin plastered across his chops. Clearly he had rallied himself and decided to schmooze the inspector into favor. I wasn't sure it would work. Bob's charm offensives tended to be light on the charm and heavy on the offensive. But before he could attempt anything the inspector laid in with the tough questions.

"Are you aware there is a fox in your meat freezer?" he asked.

Bob's grin fell. He blinked stupidly a few times.

"I can explain that," he stammered.

"You had better." The little man looked up at Bob with disapproval. "That's a serious risk of foreign-body contamination."

"The thing is," said Bob weakly, "it's got moths."

"I see," said the inspector curtly. "Well, I think I've seen and heard enough. You will be hearing from me very shortly." He glared at Bob and stepped out through the chain screen.

"Mr. Inspector, wait . . ." said Bob, following him out. I felt obliged to go with him.

It was a cold and miserable night, the rain falling in heavy sheets. The inspector, paying small heed to Bob's implorations, fought briefly with the back gate, got it open at last and walked full pelt into Glen, who was taking a shit in the alley as was his custom. The inspector was not at all keen on this latest development and shouted at the tramp, his muted voice trembling with rage and indignation, that this was a restaurant premises and did he mind.

"Do *you* mind?" Glen soggily replied. "This is a personal matter if you had not noticed. Tell the chef I'm going to need a lot of napkins today. This one is turning out a little tricky."

"Napkins?" the inspector mumbled in shock. "They give you napkins for this?"

That seemed to make up his mind and he squeezed quickly past the squatting Glen and bolted out of the alleyway in a stiff, jogging walk.

"Mr. Inspector," Bob shouted, running after him into the street. "Wait! I've never seen that man before, I swear! Mr. Inspector—"

The inspector spun around to face Bob. They were standing on the pavement a few yards from the entrance, where the last of the dismissed guests huddled under the awnings waiting for their cabs.

"This is The Swan on top of its game, is it?" the inspector shouted through the downpour. "A turkey full of pus? A fox with moths? Human feces? It's the single worst inspection I've ever conducted. This place is closed, effective immediately, as of now!"

With that he turned and strode away from the restaurant as fast as he could. And Bob, instead of following or trying to shout after

him again, fell back against the wall in despair, deflating in front of
my eyes. Personally I expected him to stomp back into the kitchen
and give us all seven shades of hell for what had happened that
night. But he just stood there in the pissing night, in the utter damnation of it all, rain or tears coursing down his massive fleshy face,
mumbling softly to himself, "I'm finished. I'm finished." Here were
the nails in the wall, here the hanging man.

Plenty of times in the course of my employment at The Swan I had
dreamed of hearing this news, of seeing Bob broken. But when it
happened I found I was not so happy after all. Bob's downfall killed
The Swan. It finished every one of us. In hushed tones that evening
Racist Dave told the other chefs that the restaurant was bound to
reopen sooner or later, but how long might that be? I couldn't wait
forever. Without a job I would be on a train north within the month.
I had not forgotten the finality of my mother's last e-mail, or those
frequent missed calls from my father. There was a reason he kept
ringing, and deprived of a kitchen to hide in I feared I would soon
know it. And I thought of what The Fat Man had shouted as he left
The Swan: how we all owed him now. This debacle would come at
a price. With Bob gone, who would pay the debt?

That night the extractor fans were silenced, the burners extinguished. The chef's whites were thrown pointedly into the laundry
basket. Then—terror of terrors—the large, glowing switch that said
IF THIS IS OFF THEN WE ARE ALL FUCKED was flicked to off.
There were no earthquakes when this happened, no planes falling
out of the sky or lakes of blood cascading through the ceiling.
Nothing. The kitchen was silent.

INTERLUDE

I. AFTER BOB

So I was free once more. Monocle the fly, at liberty to buzz wherever I pleased. To sit in the armchair that smelled of hand lotion and read "The Waste Land," complete with annotations. To pick my zits all day if I wished. To discuss the state of the neighborhood with Mrs. Molina in patchy Latinate. To trawl through the charity shop downstairs in search of bargains, nose averted from the smell of death. And to think, often, of the kitchen I had come from and the service that Bob had demanded, of the burning and mind games and long, thankless hours, where the choice to stay or quit had existed only in theory. That was no type of freedom, surely.

Racist Dave, if he hears me talking like this, will no doubt tell me to stop feeling so sorry for myself and crack on, but it occurs to me now that we tolerated it because we had no wish to be free. It was the same reason why I had spent four months at home after university, hating every minute of it, trying to clear the brambles and splintery green alkanet from the garden, my father asking me every day why hadn't I got a job, when was I going to cut my hair, why were my arms so scrawny. Freedom was terrifying. For the most part we put the yoke around our necks ourselves. Kitchens were merely an extension of our natural sense of burden. If not exactly slavery, certainly a modern shade of servitude: to work every waking hour for those with deeper pockets; to never answer back; to still, in this age of greater freedoms, have no rights of which to speak. We had all, each one of us, chained ourselves to the kitchen. Perhaps none of us felt that we deserved freedom. Perhaps our histories whispered too strongly in our ears. They will whisper louder before this story is through.

In the kitchen Bob's great shadow had contained us all. And yet, sitting in my bolt-hole room observing the days drag by, unrushed and idle, watching the street theater of One-Eyed Bruce and his motley players below, I did not feel any freer. The world was in the palm of my hand, it was my oyster and so forth, but I did not want the whole world, it was too much for one man. I wanted only a small part of it. I had seen what had happened to my father when he had tried to eat the world; what that hunger, that sense of entitlement, had done to him.

When I stood apart from others—doing odd jobs around the house that miserable summer after university, watching the Camden bustle from my rented room—my value was undefined. Was I passing through this life because I was supple, pragmatic, elastic of self—or simply because I was small: small of character, small of self? Did I, as a writer, have any thoughts worth having? But in the kitchen these questions did not arise. I knew my value at any single moment of the day. I could measure it against every item on my prep list, every order that came in. For insecure and maladjusted human beings there was no greater prize. And I saw how the kitchen had been a fine window onto the world after all, and I realized that I missed it. I greeted each morning with disappointment now, knowing there were no deliveries to unpack, no leaves to wash. Around seven in the evening I became agitated, preparing myself mentally for a dinner rush that never came. The nights were long and turbulent, the days drained of flavor. I thought of my fellow chefs, lying on their own beds, also sliding into debt. Often in those first dark and jobless days I felt worse for them than I did for myself.

I had enough money left over from The Swan to pay December's rent. After that I wasn't sure what I would do. There was the threat that I would have to quit London, to give up the whole charade and return home. It was almost too appalling to consider. Very soon I would be on the sofa next to my sunken father, watching reruns of *Classic Sports*, or between them at table as they took their meals in silence. Just silence in that marriage, and the weekly trip to Lindy Hop, now deceased. They made no attempt to fill in the gaps. Or perhaps it was just the one gap, a Sam-sized void, which could never be filled. I had not realized, until that last trip back, quite how far apart from each other they had grown. It was only a matter of time before the whole thing caved in completely. I did not want to be there when it did. That is something a child, however grown up, should not see.

Time became a thing to kill. I went for long walks, or I sat on the lock, where the canal runs through Camden, and stared into the water, letting my eyes climb over the junk below the surface. Occasionally, having nothing better to do, I went to the park with Ramilov. I should stress that this was not a picnic and bicycles sort of excursion, nor did we wander the gardens discussing the vicissitudes of life. It was not me Ramilov wished to talk to, but the monkeys in London Zoo. At first, since neither of us had any money, we could only stare mournfully at the animal houses from the other side of the fence, but Ramilov soon discovered that if you stood in a certain bush in a particular corner of Regent's Park you could see into the back of the primate enclosure, which was good enough for him.

Since Ramilov cannot be with us, he has kindly written down his instructions for seeing the monkeys without paying:

With the zoo on the right-hand side, walk up the avenue almost as far as the spiked drinking fountain. There will no doubt be some joggers about, or speed walkers working their arms like pistons, looking proper miserable. A Misery of Joggers. You may also encounter women in sunglasses looking like they expect to be recognized, or men who might be homeless sitting with their backs against the trees. An Expectation of Celebrities. A Romance of the Unemployed. Curiously, both species are native to this habitat. Wait until the coast is clear, then step over the small fence into the flower bed and pick your way through the undergrowth to the zoo fence. When you're all the way in you can see the howler monkeys sitting in the trees or swinging on their ropes. You can talk to them about all matters. Primates are the most intelligent of all creatures, especially apes, which is why their collective noun is "A Wisdom."

Ramilov's favorite topic was the inferiority of man when stood up alongside the rest of nature. *Compare Dibden to an ape*, it always began. *The ape is stronger and faster. In many ways, it is smarter. As an animal, Dibden is pathetic. Man is pathetic. How do we survive? Without medicines or machines we are nothing. We cannot fight diseases or predators. We cannot hunt anymore. We cannot fend for ourselves, or for our young. We cannot live in harmony with any natural habitat on earth. Every beast trumps us, et cetera, et cetera . . .*

Rarely, if ever, did Ramilov speak of his past. On the subject of why he became a chef, or why he had ended up in Camden, I could never get a straight answer. He'd moved around a lot—Birmingham, Bristol, Leeds—and that was as much as he'd say on the matter. He was here and what had come before was past. I have never met a man who cared, or appeared to care, so little about his own history. At a certain stage of the evening in O'Reillys, Racist Dave would often get onto the subject of his lovely mam who made the best fucking shepherd's pie in Manchester or his ex-girlfriend who he was pretty sure still loved him but somehow never had the time to visit. Even Dibden, at times, had been known to lament his privileged and cloistered upbringing. But Ramilov's loved ones or memories were never mentioned. He had locked that part of himself away completely. Of course now I can understand why. I do not condone what Ramilov did, but I have not forgotten how he saved me either.

The closest Ramilov came to discussing his past was his Albanian heritage, of which he was uncommonly proud. His grandfather had come to Liverpool after the Second World War, and from his armchair he had lectured the family men on the customary laws of the motherland, known as the Kanun. The Kanun required you to kill any man who had killed your closest relative, Ramilov told the monkeys. If someone had killed a guest in your house, they too must get it in the neck. Once the man was dead you had to roll his body over to face the sky. This, he informed the preening chimps, was a code of honor, as old as killing itself. A brutally successful code, for the cycle of blood never ended. Revenge nurtured revenge. In Albania's mountainous north there were some villages with almost as many promised killings as there were people. Now and then the chimps looked back at him and raised their heavy brows, but their charcoal eyes and small, wizened faces gave nothing away. Ramilov insisted that they could hear him and were taking it all in. I did not share his hope for primates but I could see that, such as times were, hope was at a premium, and we each had to find it wherever we could.

Mrs. Molina soon took to worrying about my rent again. The blasts of air freshener through my keyhole increased. Sweet old Mrs. Molina, with her fluffy pink slippers and her filthy mouth. From her cries of "*filho de puta*" and "*pentelho,*" I hid. From One-Eyed Bruce and his shipwrecked Shakespeareans, from their cries of "*pussyclot*" and "*please mister,*" I hid. And I had come to London in the first place only to hide from my father and his variations on the *Mr. Useless Streak of Piss* theme.

I was a stranger in the city. My few months at The Swan had made my return to solitude even more intense. Was it my imagination, or did the crowds of people turn their backs away from me as I approached? This was not a loneliness I had chosen. Strange coincidences implied that the rest of London functioned as one hive organism in conspiracy against me. That pale girl in the doorway one night whom I could have sworn called my name. A new lodger downstairs with the same northern drone as Racist Dave. Bob's voice in the next supermarket aisle across, complaining about corned beef. One-Eyed Bruce stooping to talk to a passenger in a dark, expensive car that pulled up alongside him, a passenger that looked, through the glass, distinctly like The Fat Man. He of great and joyless appetite. Around them the faceless crowds flowed.

The church next to the bookie's on Camden Road hung a new sign above its front door. Making a family out of strangers, it said. Very good, but I was now in the opposite business, trying to make strangers out of a family. It was not proving so easy. I had to keep my distance, to get money from somewhere. Yet I could not stop thinking about my parents. I would find myself in the Chalk Farm Internet café constructing e-mails to my mother—lies, mostly, about my burgeoning career—which I never sent. The thought of her in that cold study, her index fingers making hesitant stabs at the keys in reply, my father in the next room with the volume right up, made me too sad to go through with it. And though I often wondered if I had made a mistake coming to London, I knew it was better than the alternative. However much of a stranger I was here, it was somehow less than I was at home.

Books failed to soothe, tweezering brought no relief. I had to shake myself out of this malaise, get a job, earn some money, keep my fate at bay. I kept telling myself: *You cannot go back*. And yet the days rolled on without improvement. A gushing newspaper review of Tod Brightman's latest book, *A Corduroy Nothingness*, did not help matters. In fact it made me want to tear out my own eyes.

But even at my lowest ebb, life managed to wring one more joke out of me. Returning from my wanderings one night, I saw a shadow pull itself from the doorway of my lodgings as I approached. For a second I thought it was One-Eyed Bruce, at last about to murder me, but the shape was wrong, its movements too leaden, the expression of the shoulders altogether too miserable for a drug dealer in Camden Town. And as I got closer I saw the keen, testing eyes and the final gracelessness of the neck and hands, the worn spot on his jeans where he kept his keys. *Deflating* is the word for such a sight, such a visitation. In a town of crooks and deadbeats, where your soul is pretty used to getting kicked around, this man in front of me could still dampen my spirit.

"Hello, son," he said.

At first I elected not to reply.

"Saw your e-mail," he went on. "London is full of interest, eh? Looks like a shithole to me."

That was the old man to a tee. No how are you, just straight into the griping.

"What are you doing here?" I demanded. I was in no mood to play the dutiful son.

"Your mother and I are going through a patch. Thought you could put me up for a few days. What a treat—a visit from your dear old dad."

To this I did not respond.

2. OTHER WORLDS

You can't stay here," I said, fumbling with the key.

"Can you believe your mother?" he said.

"The landlady will kick me out," I said.

"All over a poxy watch," my father puffed, barreling up the narrow stairs behind me.

"There's no space," I said.

"Course there is." He took in the room without turning his head.

"I'm very busy," I said.

"Did someone murder a goat?" he asked, pointing to the umber stain beside the armchair.

"Several pans in the fire," I explained.

He was seen to eye the bed discreetly. I walked over and lay on it to stake my claim. Two minutes with the man and already this was my frame of mind.

"You should get a hotel," I said, looking up at the moldering ceiling with an expression that I suppose, to the outside observer, might have come across as pious. "You'd be more comfortable."

"No cash," he said. He kicked off his shoes, unfurled his sleeping bag and cast it out into the wedge between bed and door. "Good thing you've got that job," he added.

Was that a trace of slyness in my father's tone? Did he know? I could not bear to tell him I had lost it.

"See?" Crouching, he edged his head gingerly beneath the sink and slid down. "Loads of space."

"Your feet are in my face," I pointed out.

He grumbled, raised his head, smashed it on the U-bend of the sink and swore with enthusiasm, then shifted to face the other way.

"There we go," he proclaimed, opening his arms in an expansive what-I-have-accomplished gesture, whacking his right hand against the door. He swore again, with a note of exhaustion this time, and said he couldn't understand what I was making a fuss about. Then he paused, propped himself on his elbow and looked around.

"Hang on," he said suspiciously. "Where's the TV?"

"I don't have one."

"What?" he cried in utter indignation. "My own son, without a telly!"

Floorboards creaked on the stairs outside. The pink slippers of Mrs. Molina were on the prowl.

"Shhh!" I hissed.

My father cut short his objections. We waited in silence for the threat to pass. Further creaking came from the corridor, then fell quiet. There was scratching at the keyhole, followed by a lengthy burst of aerosol spray into the room. The ghostly smell of artificial roses descended around us. My father's face was a mask of consternation and disgust—well worth seeing. I glared at him before he said anything. The creaks began again, moving down the corridor, and we relaxed.

"Jesus Christ!" My father exhaled loudly. "What was that?"

"The landlady."

"She's a bloody maniac!" he said crossly.

And though he was probably right, and god knows I harbored no great love for Mrs. Molina, I felt suddenly angry that he should pitch up here so casually and begin throwing stones at things he knew nothing about, things that had nothing to do with him. How dare he criticize my landlady? What gall he had to swear at my chipped sink! I had not asked him to come. He was not paying for the service. He had sneaked into the party uninvited and was now complaining about the canapés. (Racist Dave, who has seen my room, says this last sentence is a stretch.)

"Dad," I asked with growing impatience, "what the hell are you doing here?"

He sighed and laid his head back on the pillow. Straightening his legs, he knocked a pile of books into a glass of water, upsetting it over the carpet. Without interest he looked down the length of his body at the sprawled books and the upended glass.

"Stupid place to put stuff," he said sleepily.

"Why are you here?" I asked again.

"She won't talk to me until I explain the watch," he mumbled, eyes closed.

"So explain it."

"You give your heart to an idea," he said in little more than a whisper. "But when you wake, it's not there anymore . . ."

"I don't understand what you're saying," I told him.

"In the morning," he murmured. "Okay, son?"

The "son" was almost affectionate, which threw me. Stretched out on the floor he looked old, careworn, strangely undeserving of the blame I attributed to him. Was that what he meant by this talk of an idea? I stepped over his low breathing and put a towel over the water at his feet. Then I switched off the light and climbed quietly back into bed. His breathing soon deepened into snores, and I lay there in the darkness, struck by how personal the sound was, imagining how my mother must have felt on the other side of that marital bed. Joined across the country, she and I, by our shared experience of this man. Perhaps we did deserve to be called a family after all. Lulled by this thought, I too drifted off.

But early the next morning I was rudely woken by a punch to

the leg and my father's voice saying he needed my help with my mother.

"The watch," he explained. "Tell her I found it in the charity shop in town. Save the Wotsits. That I bought it for her."

"Tell her?"

"You'd do that for your old dad, wouldn't you?" The night's suggestion of another, more thoughtful version of the man was gone, broken as quickly as it had been formed. This was the father I knew: wheedling, sly, on the make.

"Last night, Dad, you were talking about how you gave your heart to an idea. . . ."

"Was I?" he said blankly. "Probably sleep talk. All bollocks, isn't it? Now help me with your mother—let's work out what you're going to tell her."

"But is it true?" I asked.

"Of course it's true." Bridling now, he lifted himself to a sitting position. "Are you saying I'm a liar?"

"So why say 'tell her'?"

"It's a figure of speech, Wordsworth. I'm asking you to tell her, is all."

Thus my father moved his stealth and bitterness in and reminded me afresh of the perils family could hold: the regrettable but unstoppable habits, the sexual theories of a father that a son should never hear, the candor and obscurity, the guilt. By that afternoon I was embroiled. Shoulder to shoulder with bored minicab drivers in the Chalk Farm Internet café, surrounded by heady, foreign smells of meat and boiled grain, I wrote to my mother, telling her about his unexpected visit, asking her (it was too early to *tell* her) about the watch. Almost immediately, she called me back.

"I thought the miserable git might end up with you," she announced when I answered. "It was the only way he could avoid spending money."

"He's been talking about a watch."

She sighed.

"I'm sorry to put you through all this, dear," she said, "but the watch was the final straw."

"Mum, what happened?"

"You work yourself raw, and they fuck some whore," she informed me bluntly. It was lovely to hear her voice again after so long, though I did wish she wouldn't use such language. "In your bedroom, while you're out slaving," she added.

I wish I could say this news shocked me.

That evening in my room my father shook his head at this account. He had never cheated on my mother, he said, but—and here he paused, considering whether to tell me—only pretended he had.

"What?" I couldn't believe my ears.

"I had to give her the impetus to hate me fully or forgive me fully," he explained sadly, "though I did expect her to forgive me. . . . But I put the watch in the bathroom. Even got a barmaid at the pub to call the house a few times. You don't know what it's like, living off someone. It broke my heart to lie to your mother about it, but I had to let her make a clean break of me. I've been a burden on her too long."

"If you felt that way," I said, "why didn't you just leave?"

"Because I love her," my father replied. "I don't want to leave her. I just couldn't stand being in the gray area. I thought a nudge might push it back. Everything out in the open. Acceptance, you know?"

A wild, tragic gesture, if it were true. But my mother did say the watch in the bathroom had the name "Kirsty" written on the back of the strap, and that those sheets had not stained themselves. What was the truth? What was the lie? Perhaps a man like my father could never exist with both feet in either. Even when I was arrested, a whole grim chapter we have yet to tell, his appearance at the police station was marked by ambiguity. "It should've been me in there—not you," he told me. A touching sentiment on the surface, and most probably accurate. But had it come from the heart or the spleen? Was this, even now, another dig, another put-down, for his second-favorite son? Like I had made a hash of being in prison. Like I couldn't get arrested of my own accord.

My father was a deeply frustrating man, and trying to organize his truths from his fictions threatened, in that first week, to become a full-time job. It might have been my fate—the pauper and his grubby son, cheating the Camden gentry—if *she* had not appeared before me again, reminding me of what life could be. My crutch, with none of her kitchen trappings, yet unmistakably her. One evening, as my father snored beside me, I saw her again. It was late and I was at my window, putting off sleep. I heard her voice first, coming from the stretch of road directly beneath me. Craning my neck against the glass, there she was, a vision in the Camden mire, still fearless even without the kitchen around her. I had forgotten how beautiful she was. She stood at the bus stop in conversation with one of the shuffling street faces, one familiar to me though not yet christened. Thanks to the snoring lump next to me I couldn't make out what they were saying, but the gist of it was apparent from the series of mournful, imploring expressions on the street face. Poor devil, I thought, he doesn't know what he's up against. Once upon a time I had made the same mistake. Throw yourself under the bus, you poor fool! There's more chance of finding sympathy there than with beautiful, hard-hearted Harmony!

Harmony said something to the man that was lost beneath my father's snores, then walked across the road to the supermarket. The man just stood there, not bothering to beseech other passersby, as if all the fight had gone out of him. I recognized that look. We shared the same heartache, he and I. She returned with two sandwiches, which she handed to the man. He looked somewhat confused, and perhaps momentarily a little disappointed, but soon his face cracked into a smile. He thanked her profusely and moved on. Harmony boarded a bus and was swept away. And I went to bed and lay there for a time, I could not say exactly how long, thinking how I might have been wrong about her after all. Even her sharpness, of which I had so often borne the brunt—*That's not good enough . . . I need it now . . . You're taking too long . . . Don't just stand there, do something*—seemed suddenly clear and to the point, a blessing after all this familial murkiness. Certainly I remembered the sharpness more fondly than I had experienced it. For the first time in months I tried to hold the thought of her again: the arch of her back, the cool olive skin. It felt good. And she took my hand in hers and guided it across her slender body, smiling gently, and, looking straight at me with those quiet dark eyes, she said—

At this moment in the reverie my dozing father let out an almighty snore that shattered all to smithereens. So I dropped my foot heavily onto his chest, causing him to cry out with the pain and fury of a newborn babe.

"Stop snoring," I said.

"I wasn't!" he insisted groggily. "I was awake. You were the one snoring. You must have dreamed it was me."

Seeing Harmony again reminded me of how serious my situation was. I was unemployed. I was hungry. And I was bored of these feelings and longed for new sensations. Day by day I was slipping closer to the shipwrecked Shakespeareans. Mrs. Molina's pink slippers at the top of the stairs generated an unreasonable amount of panic in my soul. A week of my father's conversation was making me homicidal. His eventual discovery of my unemployment, a truth I could no longer hide, had not improved our relations. I could not become like him, I had no more money for rent—I had to get back into work. Knowing nothing else except kitchens, I took to the streets of Camden, looking for another Swan.

It was far easier than I had expected to find a pub hiring staff: The Brewer's Tap needed a kitchen assistant to start right away. Two days after my sighting of Harmony I was back in an apron, poised for service, while Kevin, the kitchen's only chef (overly firm handshake, one earphone still in) gave me my instructions.

"It's a piece of piss, mate. Chips are frozen, you drop them in the fryer. Pasta's already cooked, sauce is bought in, microwave four minutes. Chicken sandwich, straightforward. Soup is bought in. Burger is cooked but frozen, you microwave. Fish cakes are bought in and frozen, you drop them in the fryer. It sounds complicated but you'll get the hang of it. Salad is in a bag in the fridge. Don't use more than three leaves per plate, no one eats it. Hummus and mayonnaise are in the big pots over there. Monday to Thursday you'll be lucky to get any orders for lunch, a couple for dinner, people aren't drinking enough. Friday and Saturday it gets busy, Sunday everyone wants roasts. We do roasts a special way. . . . I've done a hundred Sunday lunches by myself before with just this and this"— he slapped the microwave and the fryer affectionately—"and you will too. As for prep . . . You mix ketchup and mayo for the special sauce, roast the chicken breasts for chicken sandwiches, check nothing's gone off in the fridges, er . . . There's other stuff too. Just make sure you're here when lunch and dinner start. In between, do what you like. I play online poker in the office. Rolling in the Benjamins. Won't need this job in a few weeks. . . . Any questions?"

"There's no grill," I said. "Do you cook the steaks in a pan?"

"Deep fryer," smiled Kevin. "You'd be amazed what it can do."

The Brewer's was a dismal barn of a pub that caught the high street workers as they spilled out at six o'clock. People arranged themselves on roomy sofas or in large armchairs opposite, and once the house music reached its evening volume it was impossible for anyone to hear a word anyone else was saying. You could not help but admire the sleekness of the long marble bar while you waited indefinitely to be served. To drink in The Brewer's made you need a drink; to socialize in The Brewer's made you want to scream. Yet the place had no such effect on hunger. Mostly alone in the tiny basement kitchen, I watched the hours pass. A burger here, a suspect chicken sandwich there. I thought often of The Swan, of its hand-made pastas and freshly baked breads that I had taken for granted. There, we had controlled everything that went on the plate; it was all, more or less, from scratch. Here, we controlled nothing. It was all out of a packet. Gray mince patties shipped in icy blocks. Frozen roasted potatoes reheated in the fryer. A barrel of cheese sauce. How had it come to this? And Tod Brightman, man of letters, my age, flew around the world giving talks to aspiring authors.

I fumed over the ascension of this young writer whom I hated, this tawdry scribbler who spent life at lunch with his publisher or explaining Maupassant to beautiful women, who had no scars on his hands or bags under his eyes, who woke late and counted his lie-in as contemplation, had no vegetables thrust against his rectum unless requested, no sapping father, no unrequited passions, no One-Eyed Bruce. I prayed he might destroy himself with a novel of staggeringly poor judgment or a tell-all memoir. Oh Lord, for another *Answered Prayers*! And I would be there at his end, as Gore had been for Truman, to proclaim his death "a good career move." Yes, they were bitter thoughts—the boredom of my new job reviving bad old habits—though I cannot pretend I did not take pleasure in them.

I imagined my own literary triumphs. Walking into a meeting with the bigwig publishers and throwing a single sheet of paper down in front of them. The first page of the book I would one day write, which they would read aloud with tremulous wonder. I would sit there casually, examining my fingernails for dirt, while they bid themselves into a frenzy. We would settle on a million, a nice round number. Out of modesty I wouldn't let it go any higher. The publishers, overwhelmed with gratitude, would raise me up on their shoulders and carry me aloft from the meeting room, to cheers from the chief execs. Rachel Parker, who had managed to scrape an unpaid internship at the same publishing house, would look up from her photocopying to see me riding past, using her superiors as a divan. I would smile at her, graciously, to let her know I had forgiven her for the harsh and foolish things she had said to me on the university bus. Then I would buy a suit of the finest material, and a monkey for Ramilov, and stride purposefully into the kitchen and whisk Harmony away to the restaurant on Parkway I couldn't afford where we would order everything on the menu and feed each other quail. When the bill arrived I would show the pretty waitress the first page of the book and she, with tears in her eyes, would insist I should not pay. She would try to kiss me, but I would politely refuse, explaining that Harmony was the only one for me. . . .

Then, a few days into the job, a phone call out of the blue. The hoarse, hysterical voice of Ramilov, carrying the news I had been waiting for.

"Is that the residence of An Extraordinary Cunt? The Swan is rising from the ashes and we need our trusty bitch."

"It's reopening?"

"*Correct, numbnuts. We're putting the band back together. All except that fat fuck Bob anyway. The brewery's made Racist Dave head chef, and I'm sous.*"

"Are we all getting promoted?"

"*No, you're still the bitch. But a loved bitch. I'm calling all the waitresses too.*"

"Everyone's back in?" I did not mention Harmony, though I was thinking it.

"*Yeah. Bunch of unemployable cunts apparently. Everyone except Dibden, believe it or not.*"

"Dibden said no?"

"*He's got a job in an S&M café in Euston. He thought it stood for sausage and mash but it stood for S&M. They've got a torture dungeon downstairs. You can get whipped while you drink your coffee. If you want you can get your coffee poured on your nipples. They've got all the extras on the menu.*"

"That sounds awful."

"*No shit. Dibden doesn't know where to look. He hates it. Poor bastard craps his pants every time someone orders a jam doughnut. But he made his choice. What do you choose?*"

PART II

TO FOLLOW

The back gate is unlocked. The chain screen is reintroduced. The lights stutter and glare. The switch that says IF THIS IS OFF THEN WE ARE ALL FUCKED is flicked back on. The stoves are fired up. The fryers are filled. The steel-toed boots are unearthed. The laundry is found, unwashed. The accounts are reopened with the suppliers. The mats are laid out. The deliveries are put away. The fridge is restocked. The bins are lined with new bags. The fans whir. The hi-fi is resurrected. The knives are sharpened. The fox is brought back from its Siberian exile. The kitchen returns to life.

Lovely bit of bream.

You're holding it the wrong way.

They should put you on TV, middle of the night, for people who can't get to sleep. They could just watch you chopping that carrot.

Have they unlocked the doors out there?

Took home a dyslexic bird last night. Got my sock cooked.

Like all life, it was order in a system of disorder, a stumbling through, an ignorance until proven guilty. But compared to the reign of Bob, where we toiled in fear of everything, or The Brewer's, where there was neither toil nor reward, those first few weeks back at The Swan were heaven. There was Racist Dave chopping and filleting with aplomb. Here was Harmony, still beautiful and unreadable. In the plonge, Shahram was doing his skittish dance and singing his Hindi songs while Darik squealed with laughter. There was no Bob to silence them. Rumor had it he was working as a line chef in the Leicester Square Garfunkel's. As for Ramilov, the pro-

motion to sous chef was a proud moment, and he announced to
what remained of the kitchen staff that from now on there would be
no more easy listening or "Cage of Pure Emotion." We would sub-
sist on a nutritious diet of musicals and rap.

Racist Dave moved into the flat above the restaurant that Bob
and his terrible wife had shared. We climbed the stairs to look
in wonder at the palace of the fallen emperor: the silver curtains
still hanging in the living room, the portrait of a dog's ear above the
mantelpiece, the little reminders stuck to the fridge that made Bob
seem almost human, and the mirror on the ceiling of the bedroom
that sent a shiver through all who saw it. Ramilov also took a souve-
nir of the old tyrant: a pair of Bob's wife's knickers discarded beneath the bed.

"Trowelface," he said solemnly, clutching the knickers tightly in
his hand.

Business was slow. Even Glen had tramped on, leaving the alleyway
for pastures new. Word had got around about the restaurant inspector's report and the pusbucket Gloriana. When a restaurant is "in,"
diners swarm around it unquestioningly. They will tolerate fantastic
rudeness and two-hour waits for food without a murmur. Mediocre
signature dishes will send them into raptures. When that restaurant
loses its sheen, however, they suddenly recall those waits, the rudeness, the mediocrity of that dish after all, and use it as grounds to
trash it. *It was always awful*, they tell their friends. On top of all this
it was winter—a lean time for any restaurant. When it is already
dark at four P.M., snow and slush underfoot, when there is a sharpness about people that reflects the weather, few think of going out
for dinner. The Swan was desperately quiet. Fish clouded over in
the fridges. The perfume of the lemons became hoochy, illicit. This

was a shame in The Swan's case, as Racist Dave was cooking out of his skin, trying to prove that the brewery had not made a mistake in reopening the place, or in promoting him.

Without Dibden the pastry section was disbanded, with just a few ice creams left on for Ramilov or me to put up. And though I remained the bitch in all senses, as Ramilov had promised, I found myself taking care in my work for the first time. I began to clean up my section as I went along, to save the scraps for the stockpot, to label containers correctly. I tidied up when I was not busy. If we were low on something I made a note of it. And more than that, I started to notice the food. Real food, which had been so scarce at The Brewer's. The dry skins of the onions crackling as I handled them, the scent rising from a crate of oranges, the bouquets of herbs releasing their essence between forefinger and thumb. I marveled at the darkness of the meat hanging in the walk-in, at the brightness of a fish eye, at the flavor a few bones could impart to water. I noticed how the vine of the tomato had a stronger smell than the fruit and saw the wisdom of leaving it in soups and sauces as they cooked. I learned the language of food: how you "gorged" onions and "tempered" chocolate, how pasta became "claggy" unless you "let it down," how "brunoise" was a French specification of size referring to the head of a match.

It seemed there had never been time to see these things when Bob was in charge. In those days there was only ever the service, blind and unquestioning. Now I saw the greater purpose, and the greater purpose was food. How it looked and smelled and felt and tasted, the excitement and luxury and abundance of it . . . Once, when ordered to add white wine and herbs to a fish soup, I caught a smack of aroma so good I was compelled to stick my head into the pot to keep on smelling it. Harmony caught me doing this, my whole head obscured from view, my eyes closed, savoring the aroma,

and asked me what the fuck I was doing. How I'd missed that
sharpness! "What the fuck are you doing?" Wasn't that an eloquent
way of putting it? No fat on that statement, nothing wasted. A
Hemingway statement. Literature when it came from her mouth,
not so much when it came from Racist Dave's. Embarrassed that
I had nothing smarter to say to her, I mumbled that I loved the
smell of it.

"Oh," she said. "That's all right, then." She looked surprised—
another expression, like happiness, that she wore agonizingly well.

I tasted everything. I watched everything. When I was given a
long and monotonous job to do such as chipping potatoes or chopping carrots I would pretend to be Ramilov or Dave and stand with
my legs wide apart, sharpening my knife until it sang, my section
spotless. Then I would slice with brisk, precise movements as I had
been shown, the first set of knuckles against the blade, the fingertips always behind, rocking the steel on its curve in a bowing motion, letting the weight of the knife do the work. Ramilov noticed
my new enthusiasm and commended me.

"The person who abuses the vegetables is the arsehole of the
kitchen," he explained. "You're still the bitch, but you're not an arsehole anymore."

This distinction made me uncommonly proud.

"Of course," Ramilov went on sadly, "Dibden will always be the
true arsehole of this kitchen. No one could hold a candle to him."

This was undoubtedly true. Dibden was much missed by
everyone.

With my new hunger came new responsibility. Twice a week, on
busy nights when no one else had the time, I was given the duty of
preparing the staff meal. I am sure this doesn't sound like much,
and perhaps it wasn't, but I fell upon it with zeal. I would plan my
menus days in advance, thumbing through the kitchen's cookbooks

and sauntering in a self-important manner around the fridge and the dry store. Scallops wrapped in Parma ham could be nice. A leg of lamb slow-roasted with vadouvan spices until the marbled fat around it was a hard gold and the meat fell apart with the gentlest insistence of a spoon. Great bowls of crisp French beans and toasted hazelnuts in a light, sharp vinaigrette. Grilled sea bass, their skins blistered with salt and heat, on a bed of garlicky greens. The slick, unctuous richness of an oxtail stew. The seductive wobble of a lemon pie. I dreamed of food, dreamed with my eyes open, and everywhere I looked the dream seemed to be real.

Not that my lavish schemes ever got off the ground. There was no time or money for such luxuries. Staff dinner was usually constrained to whatever mise Dave had decided could no longer be fed to the customers. Rubbery roasted potatoes that tasted of the fridge. Limp salad. Cucumbers that were all seeds. Pork with a metallic undertow. Anonymous sauce. Still, I loved more than anything else those moments when I stood at the solid top, Harmony on my right, Dave to my left, mimicking the professional ease of my fellow chefs, their casual flicks, their fluidity, their gestures I had watched a million times. I liked to see myself cooking, part of the machine. For the first time I could see the joy of assemblage.

"Well done," said Ramilov. "You've finally earned a promotion to a job no one else wants."

Ramilov was right on this point. It was a lowly and thankless task, but I did not care. It was mine, and in this new operation I took immense pride. I was forever asking people what they thought of my food, pestering the eternally hungry dishwashers who would have eaten anything, inquiring of the waitresses who hid their food distrustfully beneath the condiment station until they were less busy. Had they enjoyed it? Did they think there was too much tarragon? But the harried waitresses had not tried it and Darik and

Shahram did not care, did not know what tarragon was. I did not
dare ask Ramilov or Harmony or Dave, they were still not in my
orbit; yet I felt that I had taken a step closer to them all the same.
Thus began a new era, the era of flies.

It should have been an era of greater freedoms—yet always the
past was at our backs. We were barely up and running again before
history poked its face in at the door. One afternoon, as I attempted
to tunnel-bone a leg of lamb (a recent addition to my tasks, which
Dave had reluctantly allowed me), my concentration was broken by
the silky touch of Camp Charles's hand against my buttocks.

"Having a little *perv?*" he asked. A strange question, when it was
his hand on my arse. I told him I didn't know what he was talking
about.

"I saw you," he whispered, "looking at *her.*"

Was it that obvious? I suppose I had been staring at her a bit.
Only to break the monotony of the mise, you understand, for the
benefit of my eyes, as such. I didn't think anyone had noticed.

"What do you want?" I asked.

"Your *dad* is at the bar, Monocle," he said coyly. "He says you'll
pay for his *beer.*"

Ramilov overheard this and began cackling, asking was my
father called Glen, did he shit in the alley, et cetera, and Dave was
of course delighted to join in, adding a few thoughtful interjections
of his own. *Bum. Crapper. Gash dad.* If their suggestions had been a
little further from the mark, perhaps we could have laughed about it
together. But they did not see him as I did, the well-thumbed betting slips that fluttered from him every time a pocket was turned
out, the pronounced disgust for the dirt and desperation and loose
virtues of the city, in perfect counterpoise with the hopeful packet
of Blue Zeus beneath his pillow . . . Did he think I hadn't noticed?
Even then, in the singular confinement of Mrs. Molina's guest bed-

room, I tolerated his ways; but this intrusion at work, the one place I was able to forget him, was not a laughing matter.

I stuck my head round the corner of the pass and took him in. Squinting closely at the *Racing Post*, in anticipation of gratuities. Checking dentures of gift horses. Memory, reaching forward, always threatening to derail me. Yes, officer. That's the man. Already known to you, is he? You do surprise me.

"Just one," I told Camp Charles. "But that's all."

"Aren't you going to *come out*?" he said. The man was a veritable factory of innuendo.

"No."

Ramilov and Dave, when they saw I wouldn't go out to greet my father, stopped laughing and tried to take me out into the yard for a man-to-man talk about "family shit" and how they all had it. So keen to dispense their dubious wisdoms, those two. For once I believed their intentions were good, but I didn't want advice on the subject; it had kept me company all my life. No thoughtful chat was going to make the man at the bar, with his great appetites and empty pockets, disappear.

But as my gruesome editorial duo remind me today, my father was far from the worst thing at our backs. London was full of people looking to take advantage, as my mother had warned. Other, darker forces were beginning to circle us, forces that would threaten all our freedoms in ways we had never imagined.

2. SHOW HOME

Food never meant anything to me. There are no Proustian trip wires in my past. Mother was a lousy cook and father ate what was put in front of him. The man could argue with his shadow, but as far as food went he had no complaints. My mother, back from the day shift at the care home, would always serve. Beans and chips. Sausage and mash. Egg and hash browns. This chore caused the lines about her mouth to deepen, her classical beauty giving way to a barmaid's hatchet face. *Protean* is the word. Her eyes trained on the plates. In her pale blue work tunic, she shoveled potato derivatives for my father and me. I have quiet memories of those days, the sound turned right down. I wish I could turn these recollections off altogether, but if I have learned anything from the later events of this story—the blood, the confessions, the police holding cell—it is that history has a way of seeping through the gaps.

After Sam, I remember expecting change. Steps would have to be taken so the same thing did not happen to me. There would be commands to stay away from roads and bigger boys, rules enforced. Perhaps Mother would suggest I play only in the garden from now on and panic if I made the slightest sniffle. Good. I was scared of the traffic and tired of being pushed around by the bigger boys. But instead, to my great outrage, I was left to roam free. My thoughtless parents let me do whatever I pleased—even encouraged me to go out and play with my "friends." Appalled by their negligence, I contrived various ways (that reckless inclination toward fantasy even then!) that I might endanger myself: to run away, to climb the huge garden oak, to stand out on the ring road, to find another wasps' nest. Then we would see what they held dear. I never went through with it, however. What if they did not try to save me? Greater than my outrage was the fear it might be justified.

My father's attitude could be even more extreme. His face darkened if I came back in clean or carrying a book—I should have been grubby from roughhousing and adventure. He wondered pointedly why I didn't have any friends, why I couldn't fix my own bike. Time and again he implied, in a variety of sly and petty ways, that I had failed to meet his expectations. He wanted me to lead the neighborhood boys through the backwaters, to take my brother's risks. But I was not that person. I did not understand the roughhousing, when it was serious and when it was play. I am sure my father knew, on some level, that I could never be like my brother, but he was a proud man, never accountable for his errors of judgment. Caught in that pride, he raged against his callous and uncaring family, against his straggling son.

Father made me a substitute, mother made me a ghost. Her love for me I could not question, but after Sam she seemed to pull some part of it away, to abstract it in order to protect it from further harm. Children had proved they could not be trusted with love. They were too fragile, and their fragility broke hearts. And though she slipped me sweets and told me not to worry about my father, though she held me every night in her arms, she performed these acts with a new sense of caution. Despite my best efforts I could not get her to commit the same focus to me anymore. When she pressed me to her it was tentative, as if I were a life form fallen from the sky, who at any time might choose to go back.

What else trickles in from that time? Thoughts of Grandmother, stirring trouble. She would bring news of my mother's old suitors: how well so-and-so was doing in the steel business, what's his name's latest car. She recounted these details loudly, projecting them toward the sofa where my father lay. Her eyes milky, nearly blind, shifty despite their attempts at innocence. And Mother, though she said nothing, absorbed it all. She had been much admired. If she had not married my father, who could say where she might be now. One of those new villas with the columns on the other side of the ring road perhaps. No care home drudgery. Private health care when it might have made a difference. Grandmother hypothesizing, eyes sly.

Slowly, I think, my mother came to see her marriage as a trap. She had been young and impressionable. She had been tricked. Now, between the care home and the show home, between the family she had and the family she'd lost, she was a prisoner. Her outward bitterness toward my father grew. He had known only one thing and now he did not even know that. When I think back I see her wiping those poor catatonic mouths and try to imagine how she felt. She did not do it, surely, to keep the family together, but perhaps to keep a dream intact, of a life she once had. Even though Silver Hills had lost its sheen and the bland quirk of the show home furnishings no longer comforted or amused, she was determined not to give these things up. They were links to a happier time. Thus principles will cloud a person's mind, and part stands in for the whole, and folk will fight tooth and nail for something they did not really want in the first place.

Not that it was ever as simple as that. She had fallen so heavily for my father, once upon a time. I'll admit I don't know much about romance—I have never burned a letter or argued tearfully in a railway station—but I imagine those feelings don't disappear overnight. What had happened with my brother, that was a tragedy for both of them. She knew how much it had torn my father up. She appreciated also the personal catastrophe he had suffered with his golf. Like him, she mourned for the personality she had first met;

she looked with sorrow on the couch-bound figure before her, the toothless crocodile, the clean rat, its impulses denied. Was she really going to pull away from him now, after he had already lost so much? *Because* he had lost so much?

Yes, I think this was my mother's dilemma. She felt for the man she loved . . . had loved. Her dramatic face, prone to its sudden weather pattern shifts, was impossible to read. Wars came and went in our house. Battle lines changed fast. There was the night I stumbled upon her and my father's tangled limbs, their half-secret lovemaking. I was not trying to look, but the door was ajar and I could not sleep. At the time my nine-year-old brain could not understand it. Not the physics, but the narrative arc. They'd been frosty with each other for weeks. Another time I found the blond woman's picture that had come with the house, the picture my father used to kiss good night, in the kitchen bin. What did it mean, after more than a decade of looking at that photo of another woman, laughing about it, to throw it away now? Certainly my mother was conflicted.

The truth is I do not know exactly how my parents felt back then. It was not one of those homes where everyone was constantly weeping and flinching at revelations. The arguments, when they happened, were mostly hushed affairs, considerately started after I was supposed to be asleep. And though my father could be cruel, and sensitive to any perceived slight (certain topics—gambling, golf, employment—were off-limits), he still displayed fleeting moments of charm. An unexpected gift for my mother that we could not afford, a roguish smile, a trip to the bookie's for his awkward young son—don't tell Mum. Even as I resented him I craved his attention. Even as my mother toiled and fretted she let him whittle away the days polishing his silverware.

Nor is it fair to say it was only a time of turmoil. There were times when our three-wheeled vehicle was happy, and no one was left out. That whole week before the camping holiday, for instance, when my father bristled with excitement, telling us what to do in a hurricane, what berries you could eat and how to make smoke signals. Beneath the oak tree in the back garden the three of us pitched a tent and drank soup from kitchen cups, laughing at the impracticality of it all, at the pretense of survival. My father's enthusiasm was infectious right up until we got to the Lake District proper and he failed to get the fire lit on the first night and drove off to the pub in a huff.

Usually, however, I could feel life tearing whether my parents felt it or not; I could read the signs. The details were overtaking us. The creaks in the floorboards, the oak tree slowly blocking out the light, the kitchen table wobbling as my parents hunched over the bills—this was the sum of our existence. The fading show home, decorated with someone else's taste, grafted onto us. Sometimes the bodies of transplant patients reject their new parts. The unknown liver dies, the impostor hand turns gray, and the host goes into toxic shock.

Yes, it was a time heavy with vague, suggested meaning. The loose bathroom taps leaked symbolism. The front door jammed with feeling. Our neighbors ignored us passionately. Oh, our Silver Hills community was exclusive, all right. The other kids used to run when they saw me, as if czarist blood and sporting blunders were contagious.

I remember spending a lot of my time in front of my mother's hinged mirror, reflecting and being reflected. Pulling the wing mirrors around me, it was possible to make an endless hall of mirrors with my little listing face at the center of each one, a kaleidoscope of me. I would stand there for hours, transfixed, moving the side mirrors in and out, watching as I multiplied and divided. I felt sure that each version of myself was subtly different from the next; whichever

one was in the corner of my vision always seemed to be making a different expression to the face I was looking straight at. When I changed
my focus to the one I had seen obliquely, its expression seemed to
change again. But I could never tell whether this was because I had to
angle my head differently to see this other version, or whether there
was some deeper magic at work.

I found other versions of life in books. I fought rats the size of
mastiffs with Gulliver; I despised that vengeful court dwarf. I swam
in the language of the Mississippi with Tom Sawyer, though I could
not chew long blades of grass as he did, they gave me a rash. In *To
Kill a Mockingbird* I saw a strong and noble father, a concept more
alien to me than any science fiction. But the book I loved most as a
child, which I read until the spine broke and the pages came away
in my hands, was *Pinocchio*. The story of a wooden boy who under-
took a campaign of impudence against his father, who ran about the
country as he pleased, refusing to obey, throwing himself into
scrapes and always managing to slip out of them. It is possible, I
now accept, that I took the wrong message from this tale.

Reading was not an escape, you understand. I did not dream of
fantastical worlds or get misty-eyed with wild possibilities. It was an
embroidering, an embossing, an overlaying of the life already there.
A lesson. Books taught me how to feel. They gave me words and
showed me company. Sometimes I have to remind myself that I do
not know Geppetto personally, that I have never had a conversation
with Huckleberry Finn.

Alas, books have never taught me how to be among people.
Sometimes they have been downright misleading in this regard.
When one of those oily neighbor children taunted me about my father I felt time stretching itself very thin and my anger building
slowly, piece by piece, almost in sentences, as a character grows irate
in a novel. I thought it perfectly normal to huff and puff myself

gradually into a rage like this, just as I thought it quite normal to do what I did next: I whacked the oily neighbor child over the head with a spade. When Pinocchio hit the talking cricket with a hammer he was chatting again in no time. To my disappointment, the oily neighbor child was not so forgiving. He told on me and my parents were duly informed. I told them it was only roughhousing. Apparently it was not the correct sort of roughhousing. My father marched me round to the neighbor's house and apologized for me. *He apologized for me.* For a better example of my craven, sad-sack father, you need look no further.

"It's been hard for the boy," he explained. "He was alone with him when it happened, you see, when Sam took so sudden."

I remember looking past the neighbor into the house behind him and seeing its layout, exactly the same as ours except in mirror image. Exactly the same, but not quite. They had no tree blocking the light into their living room, no father on the sofa eating corn-flakes, no empty bedroom at the top of the stairs with peeling posters. It was not our life after all.

"No major harm done," the father of the other boy kept saying. *No major harm done.* He wanted us off his doorstep. But my father, swept up in his noble bit, did not notice. Every second he stood there mumbling his apologies my respect for him faded further. He offered no strength, no pluck. So I spent more time staring into books and mirrors, looking for other teachers. He drove me to fiction. You could say he drove me further still, to a life beyond it, to the kitchen and its teachers: Racist Dave, who for all his bigotry and bad grammar leads us forward with a steady hand; and Ramilov, who, though he raked the fire under his own pot in more ways than one, also taught me the meaning of sacrifice.

Yet my father is still in the picture whether I wish him to be or not. Still lying, on my floor or otherwise; still standing, now at the bar of The Swan, panhandling for beer. For all the man's faults, I cannot deny his tenacity. If I lose my temper with him he tells me he knows how I feel, that we shouldn't blame ourselves for Sam. He lumps me in with him and puts Sam up on high, looking down on us, the source of all our love and joy when he was among us, all our frustrations and troubles now he's gone. My father will tell some version of that to anyone who will listen. By now, every diner and drinker in The Swan has heard of Sam. Stand at the bar for two minutes and you'll have my brother's entire life story. My father knows how much this annoys me. What he doesn't know is why. I do blame myself for what happened to Sam, and with good reason.

3. ORTOLAN

I, we, just wanted to escape the past, to step out of the hollows worn by other souls. But there were those who didn't want the same as us, those who wished to harness us once more, and they were worming out of the shadows again, pouring their poison in our ears, confounding our intents. My father, of course: his mention in this company is deserved. But now another, greater shadow is rising up. The flies are beginning to swarm, a black and glittering mass, a sickening drone. What exactly is it they cover? What is the rottenness at the heart of this story? We are getting to it, I promise. We are getting to the dark heart. Ramilov says I know what I must say: "the greater truth," as he puts it in his letters, the one all of us went with. He says it is not so bad where he is now—and no one there is as bad as Bob.

Bob will always be the yardstick for this restaurant. His bellowing laughter when he burned someone, his sneer of contempt at the plates of food offered up to him, that sense of being stalked by his shiny eyes. In those early days and weeks after the fall, Bob was on our minds constantly. Sure, there was happiness now, but where was the center of gravity? Without Bob's weight we threatened to float away. People became emboldened, brazen; they acted the fool. With both Booboos gone our mise was left untouched. The *clipclop* of Bob's terrible wife no longer turned our backbones to jelly. It was a time of uncertainty, of self-doubt. Without suffering, how could we be sure we were still alive? Without a master, who else might subjugate us? Had Bob, in all his petty, weaselly majesty, protected us from something worse?

Less than a month after The Swan's reopening, these questions were answered. Who should sail in but The Fat Man, fatter than ever, his gut a few seconds in front of the rest of him, his bored and diabolical face prepared to inflict new miseries upon Camp Charles and the button-nosed waitress and whoever was unfortunate enough to serve him. He took a spot at the bar while the front-of-house staff frantically prepared his table. My father, swaying slightly on his stool (it had been a long afternoon), looked up at the source of the great shadow now cast upon him and made some observation I was glad I could not hear. They exchanged a few words, and I saw my father point in my direction and offer some explanation. What was he saying? It was not beyond him to dive straight into the murk and guilt of our family with a complete stranger. But was The Fat Man a complete stranger? It was hard to tell from the way they spoke to each other. At the pass I watched helplessly as these two worlds collided. The Fat Man looked over at me but I could not tell what was in his eyes. At last Camp Charles came over and led the great brute to his table, away from my affairs.

Here was his order: one of every starter, no salad leaves on anything, the steak blue, the steak walking, by god, a duck with extra skin, a side of pork belly, chips by the bucketload, extra vinegar on the red cabbage, six oysters while he waited, and a bowl of the crab linguine.

"Would you like a small or large portion of the linguine?" Camp Charles, very suave and deadpan this evening, later relayed this joke to the chefs, to much merriment.

The Fat Man had glared at him with impatience. Only one of those choices existed in his universe, and you had only to look at him to know which one that was. Rich and corpulent, smothered by excess, The Fat Man had no choice at all. To watch him eat those starters was the pinnacle of misery for a chef, for he smashed apart the artfully presented plates of food without even looking at them, his sloppy, slick-lipped mouth churning the delicate flavor combinations and balances of texture into one homogenous pulp, a hateful battle between him and it, a war of consumption. If the mouth of the wicked conceals violence, The Fat Man's was not doing such a good job of hiding it. That massive hole turned wine into water and made five thousand fish look like an hors d'oeuvre. The Fat Man was the anti-Christ. Ramilov, watching in horror from the pass, complained it was like watching a body make shit in front of your eyes.

"What would happen if you put a baby in front of him?" he wondered.

Mains were dispatched in the same manner. With animal violence The Fat Man hooked his broad jaw around the steak and tore off great hunks, slurping the blood through his teeth and grinding the half-chewed lumps in that gruesome gob, "his charnel of maw," as Melville said of the Maldive shark. Even with the knowledge that The Fat Man was paying full price for this meat, it seemed an undignified end to a creature's life. And when he had gorged himself on every kind of creature on the menu and dismissed Camp Charles's offer of ice cream with disgust, when the blood and animal fat stained his collar and his eyes were dull with feeding, The Fat Man raised his tremendous weight from the chair and moved hugely over to the pass for a word with Racist Dave.

"A little dinner party," I heard him saying. "A few friends of mine, prominent figures in the community, cash in hand. So disappointing for us all what happened with the Gloriana. . . . Be good to set things straight. Bob proved he couldn't hack it, but a man of your skill, it'll be easy."

I thought The Fat Man was flattering to deceive but Racist Dave was not so educated in this manner and I could see him preening at the words. He pointed over at me and I knew I was being appraised. Dave was asking if he could bring me as his commis. The Fat Man looked at me for the second time that evening. He nodded.

The Swan had no bodies to spare on its days of business, so it was on a Monday, when the kitchen in the era After Bob was closed, that Dave and I made our way to The Fat Man's house. That afternoon my father had moaned when I told him I was cooking for a "private function." Not out of any patriarchal concern—apparently I had promised to buy him dinner. I did not recollect that particular promise; moreover, I resented having to explain myself to my father at all. This parental opprobrium was entirely undeserved for a man living on my floor. The questions, the waiting up or the two A.M. minefield where I crept around sleeping limbs: all that was what I had moved here to avoid.

The address was a large and sober town house on a wide avenue lined with London planes, a short walk from the restaurant. The ghost of a once sprawling wisteria haunted the building's façade, otherwise there were no distinguishing features. No indication of the horrors that lurked inside, no forewarning. Dave would like me to make it clear here that he was never scared; he was from the north, after all, and The Fat Man wouldn't have lasted two seconds on Moss Side. I am not so sure. Even as he rang the bell that first time, Dave looked more than somewhat uncomfortable.

The Fat Man seemed pleased to see us.

"Chefs, welcome," he said, opening the door. We may have murmured in reply. Being face to face with such enormity took your breath away. Your thoughts turned to oxygen supplies and planetary resources. How could his appetite be doubted? He had built a monument of flesh. He sat at the top of a mountain of himself.

It was dark inside the house and what little light there was sloped awkwardly toward the walls, as if to avoid any confrontation with its occupants. The effect was veiled, menacing. Low voices could be heard behind a closed door at the other end of the hallway, but The Fat Man did not lead us there. Instead he took us through into the dining room, laid out in preparation, which led in turn to the kitchen, a vast room of stainless steel and black marble. It was bigger than the kitchen at The Swan. Everything in it looked new. Cold, sharp instruments were lined neatly across the wall. State-of-the-art gadgetry gleamed on the counters. Dave whistled with delight. But all these machines and devices only reminded me of the savagery of cooking, of the violence implicit in the act.

"Toys," The Fat Man said as Dave examined them. "Use whatever you like. I have a jaded palette and I like to be surprised."

"What are we cooking?" Dave wanted to know.

The Fat Man smiled.

"A special something, my boys. A special something." He leaned in, eyes wide. "Have you ever heard of the ortolan?"

We had not.

"It's a tiny, rare songbird," The Fat Man explained. "You drown them in brandy and roast them in a clay pot. They're so little you can crunch the bones." He went over to a side door and began unlocking it with a large set of keys. "Before they banned them the French considered them a great delicacy, but a sinful one. . . . A man was only allowed to eat one bird at a sitting. He had to cover his head with a cloth so God couldn't see him eating it."

At this The Fat Man opened the door and disappeared inside for a moment. When he returned he was carrying something covered in a sheet of black silk. Talking about sin seemed to have put him in a good mood.

"There's a famous story about the old French prime minister Mitterrand," he went on. "A story told to show how wicked he was. They say, at his last meal, that he ate an ortolan and asked for seconds. Well, we have no such scruples here, so I bought extra. . . ."

With a swift flick he threw the sheet off to reveal a fine wire cage full of minuscule birds. There must have been at least twenty of them in that cage, all packed in on top of one another, jostling each other with their little wings. When the light of the kitchen hit them they began to chirrup loudly. The sound of birdsong washed over the kitchen, beautiful and terrible; the birds had mistaken The Fat Man's dungeon for daylight, and the two were not the same.

"If I were you," The Fat Man said, "I wouldn't bother trying to drown them one by one. They're lively little buggers. Just fill the sink up with brandy and lower the cage in."

Dave was wearing his swagger and saying, "No problem, I do this sort of thing all the time," but I knew he was perturbed also. Then The Fat Man looked over at me and winked. Not in a friendly way, exactly, but familiar. Why would he do that? I recalled the conversation I'd seen him having with my father in the pub. Not exactly friendly either, but familiar.

"Just make sure everything's perfect," he continued. "These people have paid a lot for this meal. More than you could imagine."

He went off, quote, to entertain his guests. Dave and I were alone in the kitchen with the songbirds.

"Go on then, chef," he said. "Drown 'em."

As much as I respected Dave as a chef I would not, I could not, drown the birds and in the end Dave gave up trying to make me and prepared to do it himself.

"Big pussy," he said as he filled the sink with liter after liter of The Fat Man's brandy. "There's nothing to it."

He picked the cage up with both his hands and hesitated for a moment.

"It's just like killing a lobster, or opening an oyster, or boiling a langoustine," he muttered through gritted teeth. Dave says he was talking to me when he said this, but it sounded to me like he was talking to himself. Then a cold, dead expression came into his eyes and he plunged the cage of birds downward into the liquor and their little wings beat and thrashed about in the brandy, foaming it, discoloring it, and their agitated squawks grew submerged, turned to bubbles, fell silent. Dave held the cage down long after the liquid was still again, his face dark and clenched. When he pulled it dripping from the sink there was only a pile of small, feathered corpses where the songbirds had been, and the cage looked suddenly heavy in his hands.

"Pluck these," he said angrily. "I've got shit to do."

Of all the chapters in my life I do believe that this day, when I stood over a garbage bag with the tiny lifeless creatures in my hands, their feathers sticking to my fingers like guilt, this day is among the lowest. And let me tell you there has been some competition, Sam's final hours aside. The day my father took me fishing, for example, which had started so well, the two of us sitting on the riverbank as he told me how herrings started to glow when they died, or how the trout forced their weakest out to sea to spawn, only for the exiled to return as sea trout, bigger and stronger than their relatives. We were both excited, I think. But as the day wore on and the fish failed to bite my father began to drink and the sun got lower and the riverbank colder, and then he began throwing stones at someone's skiff and tried to make me bet he couldn't sink it, and when I wouldn't join in he said I had no balls, that I was, quote, an omen of impo-

tence and no wonder we hadn't caught any fish. A day of ugly re-
criminations in the end. It had caused a breach between us.

Or at university, when the girls in my halls guessed the un-
plucked root of my shyness and made an announcement over the
PA system in the student bar and Sally Danzig—big, lewd, loose-
hipped Sally Danzig, whom all the boys called Dirty Danzig—
walked straight up to me and offered to sort me out then and there
on the pool table. A black day certainly, but those mortifications
were at least limited to me and me alone. I could live with them.
Such assaults only strengthened my defenses. With a squint of vision, a positive could be extracted from such experiences. But I had
seen the way The Fat Man ate and the emptiness in his eyes and I
knew those little songbirds had died for nothing. I held their tiny
limp bodies in my hands. I plucked their feathers downward so I
didn't break their skin. I plucked them out in tight bunches that
turned suddenly into down in my fingers, blowing loosely and
lightly all over the room, sticking in the sink or rising to the ceiling.
There was no clean way.

Dinner was to be served at eight as per The Fat Man's instructions, and Dave was spinning around the kitchen like a whirling
dervish preparing the other items requested: steak tartare with
quail's eggs, deviled kidneys on toast, deep-fried sweetbreads—the
thymus gland, Dave explained—spears of white asparagus and a
gargantuan tray of Pommes Anna cooked in duck fat. The Fat Man
wanted the ortolans served last of all, when he rang the bell three
times. We worked quickly and quietly, the creaks and murmurs
of the house seeming to swell and multiply around us as our concentration increased. In the stillness of my thoughts it seemed now
as if the house were whispering through the walls to pluck faster,
to not let myself get sentimental. And though the occasion was unpleasant there was so much to prepare that the appointed hour

struck sooner than expected—a single mournful note from the dinner bell. Since there were no waiters or waitresses in this hateful place it was Dave and I who carried the food into the dining room.

To our surprise we found it empty. The long table in the center had been set for the occasion and the candles were lit, there were bottles of wine open and glasses half full, but no diners. The dinner bell rested on the floor beside a wide chair of polished wood at one end of the table: the chair of The Fat Man, no doubt. Four other chairs were pulled up around it, two on either side. All had been abandoned. Yet there was in that room a strong, unmistakable sensation of being watched, as if the party had not moved on but was waiting for us to leave. We put the platters of food on the table and retreated to the kitchen. From time to time, if you listened closely at the door, you could hear the clink of glass or cutlery. That was all. No voices. No laughter. A "meal of silence, grandeur and excess" is how Shelley describes the king's feast in Queen Mab, of "unjoyous revelry" and "palled appetites." "Fucking gay," is how Dave describes The Fat Man's feast and, coincidentally, how he describes Shelley.

Dave arranged the ortolans across five clay pots and slid them into the oven. They'd take only ten minutes, he said, they were tiny things. And no sooner had ten minutes elapsed than the dinner bell rang again, three times, and it was time to bring the songbirds forth. We arranged the covered pots on two trays and walked slowly into the dining room. What I saw there I shall never forget, and if I had thought about it more at the time I dare say I would have dropped my tray of ortolans and paid a heavy price.

Five figures sat around the table, the head of each one bowed and covered by a sheet of black silk. Their faces were hidden, from god or from us, from both. They neither moved nor spoke. Fun or fulfillment was not their intent. Pleasant company had not brought them here. Theirs was a grimmer ceremony: of bloodletting, of sin, of guilt and taking away. "For they [the evildoers] eat the bread of wickedness and drink the wine of violence," King Solomon said in the Proverbs. An interesting man, King Solomon, full of esoteric opinion. Among his works is a treatise on the shadows cast by our thoughts. The shadows here in The Fat Man's dining room stretched long about, looping me with dark nooses as I moved around the table.

We placed a pot of ortolans in front of each shrouded figure as we had been instructed. It was easy to tell which one The Fat Man was; of the others' identities we could only guess. They might have been doctors or politicians or criminals. There was no type that ate illegal songbirds. Only one small detail struck me as familiar: the cut and calloused fingers of one of the guests, that livid purple burn on the back of the right hand. It had to be . . . Yes, it was Bob, surely, under the black sheet. After what I had seen between those two huge men, the abject terror of one and the utter contempt of the other, I could not imagine he was here of his own accord. Some debt was being squeezed. Whatever The Fat Man had on him, he was not letting it go.

Part of me—the tweezering, zit-picking part of me, no doubt— wanted to see this ceremony completed. But as long as Dave and I remained in the room none of the figures at the dining table moved. Neither of us dared speak. The silence was thickening into something quite peculiar now. I tried, in vain, not to think too much about the world we had walked into. Where had the songbirds come from? Who were the other guests? What other tastes might The Fat Man have?

After a time the figure at the end of the table spoke. From his circumference, that of a middle-aged oak, it could only have been The Fat Man.

"Here is your money," he said, pushing forward a stuffed envelope. "Take it and leave."

Dave leaned forward for the envelope and inspected it quickly. The notes flashed crimson beneath his thumb, far more than either of us had expected, a sweetener for this bitter scene.

At the door of the dining room I turned one final time and looked back at the figures seated around the long table, the black sheets still draped over them. Then we hurried away from that place of death and silence, Dave and I, and looked back no more.

4. THE SEXY POTATO

My editors, Ramilov and Racist Dave, have reacted quite strongly to this first description of The Fat Man's shadow world. Dave says I am making us look like a bunch of pussies, while Ramilov writes to say we could have warned him before he went careering in there himself. He's right—we should have told him. Things might have ended differently. Of course, at the time we thought any debt incurred by the rancid Gloriana had been expunged. Bob's attendance at The Fat Man's dinner party suggested he was paying in his own way, for that embarrassment or some unknown other. We assumed we had appeased The Fat Man. For those assumptions, Ramilov paid more than anyone.

In recompense, he asks that I write about the waitress at the Christmas party. He is concerned that, the way this story is headed at the moment, people might think him otherwise inclined. Proud as we all are of Ramilov's achievements, I remember the event for another reason, an act of almost unconscionable wonder, a Christmas miracle: Harmony smiled at me. I am prepared for the teasing this admission will provoke in certain quarters, for it is the truth, as plain as the glove on a chicken's head, as my father likes to say. After all those months of working together, she finally showed a warmth toward me. It did not last long, only a moment, but the hope it gave me lingers to this day.

The Christmas party very nearly didn't happen. After the brewery had sacked Bob and granted The Swan a stay of execution, no one expected a party. But obviously they had certain milestones they felt they could not sacrifice. Perhaps they understood how hard the service industry could be on a person, and how we had to play at being on the other side of the fence now and then if we were to remain sane. Perhaps they felt we deserved it after everything we had been through with Bob. All that wolfish watching, all those sly inflictions. Clearly the staff agreed. The belated Christmas party, finally held in early February, turned out to be a momentous occasion. An explosion of tensions that had been brewing for months. Chefs owe more to alcohol than anyone else does.

On a crisp Monday night, when the kitchen was closed and the footfall was minimal, Camp Charles locked the door and drew the blinds. A sign was put in the window announcing that the pub was closed for a private function. Large bowls of cheap rum and orange juice were engineered. For one night only the bottles of expensive continental beer were removed from the chiller cabinets in favor of supermarket brand lager. At six o'clock the chefs and waitresses began to arrive. The preening, in those few short hours since the end of Sunday service, had been intense. Each girl was scrubbed and sweet-smelling, wearing her newest and very best clothes. The men's hair shone with gel. They tugged at their crisp shirts. Ramilov, suddenly small and unremarkable when removed from his natural habitat, positively quiet when there was no brutality to be had, was trying to counteract the effect by wearing a shirt with two collars. An economics professor making thoughtful sips at an orange juice turned out to be Shahram in spectacles and a dark suit, while Racist Dave was modeling a low-cut T-shirt with sunglasses and a diamanté earring.

"Fuckin' hell, Dave," said Ramilov. "Did you spend that Fat Man money on earrings?"

"Some of it," a sheepish Dave replied.

"You boys are on to a nice little earner there, aren't you?" Ramilov said to both of us. "What did you have to do for him, anyway?"

Dave and I looked at each other and then away. We had agreed
on the way back from that haunted house that the hooded figures
and tiny corpses would remain between us. Dave had also seen Bob
and felt the incident bore no repeating. We had agreed we would
never go back there again.

"The usual shit," Dave mumbled. "Bit of offal, bit of game."

"A nice little earner," Ramilov said again, shaking his head in
appreciation.

"What the fuck is your shirt, Ramilov?" Dave changed the
subject.

"This?" said Ramilov. "This is timeless style."

"It's fuckin' gash. Isn't it, Monocle?"

But I wasn't looking at Ramilov's shirt. In the corner, in a dress
of shimmering silver, stood Harmony. No doubt Ramilov and Racist Dave will mock me further for saying this, but her legs, which I
had never seen before, reminded me of the banisters in my parents'
house, the curve of the calves swooping elegantly into thin, fine
ankles. I'd spent a lot of time at those banisters, listening to my
mother and father's quiet arguments, so I know what I am talking
about. Her hair, no longer hidden beneath a chef's hat, spilled
gracefully about her shoulders. It was the color of her eyes. *Inky* was
not the word. No, it was like a river at night: looking at it filled you
with mystery and sadness. Truly, it was quite painful to look at her.
But at least the pain was fresh. Those memories of Rachel Parker
had become so dog-eared over time.

"I could go over and fucking talk to her for you," said Dave.
"Ease you in, like."

He had seen me staring. At this rate I was going to get a reputation. But even I did not deserve Dave as a wingman. I lied and said I wasn't interested, which provoked loud cackles from my idiotic companions. They spent the next few minutes prodding me in the ribs until Ramilov spotted Shahram in his suit, talking to Darik at the bar.

"Hey, Shahram!" he shouted. "You are looking *sexual* this evening! We are going to have a party, yes? You and me, dancey dance, and then I will pound you in the arse. Okay?"

"Okay," said Shahram, looking confused. "What time, please?"

"All night," said Ramilov. "At intervals."

"Okay," said Shahram again, turning to Darik for explanation.

"Not Darik though," Ramilov added. "He like too much. Gay boy."

Darik raised his big boulder head.

"Hey, I not gay." His voice was high and nasal and angry.

"That's your secret, isn't it?" taunted Ramilov. "Gay boy?"

"Stop saying I gay!" Darik howled. He tried to grab Ramilov but the chef was too quick for him, shimmying away into the crowd. Some quick thinker put a drink in the big man's hand before he could realize his anguish.

The sight of everyone freed from the prison-regulation blacks and whites threw people somewhat and for a time the only subject of conversation was shop: what a customer had said last night, the panic over a table's missing starter relived. The waitresses formed an excited cluster at the near end of the bar, close to the pass where they had so often waited. They made small movements, keeping their arms close to their sides as if they were still serving. The chefs gathered at the far end to argue over the best way to roast a chicken, the tastiest cut of pork. Someone had heard that Bob was testing meals for the Wetherspoon pub chain and this information was celebrated whether true or not. Cigars were handed round. Ramilov and Racist

Dave made a point of leaning on the counter with exaggerated casualness, blowing smoke at the ceiling, and on occasion one or the other would throw in a raised voice, perhaps an obscene gesture, so they and everybody else knew who the customer was tonight. And there was me, loitering on the edge of it, trying not to look at the girl in the silver dress. Trying to be invisible, and succeeding.

It has always happened, ever since I was a boy. In groups of people I tend to shrink and wither. I do not mark my territory or sound loud like the other animals. I find a corner and fold myself into it, folding inward on myself, aware of how I must look, that scrawny figure with the wide face. I do not possess Ramilov's elemental drive or the plasticity of my father. I cannot sprawl on top of life and smother it with personality. In that sense I have never been a part of it—the anger and loving and fighting and fucking—but standing beside it, apart from it, has its advantages too. What did Nabokov say? "I was the shadow of the waxwing slain."

Racist Dave, his editor's cap on (if askew), says he will personally wound me if I name-drop another author. He observes, with trademark wit, that I am the pube stuck in his teeth and that we must push on to the party, where now the chairs have been pushed aside and the music turned up. A happy scene: the waitresses dancing giddily, throwing themselves around with loose, marionette limbs, cheeks flushed, eyes sparkling; the males of the species reclining, mammalian, like seals waiting for a fish, their warm soft bellies puffed in pride, their mouths wide, a row of dark eyes drinking in the movement of the girls. Yet despite this bravura the men's smiles were shy, for it had been so long, and they had forgotten how this game was played.

From this swelter of music and hormone the Polish KP emerged. Darik looked uncomfortable as he approached the chefs. The sharp-eyed observer might have noticed he wore blue velvet shoes instead of the usual crusted steel-toed boots. He opened his mouth as if to speak, but no words came out. The chefs braced themselves. Finally then, here it was, the awful secret they had all pinned upon him. Scars ran the length of the big man's arms; his head, shaved to the sheer scalp, was an unfinished boulder. Those huge hands of his could have done anything. If he admitted murder, what then? Did you get the man a drink and carry on? Did you try to throw him out? Every man in that kitchen had made mistakes. Most talked about them openly. What had Darik done that inspired such silence?

Standing a little way apart, he arched one foot, cocked a knee and suddenly he was Darik the kitchen porter no longer but a fluid Latino hip merchant, sashaying across the dance floor, taking hold of one waitress at a time with his giant meat hands and spinning them expertly this way and that. Mouths hung open all around him. Ramilov looked pained by the gift he had been given. But slowly his expression twisted from suffering into ecstasy, his mouth yawned wider still, and a hoarse, delirious cry escaped him. Dave joined him with a low animal gurgle and soon we were all howling. The joy! The great collective joy that can wash over a kitchen! Darik beamed with happiness, basking in the music, and we roared back at him, wild, incredulous. Ramilov and Racist Dave, so often cat and dog to each other's philosophies, draped themselves across each other, weeping with delight. I looked at Harmony and saw she was laughing too. And she caught my look and it was like we were both laughing together at something that was ours, at something we had made. Laughing like lovers, or friends at least. Her dark eyes opening up to me, putting a warmth on me that had me jumping out of my skin. The joy!

It did not last, however. Before a sweaty, triumphant Darik could be congratulated and scolded for hiding his talents, Racist Dave started in on the subject of Africans and Ramilov stormed off in disgust. I found him at the bar, necking the last dregs of rum punch from discarded glasses.

"He's an arsehole," Ramilov said bluntly. "Wasting perfectly good anger. There's so many things in the world to get angry about. Things that deserve it . . . and that numpty pours all his rage into what bit of soil someone was born on, and if they eat bacon."

Here Ramilov gave a shifty look right and left, then reached over the bar and poured himself a pint of the expensive German pilsner we were not allowed to drink. He quaffed half of it in one motion, straightened up and continued.

"We're getting shafted from all sides by governments and banks and wars we didn't agree to and religious nutjobs who want us dead and famine and poverty and apathy and selfishness. We're being bled on the altar here, and all he's worried about is someone from another part of the world living next door to him. There's people getting their throats cut"—Ramilov's voice was cracking to be heard over the music—"people getting sold into slavery, people who are too weak to stop the flies eating their eyes, people losing everything, every day, people getting shafted generally. . . . But what does he want to know? What does he care about? Whether they speak fucking English or not . . ."

Not for the first time I sensed there were unknown pools of empathy in wicked Uncle Ramilov. You might almost say compassion. Hidden under many layers, certainly, and only reluctantly exposed. A tidy irony, given his enthusiasm for other kinds of exposure.

"You know," he began, "I sometimes think . . ."

I leaned in to catch more unexpected wisdoms. But Ramilov had caught sight of the waitress with the button nose and the statement was abandoned in midair, possibly truer than if he had finished it.

"Oh, fuck it," he said.

He downed the rest of his beer and threw the glass over his shoulder without looking round. Then he was off, shimmying grotesquely toward her. This was not a dance, surely, that he was inflicting on her. An elaborate courting ritual perhaps. It involved vibrating one leg at a time in her direction at a very particular frequency. The rest of the waitresses and Harmony, who had been dancing with them, scattered at his dystonic approach; but the button-nosed girl, by some quirk of nature, was responding to it. Throwing her head back, running her fingers through her pale hair, she glowed provocations, her soft features painted with fire. Ramilov stalked her with his odd little dance, closing in on her, until his zombie chef hands were clawing at her thighs and his nose nestled in her neck.

Harmony, a short distance away, was shooting disapproving glances at this unlikely couple. Of course I could understand her problem with the situation, what with the waitress being her friend and Ramilov an unconscionable pervert, but in that moment it was they who seemed contented and pursuing the right path, not her. She looked a little lonely, I thought, and the idea came to me that I should go over and talk to her, seeing as I was lonely too and such coincidences were ignored at one's peril. I took a few more sips of punch. A little more and I would be ready. I finished the glass. What would I say? Perhaps I should ask Darik for some moves first. I'd get a beer, and then I would go, whether I knew what to say or not. Just launch myself over the dance floor. In my head, pitching over my own thoughts quite uninvited, I could hear the voice of my father. *No balls, have you? An omen of impotence . . .* What was this obsession with potency and balls? Did you have to hump life to get what you wanted? Weren't there other routes to happiness? I tracked round the bar and pulled a beer from the fridge and looked again at Harmony. She had folded her arms in disgust and was prizing the happy couple apart with her eyes. Even in abhorrence she was worlds above me. I wondered if I could launch myself that far.

As I considered this, a shout went up from the other side of the room and Camp Charles, pouting insanely, steamed onto the dance floor, taking Harmony by the waist and gyrating around her as if she were a totem in a West End musical about savages. She was a totem, to me, but I would never have treated her in such an ungentlemanly way. I could only watch as they danced, pained that I might have missed my one chance, agonizing over whether Camp Charles had been telling the truth when he'd told Ramilov that he'd sucked enough dicks to know he was straight. I have been reliably informed by several parties since that nothing happened between Harmony and Camp Charles, but at the time the worry rendered me quite speechless, and after a few fruitless attempts at conversation with a squiffy Racist Dave I made my excuses and went home. Home to my father, who in my absence had cultivated strong feelings that if there was free booze he should have been told about it. Such was my fate.

Ramilov's fate we learned the next morning, when the man himself, with immense, unsavory relish, recounted his adventures to the kitchen.

"Well, now, have I got a story to tell you gentlemen," he said. "Herculean. Someone should give me a medal."

"Get on with it, Ramilov," said Racist Dave. "Did you bang her or what?"

"*Bang* is not the word for such artistry," Ramilov replied. "No. This was seduction, pure and simple. A big fucking pile up of pheromones. I put the moves on her, and when that happens, few can resist. Before I knew it she was pulling me into the dry store by my shirt and snogging my face off. She jumped me, boys. Like a beast unchained. Yours truly was caught off guard. Took me a moment to find the appropriate response. But I did find it, and I was going to give it to her right then and there on the flour bin but she said no, not here, let's take our time over this. Who was I to argue? We got a cab back to mine and she was biting my lips and scratching my neck the whole way and I was thinking, Steady, mate, this one might be trouble, you could be out of your depth here. Oh, she was fiending for it. I think that cabbie had a hard-on watching us. I fucking would have. . . .

"So we get back to mine and I tell her to wait in the bedroom while I get us some drinks. Then while I'm in the kitchen I remember my bedroom is a fucking state and she'll probably freak out when she sees it and fucking dry up completely. And so I'm pouring the drinks, cursing my luck that I've lost my first bit of muff in months because of a wank sock or a dog collar"—at this stage in the telling Dave's face clouded with questions—"but when I get back to my room, guess what? She's totally stripped off. Naked in my room, immortal amid ruin. What a sight, boys. What a sight. I know I've sometimes said she looks plain but this was a sight."

"You said she looked like a potato," Dave reminded him.

"Well, last night she looked like a sexy potato," Ramilov continued. "The sexiest potato I've ever seen. Beautiful heavy breasts with these puffy pink nipples. Oh, boys. Her skin was so hot I almost fucking burned myself. And wet as anything. She tasted like chicken stock. . . ."

Wank sock? Chicken stock? The words were gathering in disturbing juxtaposition. But Ramilov was warming to his theme, and he was not to be stopped.

"I'd barely got my head down there and she was crying out. I was obligated to mount her. Thank god for the booze, that's all I can say, 'cause I'd have lasted all of two seconds without it. But I was in the zone, comfortably numb, as the song goes, and we were rolling all over the place, her sort of wrestling me and giving me little scratches and bites and growls and I was scratching and biting and growling right back. . . ."

Ramilov, eyes closed, hips grinding, acted out the scratching and biting.

"We were going at it so hard we fell off the bed and smashed the lamp and I thought I'd broken my cock but it turned out it was all right after a bit and we got back to it on the floor, her riding me, holding her hair up while she did it and I thought that was just about the sexiest thing I'd ever seen. . . ."

Ramilov, now in a state of great excitement, mimicked the waitress with the button nose.

"And she was whispering all sorts of filth, telling me how much she wanted it and I thought, fuck it, go for broke, so I flipped her over, licked her Gordon Ramsay and gave her a dose of my Jamie Oliver in there for good measure. . . ."

This final detail was a conflation of metaphors and imagery that no one was happy with. Racist Dave winced. I giggled uncomfortably. From the other side of the kitchen Harmony glared at Ramilov, then at me. I shut up very quickly—that look was enough to turn me inside out. The ancients believed that certain women in Scythia, if angry with a man, could kill him with a single glance.

"Yes," Ramilov concluded happily. "A wonderful night. I just wish I could remember her name."

5. PRAYER

Ramilov never did sleep with the button-nosed waitress again, for reasons he could not fathom. And though he was told her name many times, he never did remember it. She left The Swan soon afterward. This was probably not because of anything Ramilov had said or done; it was simply the nature of things. Waitresses and chefs came and went all the time. The service industry is an eternal circuit of change and renewal. Labor is cheap, and so is drama. Only a few hold grimly on. Restaurant owners regularly shut their places down, then reopen them with a new name or a lick of paint. A waiter who walks out in the middle of Saturday service might be back by Tuesday. And if not him, another like him: hopeful, uncertain, passing through. So it was with only mild surprise that news of Dibden's return was met.

"Reunited at last!" Ramilov cried when he saw Dibden's familiar gangly frame at the back door one morning in late February. "Dibden and I. A classic duo. Morecambe and Wise. Laurel and Hardy. Mice and Men."

"I read that," said Dibden entering, still very much haunted. "About the big bloke with the hamster."

"Think about what you're saying, knobber," said Ramilov. "The clue's in the title. It's not called *Of Blokes and Hamsters*, is it?"

"Oh, yeah," said Dibden.

"It's all right, Dibden," said Ramilov. "You're my colleague again and I won't hear a word said against you."

Dibden had returned to us! Dibden, with his quaint aristocratic guilt, not so different from my own familial issues. Dibden, with his hatred of foul language, such a useless, tormenting quality in his chosen profession, so spectacularly uncomfortable for him. The S&M café had fired him for decency, he announced sheepishly, as if the grounds for dismissal had been fair. Always with Dibden it was a question of the world acting upon the man, never the other way around.

Yet with his return, balance in the kitchen was restored. A gentle counterargument to the excessive machismo of Ramilov and Racist Dave. He was still shit, of course, but it was testament to the indomitability of the human spirit that he carried on being shit. And though Ramilov (who was now second in command, god help us all) continued to mimic buggering him with the donkey carrots, it seemed now to be done with a certain fondness—almost, you could say, a gentleness. As a team we had been through much already: Bob's violence and subsequent collapse, the crows in our bellies at Mr. Michael's, the blarney of O'Reillys . . . Nothing like abuse, self or otherwise, to cement a camaraderie. Rubbish though he might have been, Dibden belonged here with us, and I was glad to see him back. When people fall out of your life it tends to leave you lopsided.

The other consequence of Dibden's return was that desserts were once more taken care of and everyone could move up a spot. Ramilov started doing shifts on the sauce section so Racist Dave could stop doing hundred-hour weeks. On quiet days Harmony worked Ramilov's section and I was trained up on the fryer section to take her place. As a result of this reshuffle Harmony and I became a team. She taught me how to prepare the dishes, how the section had to be set up, how to organize the fridges. We left little notes for each other detailing the mise that had to be done on the other person's shift. And though I had always watched her closely, I began to pay even greater attention to the speed and agility, the sheer professionalism, of her thought and movement. When orders were building up on the fryer section and people were starting to shout I felt defensive toward her; if she strained while lifting a pot off the stove I would strain along with her in sympathy. At changeover we talked, seriously, about how the section was looking for the night ahead and I would try to read her eyes for another sign of the warmth I had seen at the Christmas party. Only once did I see a flash of that other Harmony: at the end of a hectic lunch service I watched her take off her chef's hat and shake her lustrous hair free, then shyly cover it again.

Toward me, however, there was no ostensible heat. Harmony was mostly pissed off with me. I was clumsy with the fryer oil and cack-handed with my plating. I forgot to mention things that were desperately needed for the next service. Every day I failed to get through my mise list. If there were more than two orders on for the section I went into a tailspin. There was no check grabber on the fryer section and I couldn't understand how you were supposed to remember everything. I had to keep going over to the sauce section to look at the checks, which pissed off Ramilov because I was in his way.

"It's like watching the plane hit the tower in slow motion," he shouted at me. "Every time I see you. I know what's going to happen but I'm still shocked when it does."

Where was all the time? Between the squawking of the check machine and the call for the plate on the pass the minutes were stretched absurdly thin. If I had to look for something—a plate, a cloth, a bottle—I got behind. If I deviated in any way from the method, I got behind. If I overthought it, like my father on the golf course, the fluid mechanics became clunky and I fell behind. Kitchen time expected half an hour of work in three minutes that felt like thirty seconds. When it went wrong these different values of time became more exaggerated still, pulling the here and now in every direction. My experience lagged—I could witness every millisecond of my shame and savor the exact, awful moment my control slipped away. Yet as I failed to deliver, the demands upon me became increasingly frantic. I needed to do more and more with less and less. And soon I could hear nothing but the cries for my missing plates and it seemed whatever I did brought me no closer, I was sweating and whirling in every direction just to tread water. It was then that Racist Dave or Harmony would swing over to bail me out. Before long I would be reduced to putting garnishes on the plates they had made, forgotten, irrelevant. Pinocchio, dreaming of becoming a real boy.

"*How are you so shit?*" Ramilov would shout over the clatter of the stove. "*How is it possible? I would say it is one of the great mysteries of the age.*"

But I was no longer daunted by Ramilov's jibes. I kept at it. Gradually the humiliations lessened. I realized the secret was all in the preparation, and if your section was in order then you were in order. Dibden likes to say that "prior preparation prevents poor performance," though it is not necessarily advice he follows. I developed little tricks to save me time and got as much ready in advance as I could. It was tactical: every evening a thirty- or fifty- or eighty-headed monster would appear and demand feeding. It was a matter of not getting caught out. I began to get quicker, to know instinctively where everything was and exactly how long it would take me to do it. I was shouted at less. And I felt a change coming over me, because when I stood in front of those fryers I knew I was part of the kitchen, really part of it, directly responsible for things the customers ate. Granted, it was soup and chips mainly, but every element of those dishes was mine, and when the bowls and plates came back empty to the plonge I could say I had done a good job. Yes, I was very proud. Often I stood at the pass as if I were Racist Dave himself, surveying the happy crowds.

To see them happy made me happy. Could I have said that before, when I lay with my rumbling belly, listening to the revelers in the street below? When I looked in at the Parkway restaurants with melodramatic yearning? Or further back, before I came to London? Was there ever a time when I could have said that and meant it? My emotional career has been a series of small melancholies adding up to a hole. I have wished misery upon Rachel Parker and Tod Brightman, upon my father and countless others. Hell and damnation have been heaped upon those who have slighted me, upon those who have what I want. I have never been generous of spirit, and I have always excused that by saying a man with nothing has nothing to give. Now I felt my bitterness easing off. Let the famous young writers be. Let the girls who have snubbed me sleep with whom they want. Let this rich couple on table 6 feed half the côte de boeuf to their dog. Let this group of Primrose Hill mothers order off menu. Let Ramilov describe me as "a wubbering fucktard" to the fish deliveryman. Let my father wallow and snore. Let them all exist without my harping.

And this was just the beginning. Soon this progress would translate into other areas. There would be a lot of people to thank when I won my first literary award, a lot of things to do. First I would console poor sobbing Tod Brightman in the front row, who had bought a satin trilby especially for the acceptance speech he never got to give. Ramilov would get an honorable mention, for all the dishonorable mentions that made me the man I am today. With the prize money I would ship my father off somewhere warm, somewhere pleasant without mobile phone reception. I would buy a house in Perugia, or Provence, where Harmony and I would summer—good

Harmony, that is; the Harmony I had glimpsed fleetingly at the Christmas party, who had helped the needy beneath my window that night, not the Harmony who wiped my plate decorations clear with a single flick or pushed me aside as the checks mounted. I'd give lectures, the odd interview—or perhaps I'd decline them all and cultivate an air of mystery. . . .

Forgive me, London, for getting carried away with foolish dreams. Deep down I know I am no prodigy. Forgive Ramilov, for his many and terrible transgressions. They are perhaps too much for one man to bear. Forgive Camden Town, for its wickedness and merchandizing and zoetrope of sad stories, older than the hills. Forgive university, for not being all it was cracked up to be. It doesn't bother me so much that I missed out on the tender stuff. Who really knew anything about that, when it came to it? Love, sex—it was all a stab in the dark. Forgive Bob, for raging so hard against the wrong things. Perhaps in the next life, as Montaigne believed, his soul could be assigned a body according to previous conduct: lions for the brave, foxes for the crafty, hares for the cowardly. For Bob, I see an unscrupulous hog. If there is any poetic justice, he will end up stuffed above the bar of a gastropub. Forgive Bob's terrible wife, for being blessed with a trowel for a face. Forgive Rosemary Baby and This Charming Man, for sometimes life isn't so much of a gift at that. Forgive One-Eyed Bruce, who will surely kill me if he gets the chance. Forgive the brewery, for trying to serve lobster in a neighborhood where people shit on your doorstep. Forgive the shitters, for they know not what they do. Forgive The Fat Man, who now stands poised to finish this story. Yes, forgive even him. Forgive us all, for we have sinned. But who among us, if it comes to that, wears sin lightly? And who except Ramilov would take on someone else's? In Ramilov's defense, I would ask you to remember that.

Last, forgive my father. I'm not sure if I should specify what for.

The list is a long one. Forgive him for the way he talks about my mother, her sexual proclivities that I shall not repeat here, the shape of her body—*oh, those hips, you could have rested a pint glass on those hips, et cetera.* Forgive him that he has not worked in so long he cannot countenance the thought of a toilet other than his own. Forgive him for his feet, if that is within your power. Forgive him for his snoring. Forgive him his utter purposelessness that keeps him here with me. His reasoning: "Why should I go somewhere and pay when I can stay with you for nothing?" A gauntlet thrown down, if you like. If I wished my father to leave, I would have to pay for it. So I gave him the money for a room and told him I'd visit very soon. But he was back by the afternoon. "It got spent," was his response. "You shouldn't have trusted me." A lesson learned. Who said he taught me nothing?

Forgive him for pitching up at The Swan most days, angling for free booze, joking about me with the front-of-house staff even as he trades on my name. Forgive him for the embarrassing memories he insists on dredging up so publicly: that I was a fat baby, that I wrote a will when I was eight bequeathing my collection of rocks and pebbles to my mother. Forgive his frequent requests for money, which I am too weak to refuse. I worry about him, the lone country lad in the Camden Town bookie's, mixing with the wrong elements. I see the fistfuls of betting slips he pulls from his pockets and fear I am not the only one he asks for money, that he may have found other, less forgiving financial backers.

Forgive him also for whatever part he may or may not have played in the disappearance of the antique silver swan statue that sat above the till of The Swan. Dave has shown all of us the surveillance tapes of that afternoon and, although the camera's view is poor, and the statue too small to be properly seen, my father is the only one at the bar within snatching distance. Besides Camp Charles and a terrified-looking teenage bar hand, there are few places to point.

"They've asked me what I know about it," I told my father. "You can't imagine the shame."

"You shouldn't blame yourself," was his response. His trademark response to all my woes.

"I'm not blaming myself," I shouted. "I'm blaming you!"

"Don't even trust your own father," he grumbled. "Some thanks I get for raising you. You think I'd come to your place of work and put you in that position? You think me so cheap? Well, go on, search my stuff. You'll find nothing. I'll bet money on it."

I did not like his phrasing. Why not bet he didn't take it instead of whether I would find it? Why not leave the betting out of it altogether? I refused the wager. Truthfully, I did not know what to think. But furtive searches of his possessions revealed nothing, and the missing swan never turned up. I had to go back to Dave and declare the evidence inconclusive.

Forgive him for the shame he has brought upon me, even if he did not steal that silver swan. Forgive him for the smell of home he has brought with him: of wet elderflower bushes and cornflakes, of varnish reapplied. Forgive him for his thin, sad face so like another's, for his occasional bursts of charm. Forgive him for reminding me of my brother.

INTERLUDE

I. CHORUS

The days roll by. An earthquake in Japan. Portugal collapses. A Tory MP posts pictures of himself in Nazi uniform on the Internet. Nazis everywhere complain. The wheels keep turning. Builders open a long derelict house on Eversholt Street and find hundreds of dead pigeons inside. Let gentrification commence. The flower seller on Parkway is moved to beside the ladies' public toilet. Somewhat displeased, you could say. One night my father finds me scribbling thoughts about the city, and for a few days is convinced that I should write a book about him, his sporting triumphs and so forth. I don't think this book will be what he wanted. Roadworks finish on the high street. Roadworks begin on Camden Road. Traders sell, tourists buy, tubes strike and traffic roars. This is how time moves for a chef. A jumble of events in no particular order. Are we taking great leaps or are we treading water? Unless the menu changes, how do you measure the passing of time? The monotony of the chores, the daily routines. Weeks turned inside out. Whole months lost. No seasons. Hot or hotter. Tangled streams of consciousness. Spuds, stocks, bones, blood. Most of the last not mine. When writing of the kitchen, it is important to remember the blood.

What else do I remember? Only moments, voices . . .

Shahram and I out on a Sunday morning, pushing a shopping trolley full of milk through the streets. All the well-to-do Camden couples with their prams. Shahram's trousers in rags. Shaky Shahram, jiving gently. An odd couple, he and I. Our baby not like the rest.

Fucking knew you were a pastry boy.

Running up the stairs with oranges in my apron. Deep gastros of confit lamb breast pulled from the ovens and stashed underneath the benches for later. Fat bubbling where the foil was torn. A delivery of game on Saturday evening before service. Hind legs poking from potato bags as we haul them to the cellar. Deer among the beer. And pheasant too: eyes closed a little too tight, feigning sleep, still in their feathers, red collars around their necks.

There goes my day off, said Racist Dave.

Shouting, swaggering, elaborate rap bragging.

Chinchilla coat is my dog's bed.

Greasy laminate of the kitchen bible. Every recipe The Swan has ever known. Bob's mum's Victoria sponge. Pasta dough revised. Consistency the watchword. Smells competing. Doneness. Her dark eyes, unreadable.

You got any other stories?

The sarcasm.

Oh, chef, don't cut yourself with that knife.

Racist Dave on quality control.

Why is this lemon curd bitter?

Dibden taking the pith.

Ramilov putting words into the kitchen porters' mouths.

What Shahram is saying, in his own little way, is that he wants to see a good hour of mise out of you.

The film actress coming to eat one day and we, the chefs, sneaking out to catch a glimpse. The scene framed through the doorway. Another world. The starlet, laughing easily with friends.

I'd fucking break that in half.

Racist Dave confronted by beauty.

Two worlds always in tension. Each choosing to forget what the other is like, or else the whole show falls apart. The art of forgetting: something my father never learned, something I am still mastering.

A forkful slipped into a diner's mouth.

Oh, my, have you tried? Utterly delicious.

The same plate coming through the kitchen.

Let that sauce down, chef. It tastes like my ring piece.

The leisure at table.

Would you like any coffee, petits fours?

The haste at stove.

Coming up fast on a rav chaka. Whenever you like next thirty seconds.

The aesthetic appreciation of one.

Look at those swirls of sauce. A picture.

And the other.

See that last plate? I proper gayed it up.

The manners of the front of house.

Absolutely, sir, that shan't be a problem.

The manners of the back.

You've got the fattest arse I've ever seen. We should get your arse in a pan and render it.

Those groomed and glowing customers, eyes sparkling in full faces. Sweeter, neater, cleaner, greener. Satisfied. Indulged.

Casting imperious glances toward the pass.

Absolutely famished.

Literally dying.

From outside our kitchen appears quiet, thoughtful. Inside it is a cauldron. Smashing pans, blazing jets. Manufactured grief. Little wailing, much gnashing of teeth.

You've split the béarnaise.

Run it through the oven.

More chiff on this bass!

I don't think Darik likes you today. I think he thinks you're a fat prick.

Late-night frenzy of the clean down, wanting to be done. Sniffing the mise, throwing stuff away. Cling-filming the containers. Rolling the fridges.

I want that all pulled out tonight. Get behind it.

Oui.

And you better be using blue spray over there.

Dave assembles the order lists, retires to the office to phone it in. The kitchen relaxes. Music climbs. *Gotta get up, gotta get out.* The chefs singing along, painfully keen. Extraordinary rendition. An envoy is dispatched to make peace with the much-maligned front of house. Camp Charles looks to the heavens and forgives. Now ask.

Please, sir, may we have some beer?

The slack fooling that follows. Chefs stinging one another with rolled-up cloths.

Don't move away, you pussy. Stay still.

No, you'll get me in the eye.

I won't get you in the eye.

You did last time.

I won't.

Drinks after work in O'Reillys. Shattered but you will have one. Rude not to. Is Camden an island, or a bigger creature that we're living on? *Epizoon*, that is the word. Second always goes down easier. Spirits rise. Nora the landlady watching crossly as Ramilov, demonstrating a sexual activity illegal in the state of Texas, spills lager on the tired carpet. Dibden red-faced, ashamed he is laughing. Those powerfully sad Irish and their songs. Chefs discussing love.

True love is sticking with someone no matter what.

That's blind love.

No.

Yeah. Like a dog.

Ramilov asking one of the old boys if he can make a brass rubbing of his face. Throwing oneself out, a sign of good grace. Cold air hitting, winter's blade drawn. Shivering, a young fox sprawls in the street. Hit by a car, they reckon. Do you call a vet for a wounded fox? Not so big beneath that fur. Not so wild up close.

The regrettable Sunday-night conversations in Mr. Michael's drug den.

In Camden, the corner shops sell individual steel scourers especially for the crackheads. That's recognizing your market.

Too busy listening to listen, too caught up telling it like it is to tell it. The chefs talking about their dreams . . . of owning a pig farm, of running a ten-cover place with the wife as front of house and no choices on the menu. Like it or lump it. Open tomorrow if they only had the money. Mr. Michael's midrange Charlie vanishing up the nostrils. Where does it all go?

For they, the sinners, reasoned unsoundly, saying to themselves, "Short and sorrowful is our life, and there is no remedy when a life comes to its end, and no one has been known to return from Hades. For we were born by mere chance, and hereafter we shall be as though we had never been, for the breath in our nostrils is smoke, and reason is a spark kindled by the beating of our hearts; when it is extinguished, the body will turn to ashes, and the spirit will dissolve like empty air. Our name will be forgotten in time, and no one will remember our works; our life will pass away like the traces of a cloud, and be scattered like mist that is chased by the rays of the sun and overcome by its heat."

Dibden speechifying to the moon-eyed masses. While I, tight-jawed, lecture mute Rossi on *Crime and Punishment.* Carrying my shame home on Monday morning past school-bound kids. Appalled by my own banality, the uselessness of my remarks. Praying I don't meet Mrs. Molina on the stairs.

Good morning, Mrs. . . . . Yes. Popped out for a stroll. My eyes? Must be the fresh air.

Or worse, my father.

You didn't come home last night. You didn't . . . you didn't get some, did you? His disbelief at once affectionate and infuriating. Because I could if I wanted to: a number of doorway shadows had suggested their enthusiasm. And all the while unraveling under his gaze, having my soul picked loose, terrified of his suspicion. So we spend the best days of our life. At the end, day or night, he is always there, curled around a kebab or the *Racing Post.* Pride and self-pity jostling for pole position.

I should get the bed. Seniority.

If I could get a hundred on him ante-post, trust me, I wouldn't be asking you for cash anymore. You'd be asking me.

Detritus of cornflakes and toenails encircle him. Perhaps he fears my intentions. To hear attackers, those at risk of assassination are advised to surround their beds with newspaper when they sleep.

Sometimes he pierces my dreams to ask if I am still awake. It seems we are forever at opposite ends of time, he and I.

Any word from your mother?

Dad, it's late.

I know that. You think I don't know what time it is?

Over time I stopped answering him. Letting his questions fall on the night.

Son? Son?

Occasionally, an emotion creeping in.

2. THE FAT MAN'S SECONDS

Racist Dave says this story is too much about me and my issues. He says I'm telling it all wrong and asks—insists—that he be allowed to contribute. Well, this is a chapter about Dave, one that only he can tell.

It is March and The Fat Man casts his shadow over us once more. At the pass one evening he leans in for a word, and Dave, though quite adamant he would never go back, hears something that makes him change his mind. Another dubious dinner party is on the cards. Another mysterious dish. This time a commis is not required. We are getting closer to the night everything changed. Beneath the glittering mass of flies a shape is slowly appearing. A skull of some kind, not quite human.

Where possible, I have tried to remain faithful to Dave's consideration for grammar.

I didn't just become a vegetarian overnight you know I'm not a fucking twat. People give me shit about it now because I share the veggie meal with Shahram and I used to say only terrorists and rabbits ate that food well those people never had to do what I had to fucking do so what do they know. Long story short The Fat Man is a disgrace he got what was coming to him good job our boy. This was not so bad as that but still fucking gash you will not catch me doing that again in a hurry or ever. Understand this I weren't scared at any point just fucking gagging over it really cos it were wrong I knew it were. Some cunts are going to say why d'you go back after you had to drown the birds Dave well killing little birds is one thing but this were something else. You should have called the Old Bill they'll say but I ain't that type of guy. Besides it were a fuckin' grand and I don't know any chef that wouldn't drown a little bird or do a bit of bad gash for a fuckin' grand. It ain't fuckin Sunday school, chefing.

Another thing too it weren't like I had no choice. Fat Man comes up to me at The Swan all matey like an' says you should do this, I'm like nah but he don't take no for an answer gets this creepy smile on his face and says it could pay off some of the debt. I don't know what the fuck he's on about and I tell him so. Oh I think you do says The Fat Man still with the creepy smile you owe some friends of mine a lot of money. Well I don't owe no one in London a fucking penny and I said that to him but Fat Man shakes his head still smiling and says not in London, in Manchester. That fucking freaked me out I tell you. How do you know about that I say. It's my business to know he says. Well I'm thinking if I piss him off and he tells those guys they'll fucking kill me straight up. So I said yes.

That day I've turned up at The Fat Man's gaff and it's the same deal as the first time with the whispering behind the walls in the corridors and the big empty kitchen. Fat Man goes through a list of stuff all pretty basic liver parfait trippa alla romana carpaccio of beef and that then he says to me oh we've got a special treat tonight you'll enjoy this. I'm thinking will I fuck. He unlocks that cupboard of his and comes out with something under a black cloth. I'm thinking oh shit already cos last time it were those fucking tiny birds and I don't want the trouble but this is worse. He's pulling the sheet off now and I can see there's a cage underneath with proper big bars and everything. Fuck me if there i'n't a baby tiger in there.

I'm like er what the fuck where did you even get a fucking tiger? Well he just smiles at that and asks am I having second thoughts about it. I weren't scared. . . . Shocked maybe. Is it legal though? I says. Davey

Davey he says clucking his tongue, what do you take me for I'm a community man.

This didn't exactly answer my question but before I can say anything he's talking again saying how I had to drown it in the sink like I done with the birds then skin it stuff it brown it off in a skillet and chuck it in the oven for twenty minutes. Said it had to be basted regular as it were very lean. How the fuck did he know that? Is there a cookbook for this shit? Then he tells me not to bring the tiger in 'til bell has rung three times. Then he leaves.

Muggins here just stands in the middle of the kitchen not knowin' what the fuck to do. Just stood there. It got dark and I still hadn't made up me mind. That tiger were looking at me dead funny and the house were giving me the creeps and I could hear the low voices comin' through the walls like sayin' stuff to me and tellin' me to do it and think about the money and how boss it would be to have it. And all the time I felt like I were being watched and this were part of the fun.

I were in a weird mood like bored but edgy and I didn't know what to do with meself. Started looking in the drawers and cabinets checkin' out the gizmos. Then I saw The Fat Man had left the door to the cupboard open and I thought why not no rule against it little peek won't hurt no one so I went in there and sniffed about a bit and I found something proper weird lookin' in a jar. At first I was like no way is that what I think it is but then I looked again and it fucking was. A finger. No lie. A fucking human finger. Pickled in a jar. I don't know what the fat bastard was doing with a human finger and I don't fucking want to know.

Finding that finger sort of made up my mind though and I fucking did it anyway didn't I. Drowned the little thing. The sound it made when it were going into the water were horrible. I didn't like doin' it but I weren't thinkin' right. I prepped it and cooked it up just as The Fat Man said and tried not to think about it. Then I bring in the other food and like last time the room is empty but empty like a knowing empty if you know what I mean. I go back and wait in kitchen for the three rings and when I hear 'em I bring the tiger in on a big silver tray and there's all people round the table with the black sheets over their heads again and I can't see none of their faces and I'm thinking oh fuck Dave this is weird i'n't it. And I remember what The Fat Man were saying before about not wanting god to watch you as you sin like when you're doing evil eating wrong things and that.

I've put the tiger down and I'm standing there thinking oh what happens now when I realize they're all waiting for me to fuck off before they start they won't move while I'm in the room. Fat Man's got the envelope waiting for me on the table. So I take my money and as I'm leaving this one bloke in a black sheet nearest the door grabs my wrist and whispers help me. He's got a good grip on my wrist and there's a big old burn on the back of his hand just like the one Bob used to have. Don't go Dave he says all quiet like and I'm thinking it does fucking sound like Bob except I never heard Bob beg for nothing. Shut up says The Fat Man under his sheet at the other end of the table. I've done my time says Bob. It's not a discussion says The Fat Man you'll do it 'til I say.

Well that just freaks me out more hearing Bob like that and wondering why he's talking so and I weren't sticking about to find out. I prized his hand off me and I walked out and I'm thinking fuck you if I'm ever coming back here again and as I walked I were saying you stupid fuck Dave a fucking tiger and fucking all that bother for a fucking grand you stupid fuck. I ain't never going back, simple as. And when someone takes the piss out of me for turning veggie I say fuck you you didn't find a finger and fuck you you didn't peel a tiger. The end.

PART III

TO FINISH

1. IN SPRING

The light twists, the air softens. We have emerged from winter. In his letters, Ramilov is reminding me to tread carefully now, to remember my promise. It would be all too easy, he writes, to get carried away in the telling and let the wrong truths spill out. A pure Ramilov construction that: "the wrong truths." But he is right insofar as that around this point in the story it becomes harder to always tell right from wrong. A number of things happened which, morally, I am still trying to get a grip on.

My father is responsible for his share of these. "Put me up for a few days," he said. Almost a quarter of a year later I am still stepping over his snores or stuffing money into his outstretched hand, still waking to his wagers or the breath of his bunions. We are close, my father and I: disgustingly, repellently close. No son should have to endure it. On the other end of the telephone every week my mother says good riddance to the miserable scrounger, she does not want him back. I tell her I understand. Even as he marks the races beside me, his rotten feet poking out from underneath my blanket, this is our conversation. We have tuned our whispers over the years, she and I, tiptoeing around his passive aggression. "Don't wake the blowfish," my mother warns me if I raise my voice. "The blowfish" is her name for him, as he is prone to alarming spikes. "How is the blowfish today?" she will ask, to which I might reply "Deflated," "Semipuffed," "Fit to burst" or "Slow puncture," depending on the occasion. I accept it may seem odd that we talk this way about the man of the house when he is right there, but he is not so much of a man, and as of this moment he is not allowed in the house.

Sometimes, usually late at night when I am trying to sleep, he despairs of the distance between her and him. Grand, catch-all reasons for the rough patches are offered up.

"I married too young, son, that was my mistake," he announced one night in the darkness. "You only work out how to talk to women when you're married, and by then it's too late."

"Is that a confession?" I asked, eyes half open. It was how my father would have done it: blithely, and distributing the blame elsewhere.

"No," he said. "An observation."

I thought of my own struggles with Harmony, how I could never tell her how I really felt, and decided that, as an observation, there might be something in it. But I wasn't going to tell him that.

"If you loved Mum you wouldn't be making these excuses," I said. "You'd be facing up to this mess and trying to move past it."

"You think marriage is where it stops?" he replied touchily. "The end of line? The happy ever after? No, son, marriage is where it *starts*. Of course I love your mother. I'm just saying it's not easy. I'll bet you any money I love her."

"What sort of a bet is that?" I said. "How would you possibly prove such a thing?"

"I can prove it," he grumbled, but I would not take his flimsy bet and told him so.

"Christ, Dad, this is your family, not the horses," I reminded him. It seemed he only ever tried deep feeling on for size.

"Don't tell me about family!" he cried. "Every day I think about Sam!"

"What about me?" I shouted back. "Do you think about me every day?"

He said nothing for a moment.

"Well, you're still here, aren't you?" he replied at last.

The pain that comment caused soon gave way to regret. He was right—I had no business claiming the same level of love. I had left the soup out of Sam's reach when the blood was flooding his joints. And he had died and I had lived. It was a stupid thing I'd said, the thinking of a small man. Not that it probably bothered my father one bit what I thought. Since my brother's death I think he saw all other emotions in negative and could only trace their outlines, a necessary vagueness that he had cultivated, or that had cultivated him, for his ducking and twisting, half in half out, only-as-honest-as-the-situation-demanded state of existence. Yet you couldn't rule his feelings out. Always with my father there were doubts over his moral orientation, whether there might be some obscure, noble undertow driving the whole thing on. The incident with the apples, for example.

One rare Saturday morning off around this time I was at my usual spot by the window, observing the street scene, when I saw Glen, Bob's sworn enemy, emerge at a clip from the supermarket, a great haul of stolen apples clutched to his chest. The apples shone against his rags. He cackled at his heist. With the color and laughter, the goodness of the fruit beside the badness of the landscape, it felt as if spring had finally come to Camden. But as Glen made his way past the betting shop, One-Eyed Bruce, who had been studiously counting his drug money in the doorway, made a grab for the apples and sent them flying. Glen rolled after them and set about scooping them up from the filthy pavement into his sweater but One-Eyed Bruce was quickly onto him, snatching the apples from him as fast as he could grab them and stuffing them into his own pockets. I settled myself deeper into my seat, savoring the spectacle of two grown men rolling in the dirt for apples, when a third ran out of the betting shop and joined in. To my horror, I realized that this third man was my father.

I dashed down the stairs and into the street where a small crowd had gathered to watch the fracas. Other pedestrians continued to walk past the scrambling figures, sometimes over them, in their hurry to get where they were going. One-Eyed Bruce had pinned Glen on the floor and was punching him in the face. His fists were still full of drug money, and every time he punched the tramp there was a small explosion of notes. My father was in the center of the tussle, gathering up money and apples as fast as he could. When One-Eyed Bruce got bored of punching Glen he lunged over to my father and began beating him. My father dropped the apples and money to fight him while Glen, back on his feet once more, shuffled around picking up the apples and money my father had just dropped. Then One-Eyed Bruce switched his attentions back to Glen and pushed him over before picking up the money and apples, one apparently as important as the other, until my father, rousing himself from the canvas, managed to catch One-Eyed Bruce in the face with a wild, swinging kick, and the money and apples went flying again.

A woman next to me in the crowd tut-tutted.

"Why is that man with all the money fighting over a few apples?" she said aloud to no one in particular. "He could buy a truck full of apples with all that."

"Because they're his apples," said someone else. "Why should he let the tramp steal them?"

"People need to have a little pride in themselves," said a man behind me. "That's what's letting this country down."

I turned to look at the speaker of these words and saw it was the man who slept in the blood-red Porsche at night, The Last Lehman Brother. With a little less pride, I thought, he might be living in a flat and not out of his sports car. But I was too churned up with the scene in front of me, too pleased with the pummeling of One-Eyed Bruce and at the same time too mortified by my father's actions, to tell the man what I thought. My father did not even like apples. Yet here he was, making a public spectacle out of himself for the sake of them. He, Glen and One-Eyed Bruce continued tussling like this until a pair of police community support officers eventually came by and broke it up.

"I was helping him!" My father kept repeating this claim, holding his sleeve to his mouth to stem the bleeding while he pointed desperately with his other arm at Glen. "They're his stolen apples! I was gathering them for him!"

Considering my father's miserly tendencies, his supine existence, I doubted he would accept injury and public humiliation for a stranger, a down-and-out. Yet it was a tempting story to believe. That a person of such profound apathy as my father could still be riled by injustice, and in his anger, rise up. It underlined the whole neighborhood, the whole nation, with potential. Perhaps fires were burning behind other faces too. And for a moment the concrete sprawl and washed-out streets were colored with their flame. One more kick in the teeth might bring about the revolution. Perhaps my father would be there at the vanguard, a quiver of golf clubs at his side.

At this moment the crowd parted. A huge form was moving through it, pushing all aside. From on high, The Fat Man surveyed the chaos of the scene. Two weeks had passed without any word from him, since the evening Dave had so kindly cooked him a tiger—I had hoped we'd heard the last. He pushed forward to the front of the huddle, just a yard or so from where I stood, and grinned when he saw me. Was that a nod he gave to my tussling father too? Was there some connection?

Of course I said nothing to him, only nodded dumbly back. By this time The Fat Man had turned his attention elsewhere.

"Officers!" he cried. "This man"—he gestured toward One-Eyed Bruce—"works for me."

The community support officers looked at him a moment, then turned back to the dispute. The Fat Man would not be dissuaded, however. Arms outstretched, he approached the two men and gathered them in close to whisper something. Immediately they corrected their posture; just like that One-Eyed Bruce was given back his drug money and allowed to go. The terms of his employment were not questioned.

The Fat Man began to push through the crowd, smug Bruce at his back, when he turned one final time and pointed a reckoning finger.

"I'm still expecting your donation," he shouted.

"Monday." It was my father who answered. "I promise."

How did they know each other? And why did The Fat Man expect anything of my father, of all people? No one else did. Charity was not his strongest suit, as I have explained. The man had nothing besides nail clippings and bad advice and the handouts I gave him. Unless it wasn't charity. Unless it was something else.

Now the officers had shifted their attentions elsewhere. One of them gave Glen an official warning about stealing while the other returned the now bruised and dirty apples to the supermarket. My father escaped a booking, though he lingered furiously on, arguing even as I took him by the arm and dragged him away.

"They're the little man's apples!" he kept saying, pointing at Glen. "He stole them!"

Yet even in this statement it was unclear whether he was trying to defend Glen or drop him in it.

Hard truths were needed. Too much rumor and uncertainty still circulated, too much fear in the bones. I was still checking Harmony's features daily for signs of warmth and finding none—no conclusive data, at any rate. And then, to top it all, Ramilov started acting strangely. He slicked his hair back with water and spit and refused to wear a hat. He stole handfuls of potpourri from the customer toilets and put them in his trouser pockets. He kept a small ramekin of fennel seeds on his section to freshen his breath.

"You smell like a toilet," said Racist Dave.

"I smell like a nice toilet," said Ramilov. "Think about that. Every woman loves a nice toilet. They spend more time in the toilet than they do in the sack."

Ramilov's metamorphosis was for the benefit of a new female at the restaurant, a beautiful young waitress called Vivien. This name he remembered. Vivien was slight and shy and terrified of the kitchen. Someone must have told her the place was full of perverts— maybe she had looked inside. But there were times when Camp Charles or one of the other waitresses sent her to fetch plates from the plonge for polishing or to pass on a message, and then she couldn't avoid the place. Then her fear made her move slower, made her dawdle in the gangways and get in the way of service.

"Get her out of here," Dibden said to no one in particular. "Some of us are trying to work."

"If you touch her I'll cut your fucking throat, Dibden," said Ramilov. "A creature like that must be free."

Racist Dave and Dibden teased Ramilov about how he had changed for a woman, how he had gone soft, how he looked like

Boris Karloff. I was tempted to join in too; but, as the pair of dark brown eyes in the corner bore witness, I was in no position to start mocking others about romantic entanglement. For some reason, perhaps out of sympathy, Ramilov and Dave and Camp Charles had been very discreet on the subject of my indiscretions. I didn't want to risk anything.

Ramilov paid no attention to the teasing.

"It's called love," he sniffed. "You don't know what love is."

He kept saying he was going to ask the girl out, that he would leave his heart on the check spike with her name on it and so on. But weeks passed and he never did. He seemed quieter than usual. For long periods he would sit in the yard with a great melancholy about him, smoking cigarette after cigarette until Racist Dave told him to get his fucking arse back inside. He rarely abused Darik or Shahram, or me, anymore. He was civil to Dibden. Seldom, if ever, did he reach for a man's perineum. I began to worry about him.

One day, while I was sweeping the yard and he was smoking, I asked him what the problem was.

"Damn it, I love her," he moaned.

"But you've never spoken to her, Ramilov."

"That's probably why."

"So just talk to her."

Ramilov looked amused at the suggestion.

"You should listen to your own advice," he said.

It took me a moment to realize he was talking about Harmony. Such was my shame that I could only mouth wordlessly.

"What about the other waitress?" I said eventually, changing the subject.

"Who?" he asked miserably.

I reminded him of the sexy potato, and the story he had told us about the staff party when he thought he'd broken his cock. Ramilov said the sexy potato was not the same thing at all. That was lust. Sometimes his hormones got the better of him.

"But this time is different," he explained. "SHE IS THE MOST BEAUTIFUL THING I HAVE EVER SEEN. She's my nemesis."

Again Ramilov was operating on his own logic. I demanded enlightenment.

"I can't get involved with someone that beautiful," he explained. "Couldn't handle it. It would destroy me."

I could appreciate his concerns about beautiful women. I thought about Harmony and the feeling I got when she asked for the mixing bowl after me, a feeling like my soul was trying to leave my body.

"Besides," he said, almost to himself, "she is quite young."

"She is very young," I agreed.

"Yeah," he said sadly. "People can get funny about that. A couple of years the wrong way and you're climbing out of a toilet window with your stuff in a duffel bag and getting a Megabus to the other side of the country, changing your name, starting again . . ."

"What?" I asked. He had lost me once more.

"No," he continued, ignoring my question, "I can't get involved in that. The best I can hope for with a girl like that is brinkmanship."

"Brinkmanship?"

"An escalation of threat, to the point where the threats become too big to imagine. At which point both sides, faced with mutually assured destruction, back down," he explained.

Here was more of that strange knowledge that unexpectedly leaked out of Ramilov every so often, cribbed from a magazine in a sexual health clinic or a TV documentary watched late one night at Mr. Michael's or who knows where. Cribbed, then turned to his own obscure ends.

"Mutually assured destruction?" I asked.

"Kissinger without the kissing."

That Ramilov modeled his sexual relations on Henry Kissinger's foreign policy was certainly a surprise. An example of those jackdaw qualities I have previously mentioned. It made me wonder too if Harmony and I were in the midst of a cold war. Since we had shared that laughter at the Christmas party, there had been no flicker. Was it because I had messed up her section with my incompetence? Or because she had seen me laughing at Ramilov's crude sexual story about the button-nosed waitress? But then, if it was a cold war, I had done nothing to escalate the threat. I was not the United States in all of this, but a tiny state on Harmony's borders that thought it was fighting a great war while she carried on oblivious. Damn it, I was South Ossetia.

"I'll bet good money you won't get anywhere with that girl," my father opined that night as we lay on our backs in my tiny, airless room, listening to the cries of the revelers and criminals in the street below.

"That's a stupid bet," I said, regretting I'd ever mentioned her to him.

"Only for you," said my father. "Because you'll lose."

"No," I corrected him. "Because it cheapens all concerned."

"See?" he said. "That's the language of someone who knows he's going to lose."

"Fine," I said angrily. "I'll take your bet. Just to prove you wrong."

I leaned over the side of the bed and extended a hand in the direction of my father.

"Fifty quid?" he said.

The sum was a lot higher than I had expected, but it was too late to back out of it now. We clasped hands and shook. Father and son. A touching image of togetherness, never seen before or since. Obtained under false pretenses, but obtained nevertheless.

"Your problem is you're scared shitless," he added.

Thank you, Dr. Freud. You've spent my inheritance in Spearmint Rhino and on the horses but no matter, your advice is priceless.

2. A TRAIL OF ANTS

First the good news.

Later that month I managed to escalate my struggle with Harmony.

Then the bad news.

I was arrested almost immediately, along with Ramilov, on unrelated but extremely serious charges, the charges that form the dark heart of this story.

Prior to the arrest, as is so often the way, life was just starting to look up. Customers were at last returning to The Swan. From the small patch of concrete where the deliveries were stacked, the sun could occasionally be seen. Racist Dave had devised a new menu for spring: grilled lamb with Chantenay carrots tossed in caraway seeds and pea shoots, scallops with sauce vierge or spiced pigeon bastillas to start. And though he still cooked meat, his newfound vegetarianism brought a lightness to the food that it had never known under Bob. Globe artichokes stuffed with broad beans, mint and feta; a simple but transcendent dish of cauliflower served three ways: pureed, pickled and fried in masala spices.

And there was that day with Harmony. I owe it, in part, to a trail of ants, or "A Colony of Ants," to give Ramilov his due. We are in the yard of The Swan. It is a Tuesday afternoon before service and Harmony is smoking a cigarette. I have come outside to take the air (though in truth I have timed it quite purposefully) and before I have a chance to formulate some lame observation *she* speaks to *me*. I cannot stress enough how unusual that is. Besides reprimands or requests for utensils or orders about what needs to be done, I do not believe this has ever happened before.

"Look at this," she said, gesturing for me to come over to where she was sitting.

I approached cautiously. My first thought was that Ramilov was behind this and some terrible trick was about to be played upon me. She saw my hesitancy and laughed, pushing her chin out and blowing smoke up into the air, a very masculine gesture that only terrified me more.

"Closer," she said, smiling.

This was a great shock to me. The only females to use that tone of voice with me were the sad girls in the Camden Road doorways and big-hipped Sally Danzig in the student bar: I ran away from all of them. *So sorry. No time.* But I could not run away from this, nor did I want to.

I inched closer and she pointed to something in the restaurant wall, a thin crack running from the ground to a hole about eight feet up.

"Ants," she said.

I realized she was not in fact trying to seduce me and felt more than somewhat foolish. She was pointing out an enormous highway of ants going in and out of the kitchen, in two frantic lanes of traffic, transporting food from one place to another.

"They're scurrying about even faster than we are," she said.

Needless to say I was very flattered to be included in this "we." But I was also overjoyed at the comparison. She saw it too: we, like the flies and ants, were the little creatures. They toiled at their own tiny lives as we toiled beneath the Fat Men of this world. Inconsequential when looked at from a distance, those little characters, but full of purpose up close, full of life. Also they were as strong as anything. "Go to the ant, you lazybones," King Solomon advised. "Consider its ways and be wise."

"And they're doing the same job," I said.

She smiled at that. Was this that warmth again, opening up? I was not sure.

"Where do you think it goes?" she asked.

I shrugged. "Dibden's pastry shelf probably."

Harmony seemed pleased with this idea. She shuffled up and let me sit next to her on the bench while she smoked. It was perfect.

The next day I brought in my copy of *The Waste Land* and presented it to her. Don't ask me why. I just felt like I had to give her something. I thought she would appreciate it.

"It's the annotated text," I explained.

"No one's ever given me an annotated text before," she said.

I blushed, though afterward it occurred to me she might have been employing sarcasm. Still, it was a warm sort of sarcasm at that.

How did it change so fast? One moment I was swimming in the clouds with Harmony, the next I was chained to the bottom of the ocean. The end is looming over us now, and Racist Dave will tolerate no literary excursions. We must crack on, he says. The skull at the center of this story is becoming clear amid the darkness of the flies; it repeats its own grim promise, and I have not forgotten mine.

One cold bright morning soon after, a stranger appeared at The Swan's back gate. We can assume he could hear music coming from the kitchen at the end of the yard, because he knew someone was home. Perhaps he heard the hoarse tones of Ramilov, echoing rap sentiments from his spot on larder. We can assume the stranger found the gate was open and decided to enter. He walked into the

yard, past the staggered boxes of meat delivered that morning. The
music got louder.

I flip scripts
On you dipshits.

The back door to the kitchen was open and I imagine the man
must have seen Ramilov at his section with his back to him, making
Parmesan tuiles. You have to work fast and fluid when the Parmesan comes out of the oven, so that the tuiles set in the right shape.
With a spatula Ramilov had to lift them one by one from the bak-
ing tray and slide them delicately onto metal cylinders to shape
them, gently pinching.

"Oi," the stranger said abruptly.

I was putting the deliveries away in the dry store when I heard
that unpleasantly familiar voice. I stuck my head round the corner
and there was One-Eyed Bruce, as large as life, his one good eye
glaring at Ramilov while the chef, quite oblivious, gave a detailed
recital on female anatomy and shimmied his body from left to right
with a slow, filthy pelvic thrust. One-Eyed Bruce was standing next
to Ramilov as he did this, right up next to his shoulder. I hung back
at the door of the dry store, mostly hidden.

Room service all night
Like to treat my bitches right.

Ramilov cocked his knees and let his arse sashay down toward
the floor as he finished the tuiles and swept the pastry remnants
into his bin.

"Oi, pussyclot!"

"Jesus!" cried Ramilov, finally noticing him. "Doesn't anyone say '*Backs*' round here?"

"Fat Man need two chef nex' Tuesday, pussyclot," said One-Eyed Bruce. "Don' matter who, he say you all as bad as each other."

"You're a charmer, aren't you?" Ramilov, channeling Camp Charles, shot back.

"You be there." Crooking a warning finger, One-Eyed Bruce turned and was gone.

Thus everything crumbled. All those new beginnings turned to ash and scattered to the corners of the earth. We thought we had escaped The Fat Man's clutches, that our pasts could not catch us. We were wrong.

3. THE LAST SUPPER

won't do it," said Ramilov. "No way."

"Go on," said Dave.

"Not for all the minge in Middlesbrough."

"Please." Racist Dave, no longer carnivorous, had lost his appetite for The Fat Man's dinner parties. Peeling tiger cubs will make a man ask questions of himself. Also there was the suggestion of his past, waiting in ambush. What if he was serving the Mancunian drug lords who wanted his head on a plate? An uncomfortable proposition. He had made his excuses, and offered another in his place.

"I shall not work for that fat fuck," said Ramilov. "He's the devil."

"You can have any days off you want," Racist Dave pleaded. "You can come in late. I'll do your mise list for you."

"No." Ramilov was adamant. "I care about food. I have principles."

"It's a thousand pounds in cash for one night's cooking," said Racist Dave.

"In that case," said Ramilov, "I'll do it."

I froze in the middle of my veg prep. Surely we couldn't let him go. He had no idea what that house of horrors held in store. I looked at Dave, who just shrugged. What did he care? He was off the hook.

"Ramilov," I told him, "I don't think you should."

"What, and everyone gets the easy money except me?" said Ramilov. "Fuck off. I had no idea he was paying you that much."

"It's not that."

"If you want the cash then you can pony up," Ramilov went on. "But I'm not sharing. Fatty can pay us both a grand."

I could see Ramilov was not to be dissuaded. Someone would have to go with him and try to mitigate. I looked over at Dibden, the only other chef in the kitchen that morning, and saw he was already wearing his spavined-horse expression at the mere mention of The Fat Man's name. Dear Dibden, still quite useless. In the plonge, Darik and Shahram scrubbed at the pans, clattering and chattering, oblivious to the fates being decided next door. Fear couldn't touch those two.

"All right," I said. "I'll do it too."

What would life be like now if Ramilov and I had said no that final time? If he had not let the coin persuade him? If I—spurred on, in all honesty, as much by the money, by the need to keep my father's debts close to home, as by my concern for Ramilov—had not chased after? Would some other evil have taken The Fat Man's place? Or would we all, to a man, be free? Perhaps it is futile to mention these ifs and woulds. Freedom is never limitless. As a concept it is always fenced in. There is always someone who comes along and puts their feet in your face.

The morning of that final dinner my father and I had a falling-out. I say this as if it were unusual. We frequently did not see eye to eye. I disapproved of his lifestyle and I missed having a floor. But the falling-out that morning was particularly bad, and precipitated, in no small part, by my mother's phone call.

"Is he there?" was the first thing she said.

"Yes," I said, looking at the man in question. He was sitting on the edge of my bed cutting his toenails, though I had asked him not to several times.

"How's his mood?"

"Not great," I said. My father was still sulking from last night, when he had woken me to bet it was raining and I had somewhat bluntly declined.

"You know that man's problem," my mother said. "He's a child. An old and very angry child . . . Chip on his shoulder the size of a fridge but emotionally he's still pooing his nappy."

"Is that your mother?" my father inquired. "Tell her I've been going to a shrink three times a week and I realize I was wrong."

Three months . . . Three months he had been asking me to put in a word, to recycle these little lies and half-truths. He had no direct contact with her himself. When he rang, she would hang up. But today, for whatever reason, I was sick of toadying to my father's requests. I'd had enough of the wheedling and wanted him gone.

"Dad's been going to the bookie's three times a week and says he's broke," I told her. My mother laughed scornfully.

"A conspiracy, is it?" roared my father, suddenly furious. "The good son putting in a word! Three months on the floor while the little shit pours poison!"

"It's the truth, isn't it?" I shouted back.

"You think Sam would have treated his father like this?" he said, grabbing his shoes.

"He never got the chance," I shouted.

"That's right," my father spat back. "He never did. Because there was a fucking awful mistake and my beautiful son was lost. And the son who's left wouldn't put me out if I was on fire."

"What are you trying to say?"

"You know what I mean," he said. "Your mother knows what I mean."

"That's so like you," I shouted. "Always hiding behind someone else. Never putting yourself forward. Oh, we mustn't blame ourselves! You hide behind Mum. You're still hiding behind Sam. Have some self-respect! Come out with it! Say it! You think the wrong one died."

"That's what *you* think of me!" he cried, throwing the door open. "*That's what you want to hear.*"

"You don't deny it."

"Any chance you get you cut your own throat!" he shouted. "I'll tell you one thing—your brother never would have played the martyr."

With that he stormed out.

"No one's keeping you here!" I shouted after him. "Just go!"

The front door slammed behind him.

"Christ, Mum!" I cried. "He's a nightmare!"

"I know, dear," she said.

"How did you stand him for so long?"

"Like I said, a child," my mother told me. She had that calming voice on, which she sometimes used on my father too. "Don't let him upset you."

I realized that she had heard every word of my father's insults. I was furious with him already, but bringing her into it . . . *Your mother knows what I mean.* I was not prepared for her slurs too. He had kicked my last support out from under me. Could it be true? Had the wrong one died? He had failed to deny it. This was his greatest failure, in a lifetime of them. My mother's placations did not help—their implication, as I saw it: there was something in his jibes to be upset about.

"I've got to go," I told her. I was too angry, too appalled, to speak. Dressing hastily, I set out into the Camden streets and paced aimlessly for hours, cursing the traffic and the endless roadworks, the tourists and shoppers and crackheads and gamblers, the giant boots above the market shops that threatened to crush us all, the tyranny of family that each child was born into, damning the whole bleak menagerie. I replayed my father's words and grafted on fresh and stinging retorts. I imagined charging him down and knocking those hurtful words right out of him.

I was still bristling when I met Ramilov outside The Swan that afternoon and we made our way to that cold expensive town house with the dead wisteria and the whispering walls. That quiet, joyless place, where god was blind and deadly sins lurked beneath black sheets.

The sleek chrome kitchen was untouched, its expensive gadgets unmoved. The pervading sense of dread had not improved since my last visit either. Powerful and imperious as ever, The Fat Man appraised Ramilov as if he were a fly in his soup.

"Ah," he said. "The chef who ruined Bob. I've been waiting to meet you."

I didn't understand what The Fat Man was talking about and looked to Ramilov for explanation. Perhaps it was my imagination, but Ramilov at this moment looked a little caught out, an uncommon expression for him. As he did not speak, The Fat Man turned to me.

"And of course," he said with booming bogus bonhomie, "I remember this one. . . . How are we today?"

My mind turned nervously and I answered a fraction of a second too quickly, before I'd had time to check myself. I don't know why I said it. It just came out.

"Somewhat overwrought," I said.

"*Some what over wrought?*" It was four words when The Fat Man repeated it.

"He's an English literature student," Ramilov explained. "He doesn't mean anything by it."

"An English literature student, eh?" The huge mouth mulled the phrase over, swilled it about and spat it out. "Go on then, recite something for us. Give us a poem."

I looked at The Fat Man's grinning face. He did not enjoy poetry any more than he enjoyed food. It was all empires and thumbscrews with him, consumption and control. But what could I say? I couldn't refuse him. Nor could I recall any lines, put on the spot like this, with him all grinning and familiar, suggesting he knew more than he told. My mind blanked.

"I . . . I don't . . ." I stammered.

"Go on," he pushed. "A little poem. I bet you've got a lovely reading voice, haven't you? A lovely *timbre*."

"He's shy." Bless you, Ramilov, for coming to my defense.

"Is that right?" said The Fat Man, still grinning broadly and bogusly at me. "Are you shy?"

"So what are we cooking today?" Ramilov interrupted. "Lungs and gizzards? Barbecued spleen?"

This somewhat kamikaze approach of Ramilov's caused me a great deal more discomfort than I was already in. I tried to nudge him quiet. But The Fat Man seemed amused by the question. He smiled horribly and shook his head.

"Oh, I think we can do better than that," he said, and ran through the other courses we were to prepare: stuffed pig's intestines, chargrilled bull's testicles with capers, monkfish livers on toast, six capons set in aspic . . . The list went on. The special course, he said, would need no preparation. We would get to that later.

So we set about the dishes as instructed, both of us working quickly, in silence, hoping to escape as soon as we could. There was no horseplay from Ramilov today; he was thoughtful, on edge.

Every once in a while we thought we heard the soft murmurings of other people through the walls, somehow directed at us.

Do it, the voices seemed to whisper. *Kill it. Cut it. Feed us.*

And occasionally there was another sound, different from the rest: a kind of low, whimpering moan, faint but unmistakable, coming from close at hand. I wondered what it was.

"I don't care," said Ramilov, who had heard it too. "We'll just bash through this, take the money and get the fuck out of here."

The afternoon passed at a clip. We felt the eyes on us and worked faster. I read somewhere that King Solomon died standing up, leaning on his cane, and his spirit slaves, thinking he was still watching them, carried on working for forty days until termites ate the cane and the body fell. It was evening when we carried the first dishes into the Mary Celeste dining room, mindful of those invisible eyes, pushing aside the half-drunk glasses of wine and champagne to make way for the groaning trays. As we made our way back to the kitchen I noticed Ramilov's jaw was clenched. He looked more like a skull than ever.

An hour or so passed. Another hour of low whimpers and dread, of angry thoughts. I kept thinking about the argument with my father. What had he meant by "Your mother knows what I mean"? Was that just his sly implication or something more substantial? It tore me up that she might think the same as him, whatever that was. But the most hurtful phrase was my own, which he could not deny. *The wrong one died.* It was true, after all. Sam was the better child. He would always be the greater force. Yet even by my own slight standards, I could have been a better son. A better brother. In those final hours with Sam, I could have been so much better. I waited and wallowed, until The Fat Man returned at last.

"So far, so good," he said. "Now the main event."

Once more he went to the parlor door and unlocked it.

"Thought of a poem yet?" he asked, leveling his cold eyes at me. I shook my head. It was the only part of my body that still seemed to work. This time The Fat Man did not lift the thing inside the parlor, but dragged it out underneath a black silk sheet.

"Still shy, are we?" he said as he pulled the covered object in front of us. "Still overwrought?"

You could not see what was beneath, but steel glinted at the edges of the sheet. Another cage. A large one. I looked at Ramilov but he was very still and quiet, and suddenly small again. His fingers, bunched in on themselves, looked like white roses. Seeing him like this made me even more nervous.

The Fat Man looked from Ramilov to me and back again. A flicker of amusement played about his greasy lips. This was his little test. We drew our breath, and he let the drape fall. We stared in horror at the large, intelligent eyes staring back at us. It stood on two legs, whimpering softly, its fingers worrying the bars of the cage. A fully grown ape, as scared as we were. Ramilov's breathing was coming short and sharp next to me. I did not look at him.

"A lot of people think only the Chinese eat monkey brains," said The Fat Man. "Not true. The brain of an ape is greatly prized in many parts of the world. But few places do it properly. The brain is soft tissue. It degenerates very swiftly. It has to be eaten as fresh as possible. And there's nothing fresher than living. . . ." Here The Fat Man paused and moved toward the counter. "Which makes your job very simple. One single chop, in fact. Just a centimeter off the top of the skull. With this—"

From a drawer he produced a cleaver, glinting sharply.

"There's some handcuffs in the drawers," he added. "I would advise you use them. Apes tend to struggle."

He turned to leave and looked back at us.

"When the bell rings three times. That's all you have to do."

As soon as he had left I turned to Ramilov.

"Ramilov, if you think I'm going to do that . . ."

I stopped.

"It's not going to happen," he said very quietly.

I needed further elaboration on this point. At this moment, five sinister figures were pulling the black sheets over their bowed heads, waiting for the bell to ring. I thought it prudent to start looking for another door out of there, a window if necessary. But all the light in the kitchen was artificial and the only other door led to the parlor of horrors, which was locked. We were deep behind enemy lines, and the only way out of The Fat Man's dungeon was through the dining room. This was not a situation we could tiptoe out of. I was very anxious for our well-being. Also I was nervous for what Ramilov might do, as he was prone to rashness. But Ramilov did not move, nor did he speak again. I cannot tell you how long we stood like this, the ape caged and whimpering beside us, the cleaver on the counter in front of us. It could have been a moment or an hour. It was the purest example of kitchen time I have ever known.

Then the bell rang three times.

"Don't worry, mate," Ramilov said. "Whatever happens, I'm not going to let that fat fuck eat your brain."

I realized he was talking to the ape. Fine, why not? But I required assurances too. Pools of terror were collecting inside me. On some deep emotional level I had sprung a leak. What were we going to do? After a long and agonizing pause, the bell tolled again. Once, twice, three times. Rung out with full force. Again Ramilov did not move.

There were footsteps in the corridor. Belly first, The Fat Man sailed in. Angry was not the word. Fuming, fulminating, effervescent, incandescent: these get a little closer to the utter fury of the man. His enormous bulk, moving at speed, was terrible to witness. You suddenly appreciated the strength it took to carry a body like

that, and the sheer force implied by it. It was the force of every animal he had ever eaten, squeezed into one spirit.

"Well, chefs?" he snarled. "What the fuck are you doing? *Bring
it in.*"

He was right up against Ramilov, glowering down at him.

"No," said Ramilov.

"*Do you want the money or not?*" The Fat Man was bellowing,
spraying food and spit.

"Fuck the money," said Ramilov.

"What?" The Fat Man could not believe his ears.

"It's evil."

The Fat Man curled his lip. Ramilov's empathy had tickled him.

"You should see what I've got planned for next time," he replied
darkly.

Suddenly I saw the months of ungodly dinners stretching into
infinity, and I could not help but shudder. Where was the line?
Morality struggled in the restaurant kitchen as it was—in The Fat
Man's kitchen it didn't have a chance. If it were acceptable to kill
an ape, what would be next? Where could you go after that? How
many months before there was a human being in that cage? How
long before we were taking cookery tips on the best way to cook a
baby? For the first time I appreciated the weight these horrors must
have put on Bob. Perhaps some, if not all, of his awfulness could be
attributed to these godless dinners. But why had he agreed to them?
Why had he not tried to escape? Why were we not pushing past
The Fat Man and breaking for freedom right now? What hold did
he have over us?

"You're not touching that creature." Ramilov had his legs set
wide apart.

"What do you know about right and wrong?" The Fat Man

sneered. "You think it's better to slit a pig's throat? You think you can smash a calf's skull at three months but not a monkey's?"

Ramilov's jaw was jutting fiercely. His eyes were like stones.

"Apes are different," he said through gritted teeth. "Apes are majestic."

"Ha!" The Fat Man cried. "Majestic! You chefs! You think you're all judges of taste! What taste have you got? The restaurants you run are tacky, the clothes you wear are tacky. Your friends are tacky, your wives are tacky, your lives are tacky!"

This was me, and my friends, The Fat Man was talking about. This was my profession he was insulting. The Fat Man was not interested in food—only in consuming, in mastery, in destruction. I felt sick. The pools of terror were fermenting in my gut. We had to get out of there.

"That's why you'll always be slaves!" The Fat Man spat. "You deserve no better!"

"Shut your mouth!" Ramilov barked back. The muscles in his neck were straining to attack.

"Ramilov," I said, tugging at his sleeve, "let's go. Now."

"Yeah," he said in agreement, though still looking as if he were about to bite off an ear or nose. "You're right. Fuck this guy."

He pushed past The Fat Man with me following close behind. There are Saharan plains smaller than that kitchen was just then, whole continents one could cross quicker. The open door was in front of us, the room of hooded figures at the corridor's end. If we ran now maybe they wouldn't catch us, maybe we'd be out and in the street by the time they lifted the black silk from their eyes. If we just ran . . .

We were passing the counter nearest the door, where the cleaver sat, when The Fat Man called out after Ramilov.

"Why don't you tell your little friend here why you left the place in Leeds?"

Ramilov stopped. His face, half turning toward his accuser, had drained of all color.

"The head chef's daughter, wasn't she?" The Fat Man asked with a leer.

Ramilov turned fully. Much of the earlier forcefulness had left him; he appeared quite stunned.

"How do you . . ." he began to ask.

"Amazing what you can find when you know the right people," said The Fat Man. His voice had lowered. He knew he had us hooked again. "We do live in an age of wonders. . . . How old was she anyway? Thirteen?"

"That's not true," said Ramilov blankly.

"That's what I like about chefs," replied The Fat Man. "You're all so *bent*. Each in your own little way, you can't keep your hands clean. Your friend Dave had his drug debts, that weirdo Bob had his home videos. No wonder that dog was always trying to escape. You're all so proud . . . and stupid. You changed your last name—so what? How many Ramilovs do you think there are in the system? Bob kept those tapes just lying around in a locked drawer. You people make blackmail easy. You're a gift. What you won't do for money, you'll do for fear of others finding out. . . ." His words were trickling softly, calmly. "Thirteen is a bad age, isn't it? Lot of awkward questions."

Ramilov had lowered his head. His breathing was forced.

"Tell me," said The Fat Man, "did she still have dolls in her bedroom? Did you turn them to face the wall?"

"She wasn't . . ." Ramilov began. "I didn't . . ."

"Yes, I can see—a very difficult one to explain," The Fat Man went on. "But all that can be forgotten. Just do as I say and carve that monkey up. Right fucking now. I might even still pay you."

Unsteadily, Ramilov took a step toward him. I could not tell whether he was about to yield or fight. My heart was doing laps. Was this the history of which Ramilov would not speak? I was terrified, above all, of discovering he was weak. I had no strong figures left. In that moment I hated The Fat Man more than I have ever hated anybody, for holding the past over us, for never letting us forget. People like The Fat Man and my father, forever contaminating our lives and poisoning our abilities, figures to fear, to dream of overthrowing. All the bitterness and rage I felt toward one flowed into the other, and I saw that as long as there were people like them in our lives we would never be free. There was the quaking ape in its cage, there the glinting cleaver, and here we were in the middle. "That's not how it was." Ramilov raised his head and looked The Fat Man in the eye once more.

"Oh, I know what you must have told yourself," The Fat Man said, grinning. "Everyone finds a way to make it right with themselves. When you steal something, when you kill someone, when you fuck a child . . ."

Ramilov stared at him unsteadily. He was about to crack.

"Don't listen to him, Ramilov!" I cried.

"Oh," laughed The Fat Man, turning on me. "You think this is only about him? The money you give your dad, where do you think it goes?"

What was he doing bringing my father into this? What business was it of his?

"He has a gambling problem," I said, uneasy with this new line of inquiry. "Come on, Ramilov, please . . ."

"He did have," The Fat Man grinned, "but I cured him. Turns

out he'd rather keep his fingers than play the horses. That money goes to me, for debts unpaid."

This information pinned me to the spot. I was in no mood to discuss my father, with this man of all people, but I had to know what he owed, what it would take for him to be free. This man, this constant reminder of my brother and my relative shortcomings, this tyrant to me for so long, now tyrannized by another. I cannot tell you exactly what I was feeling at this moment. My emotions were all riled up.

"How much does he owe?" I asked. No matter what my father said to me, we were still joined to each other. His debt was my debt. Out of the corner of my eye I could see Ramilov edging forward.

"Enough that he'll never pay it off," The Fat Man replied. "I'm . . . *flexible* with the interest. Best thing you can do is get that monkey out of the cage and get to work. Take that money home. Be a good son, eh? Don't disappoint your poor old dad. . . . What would that brother of yours have done?"

In his most recent letter, Ramilov says he doesn't remember much about what happened next. He suggests "A Muddle of Violences." The long and the short of it is The Fat Man received a meat cleaver in his prodigious gut. The lower intestine. A ruptured kidney. *Chop chop.* Nothing fatal, though we did wonder at the time, as he lay there bleeding out across the floor, his mountainous flesh changing color before our eyes. *Untold claret.* Ramilov suggested that we turn him over to face the sky, according to the laws of the Kanun. Otherwise his soul would enter the earth and there'd be no end of trouble. Ramilov has no memory of saying this, but I do. I can see and hear every element of those last moments in The Fat Man's house. I remember how we eventually rolled him, how I held his head to stop him from choking on his blood and felt the hair and fat and clammy skin of it, no different from a swine's. The si-

lence in that house was coming at us in waves, rushing forward and
then retreating away. Voices were gathering in the corridor. *Pussyclot*
was mentioned. Ramilov locked us in.

"Call 999!" I hissed.

"No police!" he cried. "We can't get them involved!"

"Are you crazy?" I shouted back. "He'll die!"

The Fat Man was trembling now, quite cold in my arms. His
blood was everywhere, pooling around us both. It would not stop. I
was eight years old again, watching helplessly as the life ran from
my brother. Neither of us was strong enough to stem the flow. That
awful silence returned, louder than ever. I racked my mind desperately for a way to stop it, to forget the blood, and suddenly the lines
of a poem popped into my head, I don't know why. Memory of
some first aid would have been more useful but, like I said before,
you can't choose what you remember. I decided to give The Fat
Man as much of the poem as I could recall.

> *To see a World in a Grain of Sand*
> *And a Heaven in a Wild Flower,*
> *Hold Infinity in the palm of your hand*
> *And Eternity in an hour.*
> *A Robin Redbreast in a Cage*
> *Puts all Heaven in a Rage.*
> *A dove house fill'd with doves and pigeons*
> *Shudders Hell thro' all its regions.*
> *A Dog starv'd at his Master's Gate*
> *Predicts the ruin of the State.*

I am not sure if The Fat Man appreciated my recital, as he never
said anything one way or another on the subject. Of course, Ramilov does not remember this either. He was arguing furiously with

the guests on the other side of the door. They had realized the injuries were serious and the initial threats had been replaced with something stranger: some of them seemed to be suggesting that we should let their host die. *Let it happen,* the voices whispered. *Set us free.* Ramilov was shouting back that we weren't about to kill anyone, but when he turned away from the door and saw The Fat Man again, took in the state of him, he conceded that death was a distinct possibility. Reluctantly he made the call. The voices outside dissolved when he announced that the emergency services were on their way. The whispering walls were silent.

All Ramilov remembers for certain from this time is the ape, which he says did not take its eyes off The Fat Man until the paramedics had got him on the gurney and carted him away. He says he can't prove this for sure, but he swears that the creature was smiling.

Ramilov adds that he has joined the library and there is space on the shelves for a book by Monocle about Bob and the restaurant inspector and Racist Dave and The Fat Man and everything that happened. He says there is quite a lot of space on the shelves. The book selection is piss-poor in prison.

4. THE SELECTED WISDOMS OF RAMILOV

xcerpt from Ramilov's letters, no. 1: History is a graveyard of fallen idols. You'll stub your toe on a headstone if you wander round it long enough.

Soon after the stabbing I took my father home. The handcuffs, the holding cell, the questioning—these had all been distressing, if formative, experiences for me. Those detectives certainly know how to make a person feel lousy about themselves. My night behind bars had been a long and restless one, with only Ramilov's occasional groans (of distress, I think) in the adjacent cell for company. Strange as it was, in that hard room I had even missed my father's snores. The next morning, when I saw his sharp face in the reception of Kentish Town nick upon my release, all the rage of the previous afternoon was forgotten. For a second it occurred to me that he might have been arrested too—had he stolen someone else's stolen fruit?—but no, he was here for me, he had come to take me home.

"It should've been me in there—not you," he told me somewhat ambiguously.

But I would not let him confuse me now. The minute I saw his face I resolved to do as he had done for me, as he had been asking me to do for him these three long months: I would take him home. An act of mediation on my part. After that mess in The Fat Man's house, good counterbalances were in order. My mother had not agreed to it, nor was she likely to, but I had seen enough of their fights to know there was no such thing as a clean break with them. Like two halves of an old book, one made no sense without the other. With a bit of tape, a little perseverance, they could be stuck back together. Those long years had worn them into each other. They shared familiarity, and that counts for more than you think. I believed they could work together again.

The old man pronounced it an excellent idea. This, combined with the news of The Fat Man's incapacitation, the canceled debt, lifted his mood no end. Was it the thought of a reunion with wife or bookie that cheered him more? Still, it was an improvement. He gabbled about what he should wear for the trip home, how this time meant change. He'd turned over a new leaf, he said, he was no longer the useless human being he once was. He'd changed. Oh, and there was one more thing. Could I pay for his train ticket? He'd spent the last of his money on a present for my mother. A small collector's edition of model sports cars.

"Your mother is crazy for these," he kept saying excitedly, though I seemed to recall it was he who loved sports cars, not her. Anyway, I didn't mention it. The second, less honorable part of my thinking was that if I got him out of London he wouldn't have the money or inclination to come back. An act of disposal as much as mediation.

From the train, beyond the carriage's lime green furnishings and the surly trolley steward, a great and ancient city could be glimpsed, as gray as the sky above it, carved from the same solemn temperament. And behind those stone façades: stories, flesh, difference. The land under this bridge, I once read, had belonged to German merchants for centuries, a self-governing Teutonic enclave deep in the heart of Albion. Of course my father was not interested. You could tell him nothing about London. He began arguing with the steward about the price of the Kit Kats, and I was obliged to produce my wallet once more. My father seemed to expect nothing less. As he reminded me between bites, I still owed him fifty pounds from the

bet about Harmony. I told him the book on that one was still open.
He nodded.

"Yes," he said. "Some women will take anything."

Ordinarily I might have read this for a dig, as was my father's
custom. But I don't think this was his intention.

"Your mother keeps taking me back," he continued. "Christ
knows I don't deserve it. A very kind woman. She deserved so much
more."

Was this another reference to me? The fallout from Sam's death.
The son I could never be. But all that felt so faint and far away from
us now, passing over the river, the sunlight flickering about us
through the girders. I would like to think I had grown up. There
was no reason why I could not have a civil exchange with my father
about my mother.

"She is kind," I agreed.

My father nodded happily.

"Yes," he said, turning his head to look out the window. "It's
time I went home." He breathed in deeply through his nose and
sighed.

"Smell that," he said.

I sniffed the carriage air. It smelled like a train to me.

"Doesn't the world smell great when you don't have air freshener
being sprayed through the keyhole every five minutes?" he said.

We both laughed, and it struck me, a little spike of sadness in
the middle of our laughter, that we had not shared a joke in a long
time. It had taken an arrest, a reunion and frequent dispensation of
funds, but perhaps it had been worth it, for this.

Around us the city grew slowly out, greens sneaking in among
the grays, increasing their share, popping up behind station plat-
forms, between industrial parks. Banks of ivy sprawled over con-

crete. Buddleias sprouted impossibly from the brickwork. Then we were in the still, patchwork fields and the city's populous streets and sad shadows and One-Eyed Bruces were just a dream, another version of life I had read in one of my books, and I was coming home again.

Was this right? Home? At the door my mother threw her arms around me.

"Why didn't you tell me you were coming up?" she scolded fondly, kissing me on both cheeks. I had forgotten that note of carbolic and old age she carried from the care home. Was that a little more silver in her hair, a little less rose in her skin? Still a handsome woman though, by any standards.

"I was arrested," I told her by way of hello. "I've only just got out."

Her eyes goggled a bit at that, which pleased me.

"My poor dear!" she cried, then slightly warily, with that voice she reserved for my father, "What happened?"

"An accident, Mum. It's okay. I'll tell you all about it."

She ushered me in, aflutter with big, sweeping sentiments. They stopped short, however, of the other figure on the doorstep.

"Catherine," he said. His arms came up a little at his sides, an old muscle memory of embrace, then fell quickly when she made no effort to respond. She looked neither surprised nor angry to see him. He nodded toward the front garden. "Daffodils have come up nice."

She let him in without a word. In the sitting room the old sporting trophies had been cleared away, otherwise the place was pretty much as I had left it, as it had always been. That's what I mean about my parents—not much changes. My father must have sensed this unchallenged admittance was not the same as an official pardon, for he was wise enough not to sit on the sofa where he had spent so much of the last fifteen years. He chose instead a straight-backed chair near the television that made him the center of attention. He knew an apology was required and molded himself into an appropriate shape—clasped hands, penitent stoop—to deliver it. Unfortunately, that was not what came out of him.

"I see you moved my trophies," he said. Then, seeing the look my mother shot him, he added, "Which is fine."

"How's London, dear?" my mother asked me.

"It's fine," I said.

"It's horrible," said my father. Whether it was the sight of my mother again, his hatred of the capital, the disappearance of his trophies or simply the effect of sitting upright, he appeared quite moved in his response.

"Are you all right for money?" she asked me.

"Yes," I said.

"No," said my father.

"I've missed you, love," she said to me.

"I've missed you too," my father blurted out.

"Dad"—I turned to him—"do you have something you want to say to Mum?"

"Yes," he said. "I messed up. . . ."

This was true so far as it went. No one could deny that. My mother listened as he outlined his personal disgraces, her face flickering between the hatchet and the muse. He had gambled, he had strayed. Oh, he had been so terribly weak. Here he looked at me. Was that a wink? Was he lying about being untrue? Did he hope, by talking of infidelity, to remind my mother that he was a man of blood and passion? Perhaps this was their bond: somewhere between love and hate, closer to the latter but reminded, by these unsavory proxies, of the former.

He had blamed himself for losing Sam, he went on, and he had blamed that loss for so much. He had hogged the burden of grief. He knew that wasn't fair or right, because we had loved Sam too, my mother and I. That guilt had also fallen on us and we had not given in. I studied a detail on one of the cushions and did not meet his eyes. My father said he could see his mistake now, and he could change. It was a touching speech, which struck all the right chords. And though my mother's bitterness was every bit as corrosive as my father's in its own way, I thought I saw her expression softening as my father talked, the deep marionette lines around her mouth dissolving, the blue-gray eyes taking in new light. In that moment I was filled with hope for my family. As people we had a lot to learn, yet there was some acceptance of that.

But always with my father there were doubts. His record for sincerity was poor. Country cunning lingered in those sharp features. His eyes, small and bright against his spider-veined cheeks, knew many versions of the human condition. Like the mirror in my mother's room that split the viewer into a thousand different types of self, my father possessed kaleidoscopic properties: he could be many things at once. He was the husband begging forgiveness, who had come bearing gifts. He was the con man spinning his spiel, with some toy cars he'd bought for himself. He was the penitent traveler. He was the man who stole apples from the homeless. He was the poor dupe who always got the blame. He was the only one who had been near that silver swan above the till. He was the chicken and the fox. He was the thief next to Christ who was saved. He was the thief who was left to rot.

I left the two of them to talk in the living room and wandered around the house awhile. The same pictureless walls. The same tatty show home furnishings. The same damp, unlived-in smell of the house rotting quietly when we turned our backs. The glass on the front door was frosted, not striated as I had remembered. The place was still cold. Behind an old tumble dryer in the garage I found a child's bicycle covered in rust and cobwebs, its tires flat and jaded. Sam's bike. I remembered how big that bike had looked to me when we tore through the backwaters together. So shiny, so grown up. I had dreamed of one day possessing it. Now I did not even want to touch it.

Up the stairs, past the window that overlooked the rest of the cul-de-sac, I paused outside his room but did not enter. Not yet. I was still not quite ready. Instead I carried on toward my parents' room. My mother's hinged mirror stood in the corner. I pulled the wing mirrors around me and I was back in the endless hall of my childhood, a kaleidoscope of all my many selves, multiplying and dividing according to the angles of the glass. I was the wooden child with books for friends. I was the weak brother, straggling and creeping. I was the brother who survived. Hate. Love. We learn these words so early; we read them in our mothers' laps. But little boys grow up. Experience outstrips us, and we live with the mistakes we have made. The face at the center of the kaleidoscope was leaner and older now. A man's face looking back at me: a chef's.

Excerpt from Ramilov's letters, no. 2: What is done cannot be undone.

Back on the landing I looked again toward Sam's room. The door was closed. I had not entered since the moment I found him. Now I reached for the handle. Now I stepped inside . . . There were the posters of the shows we used to watch, the teenage footballers long since retired. There were the scrapbooks he had kept and the boots he had run in and the football shirt hanging proudly over the back of his chair, torn where he had snuck under the golf course fence one time to retrieve our ball, restitched by our mother in nearly matching thread. There was the bed where he had rested before . . . Christ, could I not even say it? Before he died. Before the hemophilia took Sam, with a little help.

In fact, *hemophilia* was shorthand for what Sam had really had: thrombotic thrombocytopenic purpura. A different cause amounting to the same curse. His platelets would not clot. The blood was faulty and had to be replaced. But when the doctors took his blood they seemed to take a part of his character too: he became sluggish and overshadowed, adult. In the months following our encounter with the wasps Sam's movements grew stilted. Like his father on the tee, his hips were not in kilter. Back to the doctors he went, and they found blood in his joints, making him limp. He had never stopped bleeding. They said his blood must be changed again.

I remembered one day around this time, on the way to town, my mother suddenly pulling the car into a foreign lot. It was just the two of us. My brother was at home, resting up on doctor's orders. My father, preempting medical opinion, was doing the same. Outside it was pouring with rain, and the glum afternoon light had made the windows reflective. We sat there awhile, the wipers still slapping, as I watched my mother's strong features in the windshield wrestling with the idea. Back and forth, back and forth. Then they made a decision.

We stumbled through the downpour, hand in hand, into church. The metaphors are all there if you want them: deluge and shelter, the passing out of darkness and into light; though if I recall correctly it was pretty gloomy inside that church, more of a passing from one kind of darkness into another. A few figures sat facing the front, regarding the stigmata of the painted wooden Christ, meeting the gaze of those gaping wounds. It was the first time I had ever been inside a church. Of course I'd heard claims of god's powers, the magic tricks and resurrection stories, but I'd never been inside his house. Looking around it, I was a little disappointed. There didn't seem to be much to do.

"Stay here," said my mother. She put me in a pew at the back and went off toward the priest. They talked together in low tones. Concerned, he held his robe of deep tropical green away from the bank of candles. Shadows of a tree reached through the stained glass behind.

"Is it a fatal disease?" I heard him say.

On the walls about him, scenes from the crucifixion.

Jesus is stripped of his garments.

Jesus falls the third time.

"But you must let us know when and we shall pray for him," said the priest.

Only then did I realize how sick Sam was. So sick, in fact, that my mother and the priest were going to talk to god about it. But something about the way the priest said it rankled me—so casual, as if talking to a higher power were the same as brushing your teeth or cleaning your room. It stripped a lot of magic from the enterprise. I was furious with the priest for that. Here was my mother, ashen with worry, begging him for a miracle, and this scoundrel was waving her implorations away—"Sure, sure!"—as if it were nothing. I'm not sure what my mother thought about it. She's had a lot of practice obscuring these things.

The prayers did not work. Sam walked ever slower. After the second transfusion the footpaths and backwaters were out of the question. His bike bloomed with rust. Again they changed his blood, but Sam was weak from all the secret wars beneath his skin. Bed was the only sure thing. Piles of blankets, and the unnatural sight of my father attending. Cold palms, sour sheets, windows closed to keep the heat, color fading from the cheeks. Too frail to wipe away the nosebleeds. Stay rested, your loving brother will bring you bowls of soup.

That was my only task. The single thing I was asked to do for Sam. And yet I failed, even in that. I could not understand why my brother would not pull himself together. I felt so ashamed that he had let himself be overcome, that he had allowed this thing to become bigger than him. The boy in front of me was a toothless impersonation of my brother. An insult to the idea of him. This was why I did what I did. Not because I was jealous of him, though he was the better son. No, it was done out of love. I was very young, I know, young and stupid, but I know this much. When I brought him up those bowls of soup I left them on his bedside table a little too far away from him—because I wanted him to get better. Reach for it yourself, that bowl was saying. Have a little strength. If you want it, take it. And if you do, then I'll know you've been hamming up this illness all along. I'll take it as a sign that you're all right.

One day in high summer I came back into Sam's room to fetch the bowl and found the bed empty. For a second I actually wondered if my plan had worked; if he had thrown back the sheets and returned to health. Then I saw the leg sticking out from behind the bed. The angle of it all wrong. I rushed forward, suddenly terrified. Sam lay on the floor between the bed and the bedside table in a heap of thin limbs. His face was turned toward the carpet. A nimbus of blood already framed it, creeping gently outward. I pulled him toward me and held his head in my hands and saw the dark torrent pouring from his nose, the wasps' nest again but worse, much worse. Around his mouth there was blood also. On the bedside table the bowl of soup sat untouched, still that little bit too far away, just as I had left it. Had he tried to reach for it? How else could he have fallen? Had I done this to him?

"What happened?" I cried. "What happened?"

I was desperate to know, mostly desperate to be exonerated. But whatever Sam knew he wasn't saying. He was breathing weakly, his eyes opening and closing, trying to choose what to focus on. I grabbed him under the arms and tried to hoist him up into the bed again as his limbs spooled unhelpfully beneath him. His sick body was slight enough that I could lift it, but his limbs were like cooked spaghetti, pulling the center of gravity with them. And all the while the blood kept running and running, pouring out of him, covering us both. In the end I wrestled him back into bed. I pulled the sheet back over him and dragged the soup bowl nearer in case anyone thought to notice. Then I called desperately for my parents.

My father was the first in. We watched together as the life ran from my brother. We stuffed his nose with tissue and wiped the blood from his mouth. My mother phoned the hospital. We did our best to save him, but he was too frail, too frail to stop his own blood leaving him. We could only watch. That hot summer day Sam died. My mother kept asking how he had fallen. She was repeating it like a mantra. My father said it didn't matter. He saw me standing on the fringes of our tragedy, so quiet and pale, and said we must not blame ourselves. He opened the windows in Sam's room, but there was no breeze to relieve us, only heat.

Excerpt from Ramilov's letters, no. 3: There are only three ways out of the Kanun's cycle of revenge.

The targeted man can spend the rest of his life in his house, where it is forbidden to murder him. Or he can retreat to a window-less "tower of refuge," where he will climb a ladder to the first floor and then pull it up behind him, and where food and drink will be left outside for as long as he stays. Finally, the avenger can refuse to avenge. He will be served coffee with a bullet in his cup wherever he goes, as a reminder of his cowardice and a sign of his disgrace.

Excerpt from Ramilov's letters, no. 4: Mating shortens life.

When I returned to work after the stabbing and the visit home, Harmony came straight up and hugged me, knocking the breath clean out of me. She was so relieved I was all right. The same girl who once pushed my bleeding form aside because I was blocking the mustard, now relieved I was all right. This was an improvement, no question. A worldly betterment not to be ignored.

"It was only a matter of time before something like that happened," she said with great seriousness. "You were lucky to get out alive."

For a second I wondered if she knew the truth of it.

"A pair of arseholes," she went on. "They deserve each other."

Her understanding: I was the innocent caught between two warring devils.

"I like Ramilov," I told her.

She looked at me and shook her head sadly.

"No," she said.

I did like Ramilov, despite the terrible thing he did. Perhaps that's wrong of me, and I should now be trying to disown him. Is it possible to recognize someone's good deeds without tacitly condoning their bad ones? Though that night in the cell had twisted all my feelings, I still hoped to see him freed at the first opportunity. I decided not to push the point with Harmony, however. We were speaking; she was grateful to see me, relieved I was alive. This was the most important thing in the world right now. Why ruin it?

"If you ever need to talk to anyone," she was saying.

This was an opportunity to be seized.

"I'd like that," I said.

If she was surprised by my haste she didn't show it.

"But not here," I told her. "Why don't we go to the park?"

"All right." She smiled.

"Next Monday, then?" I asked. Excitement was wreaking havoc with the modulations of my voice and I was struggling to control it. "We can go for a walk."

Excerpt from Ramilov's letters, no. 5: Know your chefs.

A very good rule. Some chefs want fussy presentation; some want simplicity. There is no ideal form of a dish. If you put heaven on a plate, someone will always complain that it's too salty or not salty enough. Some like the risotto to be liquid, almost soupy; others want it to stand up by itself. Some will chop the top of a monkey's head off when asked to; others will not. Some bring their world into the kitchen with them; others come from far away with their possessions in a duffel bag and a past they never tell.

In the police station holding cell Ramilov said he knew what he was doing, that I should let him handle it. I was too nice for prison, he said, making *nice* sound like a dirty word, but an ugly, bad-tempered, skull-looking bloke like him could have a fairly quiet time of it.

Excerpt from Ramilov's letters, no. 6: Justice in England is open to all—just like the Ritz.

I don't think this is one of Ramilov's, but he says it. The Fat Man has employed some very expensive lawyers who are demanding the maximum possible sentence for Ramilov. But Ramilov's duty solicitor, an exhausted man of uneven stubble whose tie bears many greasy scales of justice, says they are unlikely to get it. There are mitigating circumstances, not to mention the small matter of why The Fat Man was trying to eat an ape in the first place. I am not filled with confidence. If this fellow misses bits of stubble on his face every morning, what else is he going to miss?

Of course there is a better reason for The Fat Man's lawyers to fail. That is the truth, though Ramilov will be furious with me for saying it.

He did not stab The Fat Man.

I did.

5. FORGIVENESS RATHER THAN PERMISSION

I felt the anger rising up in me. I saw his intentions to hold Ramilov and Dave and my father, all of us, in fear forever. I heard that wicked mouth bring Sam into it. I let the footprint of history trample my better judgment. I clenched my fist around the cleaver as The Fat Man sneered. I buried it into his straining side. I never wanted to stab him, but he kept shouting and needling— "Be a good son. . . . Don't disappoint your poor old dad"—he made me do it. I laid him out. Monocle. Me. The commis. The fly. On the page, blood is a smooth cleft of a word with high, protecting sides. It is a word, like bed, that was meant for lying in. But as The Fat Man ran crimson at my feet I realized the word and the thing were not the same.

Ramilov made me promise not to tell. He insisted that prison was no place for a massive-faced youth such as I; he could not have it on his conscience. It had all happened so fast anyway, he went on, perhaps he had done it. But I remembered every frame of that last argument with The Fat Man even if Ramilov did not, and I knew what I had done. No matter, he said, sometimes there was a greater truth than fact, and I would have to take his word for it. He had ruined the Gloriana, as The Fat Man said, by leaving it out of the fridge overnight to fester. And he had phoned the Food Standards Authority the day of the dinner, an anonymous call, telling them they would find grounds for closure if they visited the restaurant. He had killed The Swan, he had hurt us all. Amends were called for. Though I could not see him from my cell his voice was desperate, cracking as he spoke. It sounded a lot like he was crying, which was strange, as Ramilov was not the type to cry over a rotten turkey or a failed restaurant, and certainly not over any grief Bob might have incurred.

All that was by the by, I told him. I had stabbed The Fat Man, and I must pay for it. This was one responsibility I couldn't ignore. Ramilov gave a long exhalation of breath and was quiet awhile before he spoke again.

"You don't get it, do you?" he whispered sadly. "They've got a warrant out for my arrest in Leeds. All that stuff The Fat Man said about the girl—it's true."

I could not hear it, not then. He had become a mentor to me. I could not rewrite him.

"No, Ramilov, you didn't."

"She wasn't thirteen. . . . More like fifteen," he pleaded. "And very mature for her age. I swear I thought she was older."

"Oh, Christ."

"Very soon these police officers are going to put all this together," Ramilov continued, "and I'll be put away for a long time. I'm not walking out of here tomorrow, I know that. I deserve that. But you don't. . . . Only one of us has to go to prison. You could still be free."

"I'm not going to let you take the blame for my crime," I told him.

"You fucking idiot!" he shouted. "I'm not a good person! I've done shitty things all my life! I've never been good. I'm asking you. . . . I'm telling you. . . . Let me do something good."

Spiritually, this argument caught me off guard. The force of his words, pushed through the bars of that holding cell, threw me, and I confess I eventually yielded to his demands. Ramilov made me promise not to tell a soul I did it, and I gave him my word.

But ever since I have been haunted by the idea of Ramilov in prison. Whatever crimes he may have committed, he is innocent of one. I worry about how the wardens treat him, about his cellmate's sense of humor. His letters are always terse, reasonably upbeat—I wonder what they hide. I think of that single night I spent behind bars: the hard bed, the locked door, the stainless steel toilet bowl, the absence of belts and shoelaces, your life around your ankles, the eyes at the door, the terrible weight. Above all, the shame. Night after night, who knows what that must do to a man?

And so, finally, my guilt has won out. Guilt, you understand, for letting another suffer for my actions, for always letting others suffer for my actions—not for any pain The Fat Man might have experienced. It would have been more poetic if that gross tyrant had been attacked by one of his dishes or burst an artery laughing at someone's misfortune, that's all I will concede. On that score I have no regrets (though late at night, when I am alone, I do still see the cleaver opening him up, scoring through the soft fat and flesh, and wish I could forget it). But serving justice to one has dealt injustice to another, and this is what piques my guilt. Ramilov would no doubt say that guilt is a selfish emotion, that he is not an innocent man, that justice steers its own course, and that he'll kill me himself when he gets out.

I have given the matter a lot of thought. To ruin a man's great redeeming statement might, I think, be more brutal than putting a cleaver in his guts. I am sorry if I have thwarted Ramilov's shot at absolution, but I could not leave the truth unsaid. This is my smart apology for a savage act. Whatever comes of this confession, I shall accept.

6. TAIL END

Racist Dave thinks I have used the word *personally* too many times and the word *gash* not nearly enough. He says he would have put in less of the love bollocks and maybe more of his cooking triumphs instead, like when he did 130 covers by himself on the Sunday after our first trip to Mr. Michael's, still so spannered that he couldn't talk, or more about how he saved the croquembouche and less about how poor diddums's hand got burned afterward. He is still sore about my buzzing around the story and wishes I possessed a more constant, focused mind. He is generally appalled by the literary allusions and claims he has been misquoted on a number of occasions. He would like to clarify that he was merely stating the opinions of others when he said, "The fucking Pakis are coming through the Channel Tunnel," in chapter 3. Dave is also of the opinion that this whole story would have worked better as a musical, with a nice chorus line of waitresses, a big Pavarotti-type tenor as Bob and perhaps a choreographed dance sequence based around a Saturday night service. I respect Dave's opinion but he does not know what he is talking about.

No doubt he will consider this blather as well, but there is an interesting coda to the story of my father. A week or so after the stabbing I came across Glen rooting around in a bin at the corner of the high street and Camden Road. His thin, shambling frame was bent forward at right angles, and with his bony arms he worked the rubbish over, as a swimmer treads water, every so often raising his dark and tilting head to draw breath. Though his heavy overcoat and filthy shoes bore all the hallmarks of long struggle, his eyes were bright and keen. Winter had not diminished him.

It was early and I was not due to start work until eleven. And so, partly in honor of Ramilov, who had always treated the man respectfully, and partly in honor of Harmony, whose act of charity outside my window that night had made such an impression, I asked Glen if he wanted some breakfast. He did, and promptly ordered four bacon sandwiches and five cups of tea as soon as we sat down in the greasy spoon. I was happy to feed him for a little closure. What had really happened, I wanted to know, between him and One-Eyed Bruce that day?

Glen, between mouthfuls, said he did not have a clue what I was on about.

I realized my fictions had got ahead of me. One-Eyed Bruce was my name for him. I rephrased the question.

"The Rasta with the white eye. You were having a fight about apples in the street."

"Oh, him," Glen said without interest. "You mean Neil."

Neil? My mortal enemy of the last eight months, the adversary who woke each morning with the intention of bathing in my blood, my sworn tormentor, was called Neil? The world buckled a little under the weight of this new information. There was no One-Eyed Bruce, just as there was surely no Rosemary Baby or Charming Man or The Last Lehman Brother. The supporting characters in my story threatened to float clean away. If they left, what then? Racist Dave, Mr. Michael and The Fat Man would all expect proper names, and Darik, Shahram, Dibden and Ramilov too. And I would not be able to get away with calling myself Monocle any longer, and would have to use my real name. The thought of it was too appalling to consider. So I did the only reasonable thing: I ignored what Glen had said.

"What happened?" I asked again.

"Trying to steal my apples, wasn't he?" said Glen. "Too crooked to steal his own."

"I saw that," I told him, remembering how my father had come running out of the bookie's to join the fracas. "There was another man in the fight too, wasn't there?"

"Oh, yeah," said Glen. "I thought he was after my apples too"— he wrapped his long piano player fingers into a fist around the bread and bacon—"but the next day he came up to me in the street and gave me something worth quite a bit, said I should buy myself some more apples."

This was a shock to me. A revelation. My father, with his bent pound shop spoons and his "If you want me to leave you'll have to pay me" attitude, responsible for this act of grace? It was supernatural. But perhaps, I thought, I had read my father wrong. Perhaps he was as capable of goodness as anyone else, his heel-like qualities notwithstanding. As Ramilov had proved, the great acts of charity were not always where you would think of looking. And even though the apples in question had been stolen, it was still a noble gesture. He had fought for the little man, and with that apple money he had helped him survive the cold hard winter. Those apples had sustained Glen. A bright bushel of health amid the Camden canker, they had kept him going. Alone, the gesture did not excuse my father's conduct of the last fifteen years. Yet it opened up an avenue of possibility. It made my father a candidate for redemption.

"And did you?" I asked, almost choking with happiness.

"Did I what?" said Glen.

"Did you buy more apples with the money?"

"Fuck no," said Glen. "I spent it on booze."

"Ah."

"Yeah," Glen added, "thirty quid I got for that silver swan. The man at Cash Converters said it was an antique."

Don't even trust your own father. Some thanks I get for raising you. You think I'd come to your place of work and put you in that position? You think me so cheap? Well, go on, search my stuff. You'll find nothing. I'll bet money on it.

The lying git. Truly, the man had no shame. But even this information held a ray of hope for my father—he had chosen to give the silver swan to someone in need. It was a criminal act, but not a selfish one, and somehow that made it easier to forgive. But why was I always so keen to forgive him, this put-upon sneak, this worming pariah? In that moment I realized I still loved my father, even if I didn't always like him.

Now our northern friend is urging me to crack on. No time, he says, no time. All right, Dave, but there are more things in heaven and earth than are dreamed of in your philosophy.

At midday on Monday I waited at the Camden Town Tube station for the quiet dark-eyed girl. There was a knot in my intestines the size of a cantaloupe. Strange to say it, but I was more nervous at this moment than I had been in the holding cell, awaiting my fate, arguing with Ramilov about who would take the blame. *I will. No, I will.* It meant almost nothing that she had agreed, on her day off, to come to the park with me. Almost nothing, but not quite. Days off were rare and sacred occasions, particularly since Ramilov's detainment. She could have given me a thousand excuses for not being there. But she had said yes, and I could not imagine that had anything to do with the scenery.

The escalator brought her toward me, no silver dress this time,

no halo, but beautiful all the same, that long river of black hair released, flowing free once more. I saw her long before she saw me. As
she got closer I pretended not to recognize her, looking through her
as if she were just another girl, but the act soon fell apart, much to
my relief. Outside, sunlight poured into the streets below. It fell
onto us, illuminating our tired faces, washing away the shadows.
Yes, more metaphor if you want it. Baptism, renewal, divine love:
take your pick. What struck me was that, for the first time in six
months, I remembered there were other kinds of heat besides the
stove.

She was holding out the book I had lent her, *The Waste Land*.

"Thanks for this," she said. "He gets the loneliness in the city
right, doesn't he? When he stops poncing about in German."

So she was lonely in the city too? I hadn't thought anything
could dent her, she was so formidable to me. But I wasn't quite foolish enough to read it as a weakness admitted. That was a highly
conscious reveal. She was opening something up to me.

"Do you want to see the monkeys?" I asked.

"Am I meeting the parents already?" she said.

I would call that a warm sort of insult with romantic potential.

Up Parkway and across the traffic junction, Regent's Park
stretched out ahead of us, the vaguely military fences and nets of
London Zoo beyond. In the world again, amid all these strangers
and faces and expressions, after all those hours in the kitchen. Together, Harmony and I. Me and Harmony. For a moment, when we
reached the top of the tree-lined avenue and I gestured for Harmony
to follow me into the bushes, a trace of some old distrust passed
across her face. Only for a second though, before she was following
me through the shrubs on the path Ramilov had picked many
times. There at the fence the monkeys could be seen. A wisdom of
apes, a darting of exotic creatures high up in the English beeches,

their ancient faces—alive despite the Fat Men of this world—turned in curiosity toward us.

I had not given any serious thought to what I would say to her. The thought of "talking things over" I'd accepted as a pretext for getting some time alone. But the last week had not been easy. Now I could only think about the pool of clotting blood on the kitchen floor, the slow spread of darkness around The Fat Man's frame, his cold sweat against my skin, the cleaver still gripped too tightly in my fingers. I looked at Harmony and felt an overwhelming desire to confess. I had been through it all before with Sam; I could not go through it again. Both times I had lied to my parents, but for some reason I felt I could tell Harmony. She was the only person who might understand, the only one I would allow to judge me. Indeed, I felt I had to tell her: bottling these things up was not good for me.

"It didn't happen like you think, you know," I said. And I described the figures beneath the black sheets, the house of sighs, the songbirds and the tiger. I told her about that final night, and the cell, and Ramilov hammered to the wall for his sins in an earlier act. I told her everything. She listened without a word, those dark eyes trained on mine. When I finished she remained silent. That's it, I thought. Our first date, and I've confessed grievous bodily harm. I waited for her to make excuses and move away. But she stayed where she was.

"Well, if you did it," she said quietly, "he must have deserved it."

"You don't understand," I blurted. And then it all came out—Sam's last hours, the bowl of soup too far away, the tangled limbs, the thin impossible blood. The inadequacy of the second son. All the blame and uncertainty I had nurtured ever since spilled out of me in one long torrent, things I had never told a soul, that I had vowed I never would. Still she did not move away.

"You can never do enough for the people you love," she replied at last. "You can never be enough. You can never say enough. . . ."

I looked at her.

"It took my dad weeks to die," she went on. "I cried every night, but I never went to the hospital. Not once. We weren't close. I couldn't do all the things I should have done earlier, not then, with him barely there. That would have been worse. Sometimes you have to accept you can never do enough. . . . Then you leave that thought behind, in the past, where it belongs. And you start from where you are."

Without another word she put her arm through mine. We stood in silence for a while and my mind was silent also, for once not trying to augur great omens from the small and humble details. Gradually conversation resumed on safer ground. Yet it was surer, as we were, for the perils encountered and survived. In the trees above us the monkeys flitted from branch to branch, with one ear out, I'd like to think, for our words. They were the first real words we spoke to each other, and those creatures were the only witnesses to this historic moment. What else we talked about is between us and them.

Life at The Swan started to settle. The customers returned, and the food was the best it had ever been. Confidence among the chefs was growing. Harmony had mastered larder while Dibden, to his and everyone else's surprise, had emerged as a competent, even skilled, pastry chef. It turned out that the solitude and precision of the section—and time, lots of it—had been what he needed. In the plonge, Shahram and Darik powered through the dishes, gabbling happily in their nonsense tongue. Dave, though still dense and out of tune, was proving himself a fair and just leader. Even Bob, our unmissed former tyrant, seemed to bear no ill feelings: a card arrived, postmarked Bradford, with the message "Whoever did it, thank you." New and wonderful produce was coming in every day: nashi pears and yuzus from Japan, pillowy buffalo mozzarellas from Campania, beautiful packages of Iberico ham. Midweek lunches were booked out and a flock of new waitresses, "an ogle," was drafted in to cater for the growing demand.

Yet it was all a little too quiet. No coarse shouting, no obscure rap lyrics, no sudden and alarming violations. Less laughter too. Without Ramilov, things could never be quite the same. The innuendos of Camp Charles sounded hollow without his filthy laughter. Dibden had no reason to protest, the waitresses no cause to scream. All the success and happiness The Swan was enjoying carried a tinge of sadness for our fallen comrade. Often the conversation would turn to Ramilov and the outrageous things he had said or done (I made no mention of our conversation in the cells, of the girl in Leeds), then to how his case was progressing and whether he would be out soon. Each day we hoped he would return. When the yard gate squeaked open there was a collective pause in chopping and mixing, an anxious listening out for those next words. . . .

Hello, bitches, did you miss me?

I hoped to end this story with those words, but I knew better than anyone that this was not to be. The days rolled by and those words never came.

Every now and then I receive a letter from Ramilov. He has been having peculiar dreams in prison, he says. In one he is stuck in the monkey enclosure at London Zoo and Bob is his keeper, prodding him with a stick and trying to make him sing "Cage of Pure Emotion." In another, Bob's dog, Booboo, visits him from the great beyond, dressed in a satin frock coat and walking on its hind legs. It tells him that his Parmesan tuiles are burning. Ramilov says he continues to feel awful about his sabotage of The Swan. He says it was a selfish act that betrayed everyone close to him. It was, he says, like masturbating over the memory of a dear friend—not as much fun as you might think. We don't talk about the other stuff.

More often, however, his letters are brief affairs, at odds with the garrulous man I know. The conditions of prison he describes in plain, unemotional prose. Only the food raises his passions; he complains it is consistently overcooked and underseasoned. How fucking difficult is it to grill a burger, he often wonders. I struggle to reply to these letters, for they are weighted with such different concerns from mine. I want to talk about his survival, his wrongful imprisonment, his chances of acquittal. But on these matters Ramilov cannot be drawn. He wants to talk about the burgers. This is what means something in his world.

He will talk, however, about the book. I have sent him all but the last four chapters, up to just before The Fat's Man's last supper, and Ramilov has been very encouraging in his response, much more so than that philistine Racist Dave. He says, knowing it will infuriate me, that it is almost as good as Tod Brightman's latest book, which he has read in prison. He has a few quibbles, however: he says he never changed for love, he thinks there is not enough about Dibden being shit (there is almost a whole chapter) and he reminds me of my promise. I have been working up to sending him the final chapters. As yet, I have not stumped up the courage. Like I said, I don't condone what he did, but I can't forget that he saved me either.

In his most recent letter, Ramilov includes a list of collective nouns that he thinks are relevant to the story. He asks that I find space for them somewhere, as his contribution to the book. He expects some readers to have the same response to them that Nora had, O'Reillys' cross-eyed landlady, but hopes there might be others more interested than she was. Though I have added them to the glossary earlier on, if I can do nothing else for Ramilov, I would like to repeat them here:

A Band of Men
An Ogle of Waitresses
A Wince of Lobsters
A Tirade of Chefs
It is a Skein of Geese in flight, a Gaggle of Geese on water.
A Buzz of Barflies
A Blarney of Bartenders
A Skulk of Foxes
A Peep of Poultry
A Business of Flies
An Unholiness of Ortolans
A Slaver of Gluttons
A Snarl of Tigers
A Fighting of Beggars
A Colony of Ants
A Horror of Apes

In honor of my friend, I would also like to add a few of my own:

An Embarrassment of Wasps
A Snipe of Grandmothers
A Flail of Golfers
A Depreciation of Cul-de-Sacs
A Conspiracy of Cornflakes
A Frustration of Fathers
A Concern of Mothers

A Bowlful of Blame
A Quandary of Morals
A Singularity of Quiet Dark-Eyed Girls

So it seems this story will end as it began, with dubious nouns of assemblage and Ramilov imprisoned. An obese tyrant is still angry with us. We remain overworked and underpaid. The dinner rush is no easier. Sunlight remains a stranger. Beneath my window, One-Eyed Bruce still crooks a finger in my direction and offers up patois curses. My father is once again an unsavory, beguiling memory. The moth-eaten fox continues to snarl above the bar. Almost nothing has changed.

Almost nothing, but not quite. The supper club of the wicked is destroyed, while the restaurant of the upright flourishes. Our lawyer with the greasy tie says the detectives working on the case have provided more information on the shadowy Fat Man. In a previous and slimmer life he was a superintendent on the force, until he was thrown off it for attempting to extort money from a corrupt official. It seems when he left he took dirt on half the city, and kept a network of police contacts who passed him confidential records. The investigating team made a number of interesting finds at The Fat Man's home, the lawyer says. Names you wouldn't believe, involved in acts you couldn't imagine. The dinners he forced upon Bob and others in his debt were just one aspect of the man's terrible appetites, a demonstration of his power. He made us all complicit in these sadistic acts, and I am sure that was part of the fun for him. Records of other pastimes were also found, linking him to gambling, money laundering, narcotics, and animal trafficking. Pretty damning stuff, according to the greasy scales of justice. He shall not be missed.

What else has changed, besides The Fat Man's circumstances? There are the greater freedoms of the kitchen without Bob, and my new responsibilities in front of the stove. There are Harmony's smiles, and who knows where they may lead. Also, to celebrate a sudden decline in competition, Mr. Michael is now offering delicacies half price for a limited time only.

And there was the morning, as I sorted the deliveries in the yard, when a knock sounded at the gate. I remember thinking the morning light was roseate, so Dave must have been off that day. I thought maybe it was Ramilov out there, a foolish hope, and I opened it a little quicker than normal with a joke on my tongue. But it wasn't him. Instead it was a young guy, a kid really, standing there, looking up at me.

"Is this the kitchen entrance?" he asked.

"Yes."

"I'm here for the commis post," he said.

This was the first I'd heard about it. For a terrible moment I thought I had been replaced, that Dave had employed someone else without bothering to mention that he was getting rid of me. Then I realized this was not the way things were done. Even weaselly Bob had the courtesy to fire someone face-to-face. I looked at the boy in front of me, as green as I had been when I arrived, what seemed like such a long time ago. I was not being replaced. I was being promoted.

"Oh," I said. "You better come in."

He dawdled on the threshold, uncertain. He looked at the dark rings under my eyes and my blotchy fryer skin, the scars across my arms and the greasy forelock poking out from beneath my chef's hat. I saw him studying The Mark of Bob on the back of my right hand and the innumerable other cuts and burns that kept it company. I looked down with him and realized, with some surprise, that they were impressively fucked-up hands. His own hands were lilac white, practically perfect in every way. I noticed that he tried to hide them from my gaze. We stood on different sides of time, he and I, in different worlds. He still breathed air; in my nostrils there was only smoke. I knew he was wondering if this was right for him. . . .

To be the lowest of all creatures. To see the seasons from a square of yard.

No one has been known to return from Hades.

Was this what he really wanted?

Feast and famine. Faith and heartache. Love and violence. Dark mornings and late finishes. Savage acts and smart apologies. Death or glory every night. Those heads once squealing in your hands.

So we slave the best years of our lives: a family of strangers, a business of flies. Our works consumed and soon forgotten. Our names chased away like clouds. Our dreams burned up, at last, in brilliant blazing heat.

"Well, come on," I said. "Chop chop."